# THE WOLF'S SHADOW

---

## AN URBAN FANTASY THRILLER

## CECILIA DOMINIC

Dear Morgan!
Keep on howling!
♦ Cecilia

## ABOUT THE WOLF'S SHADOW

*Life as she knew it is over. At the next full moon, the real trouble begins...*

Epidemiologist Joanie Fisher can't catch a break. After her lab burns to the ground, her boss simultaneously fires her and ends their affair. And though she's inherited her grandfather's multimillion-dollar estate, Joanie's shocked to discover the property comes infested with werewolves.

Confronted by a ruggedly handsome shifter who begs her to continue her cutting-edge research into the wolves' physical changes, Joanie unearths a sinister conspiracy that puts her own life in danger. And as she pushes hard to find the cure, shadowy figures will do anything to make sure she never develops a treatment... including resorting to murder.

Can Joanie end the wolfish disease before she's next on a killer's list?

*The Wolf's Shadow* is the first book in the pulse-pounding Lycanthropy Files urban fantasy series. If you like strong female characters, insidious cabals, and medical thriller-style storytelling, then you'll love Cecilia Dominic's hair-raising genre mashup.

# COPYRIGHT

# LOOK FOR THESE TITLES BY CECILIA DOMINIC

**Urban Fantasy Books:**

*The Lycanthropy Files*
The Mountain's Shadow
Long Shadows
Blood's Shadow
A Million Shadows

*The Fae Files*
The Shadow Project
Shadows of the Heart
The Shadowed Path

*Dream Weavers & Truth Seekers*
Truth Seeker
Tangled Dreams
Web of Truth

**Steampunk Books:**

*The Aether Psychics*
Noble Secrets
Eros Element
Light Fantastique
Aether Spirit
Aether Rising

*The Inspector Davidson Mysteries*
The Art of Piracy
Mission: Nutcracker

## THANK YOU FOR PICKING UP THE WOLF'S SHADOW!

I hope you enjoy this tale of medical mysteries, murder, and mischievous werewolves. Look at the back of the book for a chance to sign up for my newsletter list, and as a thank-you gift, I'll send you a free story or novella.

Thanks again, and happy reading!

Cecilia

*To all who have the courage to make their own stories better and especially to my own Scottish lion, who has supported and encouraged me to follow my dreams.*

# 1

The two letters arrived the same day.

I expected the first: my official termination letter from Cabal Industries. Having it in my hands, smoothing the creases, and looking at the stark black print—Bookman Old Style font—on twenty-five pound cotton-bond paper, Robert's favorite for official business, made my heart thud. My lab—with all my data and backups—had been immolated in a fire a few weeks after the company had been sold. The destruction of the lab and the expense of rebuilding my research program during a difficult merger were the reasons given for my being fired, and no, I wouldn't forgive the pun. The company's symbol, a black silhouette of a wolf howling against a full yellow moon, cried out for me. *"Unfair! Unfair!"*

The second letter held more promise. This one came on plain computer paper with a name on top in block letters: Lawrence Galbraith, Attorney-At-Law. Two hours later, I stood in front of a two-story yellow brick building off Markham Street, just west of downtown Little Rock. A sign in the second-floor window read, "For Rent: Commercial Space." Mr. Galbraith didn't have a secretary, but a bell rang when I opened the door. After five minutes, I began the internal argument of whether I should knock on the heavy oak door that separated the sparse waiting room from what I imagined to be the plush inner sanctum.

I made up my mind and walked to the door, but when I raised my fist, a male voice yelled from inside, "That's bullshit, Galbraith!"

I jumped back. What in the world was happening in there?

"Mr. Bowman, please keep your voice down." I had spoken with this one earlier. "Doctor Fisher is in the waiting room."

"I don't give a damn about Doctor Fisher." He sneered my name. "Look, that land is ours by right, and I don't care if the old man never changed his will. And to bring that overgrown—"

Galbraith spoke over him. "How Mr. Landover felt about you during his life is irrelevant if it's not on paper. I'm sorry, Leonard. You and the others may have to find other grounds for your sport."

Leonard's next statement came out as a cross between a hiss and a whine. "It's not sport, Lawrence, and you know it. You're the only one who can help us."

"There's nothing I can do."

I jumped back from the door just before this Leonard person burst through it like a ball of energy—dark energy. With his olive skin, dark wavy hair, and brooding black eyes, he would earn a second look from most women. I barely got a first one as he snarled at me and stalked out of the office. The bell on the door jangled with the force of his exit.

I crept into the inner office and found Lawrence Galbraith, Esq. looking down his aquiline nose at me and pursing his thin lips.

"Doctor Fisher, I hope Mr. Bowman didn't disturb you." With his mane of gray hair and simple black suit with a long jacket over a white shirt, no tie, he could have stepped out of a mid-twentieth-century movie about an undertaker.

"He certainly seemed upset about something." I wanted him to say more about what this brooding young man wanted with my grandfather's estate, but he evaded the implied question.

"Most of my clients are, Doctor Fisher. If they're not disturbed about something, they're dead. Otherwise they wouldn't need a lawyer." He held out a chair and scooted it under me as I sat.

"I understand. Now about my grandfather's estate?"

I expected him to do the lawyer thing and pull out a file bursting with paper and tell me to look through it and see if I had any questions. Instead, he sat back and steepled his fingers as he studied me through narrowed eyes.

"I knew your grandfather quite well, Doctor Fisher. He was very proud of Wolfsbane Manor. You visited there often as a child, yes?"

"I spent my summers there."

"And your twin brother?"

I looked away. Guilt sprouted in my gut whenever someone asked about my brother. "Andrew never knew my grandfather —he died too young. My mother didn't have the guts to visit my grandfather again until after my parents started fighting. He and my father didn't get along."

"He spoke to me about the rift, how it broke his heart to lose his only daughter. He told me you were a lot like your mother."

I couldn't catch the rude noise before it escaped. "I don't think so." When I thought about my mother, I remembered the gentle hands that so quickly turned hard when she slapped me. I hadn't spoken to her since I had gotten my first assistantship in graduate school and no longer needed her financial support.

He ignored my comment and asked, "How much do you know about your grandfather's estate?"

The memories tumbled through my brain so fast I almost couldn't keep up with them. "It's up in the mountains and used to be really far away from everything. It took forever to drive there on winding mountain roads. There's a stream that bubbles up from underground near the top of the hill where the house is, and it goes to a river."

"Anything else?"

I tried to untangle murky threads of childhood memory and grasped at the images as they emerged. "The house is huge, old-fashioned, with a ballroom and a mural on the ceiling. I don't know what my grandfather did to earn his money, but he seemed to have a lot of it and was careful spending it."

"He was immensely careful. Consequently, his estate, with house and property and all, is worth five hundred million dollars." He ignored my astonishment and continued, "I told him he had plenty to share between you and your mother, but he insisted the bulk of it go to you. Something about your research."

"He didn't even know what I did. Really, Mr. Galbraith, we didn't speak at all."

"Ah, but he followed your career closely."

I'd sort out later whether my grandfather's secret scrutiny felt creepy or caring. "He did? He never contacted me beyond the occasional birthday card, especially after I stopped going up there when I was in high school."

"Yes, he did. He was a researcher in his own right."

And then the old guilt welled up. Like it was my fault he left everything to me. "Is there anything in there for Mother?"

He waved my concern away with one hand. "A small annuity to keep her comfortable until she passes on. It won't dent your fortune overmuch."

"What am I supposed to do with all that money?" As soon as I asked, I recognized how ridiculous it might sound.

"Whatever you want. I think you will find enough up there in the hills to keep you busy."

"What do you mean?" Oh, right, Leonard Bowman had an issue with me. "Is there a problem?"

His gray eyebrows met over his nose and gave him such an ominous expression I wondered if he practiced it. "Have you ever heard of the Landover curse?"

"The what?" This was new. But then a memory tickled the back of my brain, whispered conversations outside the room where my brother and I slept in twin beds about something wrong with Mother's side of the family.

Something about the set of Galbraith's mouth made me wonder if he mocked me. "If it pops up, you'll know. It supposedly skips a generation."

"What is 'it'?"

"You probably have nothing to worry about, Doctor Fisher. I recommend you claim your property as soon as you can. I can help you with arrangements to break your lease and move your things from Memphis."

"Okay. No, wait, what? I can't just move." My head was in a fog, still worried about the curse and whatever Leonard Bowman had been on about. But what was the curse? Insanity? Some weird genetic disease? And despite all his assurances, a worried line had appeared between Galbraith's brows.

"...will arrange to have movers pack and ship your apartment's contents to the Manor," he was saying as he picked up the telephone.

"Whoa, wait a second." I held up my hands. "This is too much right now. I can't just break my lease, pick up, and go."

He reached across the table and patted my hand. "I understand. You need a little while to absorb all of this. But I assure you, it is imperative you move up there and take possession of the property."

I didn't argue, but my eyes blurred with tears. "But you

haven't told me the most important thing. I don't know how my grandfather died."

Galbraith rubbed his temples. "I was afraid you would ask."

"Why?"

"Because I don't know, either."

LAWRENCE GALBRAITH HADN'T BEEN the only person I called when I got the letter, and I hoped the other person I'd be meeting could help me sort things out. My head was still spinning when I arrived at Bistro, a little French place in West Little Rock. The key to Wolfsbane Manor was nestled on a keychain in my purse between my cell phone and my wallet. After some argument—which I obviously lost—I signed a letter giving Galbraith authority to manage my affairs, at least when it came to my property. He assured me he would take care of everything and I could expect my belongings in a few days' time. Of course I'd objected to the hastiness of the move, but I may as well have been talking to the stone lions outside the manor's door.

Why did I agree? I didn't have the money to pay the next month's rent, so the arrangement Galbraith proposed seemed the easiest, if strangest, solution.

Lonna, my best friend, had already arrived at Bistro and sat in a booth along the wall. When she saw me, she waved with one of her long, tanned arms, which looked dark in the white sleeveless top she wore.

"Somebody's been to the tanning booth," I teased as we hugged. I only came up to her shoulder, and I smelled the orange and coconut conditioner she used in her long, dark hair.

"It's my guilty indulgence. I figure, with this career, it'll be a miracle if skin cancer kills me first." Even though she meant it as a joke, there was something serious in her topaz-colored eyes. A private-investigator-turned-social worker with the

Department of Family and Child Services, she didn't have a simple job.

I slid into the booth across from her and picked up a menu. "What's going on over there?"

"Just the typical bureaucratic bullshit. Not all that interesting, so you go first. You said earlier you had big news."

I opened my mouth to reply, but she interrupted me.

"Oh, and how's Robert? You guys haven't come over in a while."

"We're not together anymore." It hurt to remember our little road trips from Memphis to recruit research participants from the Little Rock pediatricians' offices.

"Did his wife find out? Sorry, ex-wife, but I always wondered."

"Worse. I got fired, so no more excuses to see each other."

"Ouch! When?"

"I got the letter today. I kept hoping there would be some sort of appeal or something, but no dice. I didn't want to tell you until it became official." That Robert hadn't stood up for me hurt the most.

"I wish I could understand you, Joanie. How could you not tell me?"

"You're my best friend. You're supposed to understand."

She didn't fall for the guilt trip. "So was that the big news?"

"No, I also found out today I inherited my grandfather's estate, so I've got the dinner check."

"Congratulations, but not so fast there, Fisher." She gave me a stern look over the menu. "Let's tackle one thing at a time. You got fired. Tell me more."

"It was after the lab caught fire. They still don't know what started it." For a second I could feel the heat and smell the smoke from the blaze. Sweat jumped to my forehead, and I had to take a sip of water. This was why I hadn't spoken to her about it before—the memory made me panic.

She reached across the table and put a hand on my arm. "I'm sorry, Joanie. You don't really have to talk about it if you don't want to."

I smiled at her implied question. "But details are important? You're such a private detective."

"How else are you going to figure out what happened?"

"Good point, although it's not like it matters now." I took a deep breath. "One night about a month ago, I was compiling data, pediatric charts, in our statistical spreadsheet..." Just talking about it brought me back. "I was checking to make sure the information in the files converted into the correct columns when my car alarm went off. I jumped down, annoyed because I was on the cusp of running the first analysis, and my lab coat caught on the stool. Really caught. Like the corner of it had gotten stuck in the middle joint where you adjust the height and then twisted in there. I was tugging at it when the smoke alarm went off. When I opened the lab door, the hallway was in flames." The squeeze of Lonna's fingers brought me back to the restaurant, and I blinked to clear the afterimages, which still came to my vision when I talked about it.

"You don't have to say any more."

But I had to finish, or I would do so in my head. Over and over. So I squeezed the words through the tightness in my chest. "I panicked. I shut the door and tried to go out the back way, but the door wouldn't open. It was getting hotter and hotter, and I started coughing from the smoke. Finally, I took the damn stool and threw it through a window, I don't know how."

Lonna rested her chin on her hands. "You're a tough little thing, even if you don't look it."

Caught in the story, I had to keep going. "So I jumped through and got scraped up." I rolled up the sleeve of my T-shirt and showed her my left shoulder, which had a long, thin, barely healed cut. "That one was the deepest. Fifteen stitches."

She traced it with a cool finger. "Wow, that looks nasty."

"I thought that was it. I started heading to my car to shut off the damn alarm and get to a hospital, but then I heard something behind me."

The server approached, and I jumped. "*Oui, mademoiselles?*" he asked with a raised eyebrow.

Lonna didn't even look at him, just gave the order for our appetizer and wine. "*Brie en croute, s'il vous plaît, et deux Chardonnay.*"

"*D'accord.*"

"Go on," she told me.

We were getting into the realm of nightmares. "Honestly, I'm not sure whether to believe it myself." I swallowed, my mouth too dry. "I would rather not say here."

"Oh? It's not fair to keep me hanging, Joanie."

"I'll tell you later, at your place, I promise."

The server brought our wine in tulip-shaped glasses—hers blue, mine red— with green stems.

"So anyway," I said after taking a sip. "Hmm, an oaky California. You can tell every time. You'd think they'd have French here."

"So?" she prompted.

"So you'd think a French restaurant would at least have some Louis Jadot or something."

Her arched eyebrow told me my wine snobbery hadn't distracted her.

"Fine," I sighed. "No lab equals no work. No work equals no job. And that's it."

"How can that be it? You were top in your field."

"I don't know. Maybe someone found out about me and Robert. Or maybe they blamed me for the fire, but I suspect it's more about money. They just got bought, and mergers mean layoffs, especially of highly paid staff with expensive research programs." I shrugged. "But enough about that. What's going on with your work?"

Lonna looked away and spoke so quietly I had to strain to hear her. "There's been this string of kids disappearing in this little community in the Ozarks north of Mountain View. I've got to go up there tomorrow and talk with the local social worker. As hard as I've tried to get out of the private-eye business, you'd think they'd leave me alone."

"Oh, that's rough." Hearing about stuff like that made my stomach twist. It reminded me too much of Andrew.

"Sorry, I know you don't like to hear about the kids."

"I just don't know how you do what you do, that's all. What's this little place called?"

"Crystal Pines."

I set my glass down too hard, and the wine spilled.

"What's with you?" Lonna arched an eyebrow.

"Wolfsbane Manor, my grandfather's estate, is up there. Crystal Pines—it used to be called Piney Mountain—is at the base of the hill, the manor at the top."

"That's odd." She swirled her wine. "From the files I've gotten from the caseworker who lives up near there, the locals —y'know, the ones who were there first before the weekenders moved in—are associating the 'old gentleman's house' with the kids going missing."

A shiver climbed up my spine. "How?"

"That's the weird part. No human footprints or anything. The kids just...vanish. When they call the forensics guys out, it's usually too late to get anything because they always disappear outside."

"No 'human' footprints? What about animals?"

"There aren't any big enough to take a child, so I don't think they're looking."

"Wolves? Coyotes? Bears? My parents always warned me to watch out for them."

"The only wolves in Arkansas are red wolves, which are too small to snatch preadolescents. And if it was something like that, they would at least find..." She cocked her head. "Remains."

"Point taken. It must be a boring summer for them. No hiking, fishing, swimming..."

"It is for the locals' kids. They're the only ones being abducted. If your dad drives a Beamer, Mercedes, Lexus or Volvo..."

"You're safe?" I didn't find that hard to believe. Locals seemed to get shafted in those big "developments." "So it can't be wild animals then. They're not that discriminating. What do you have to do tomorrow?"

"The caseworker, a guy named Matt, wanted me to come and check things out for myself. He's worried the board won't believe him and wanted an outside opinion."

"Is he single?" Lonna, like me, had rotten luck in love.

"No such luck. Happily married for thirty-four years."

"Too bad."

The server arrived again, so we ordered our main courses, *Coq au Vin* for me and *Moules et Frites* for her. I didn't realize how hungry I was until the food arrived, and the aroma of red wine, spices, and hot, crusty French bread rose to my nostrils. The food also gave me the opportunity to ignore Lonna's question, so she had to repeat it.

"Earth to Joanie." She poked me in the arm with a mussel shell. "What happened with Robert?"

"You would ask."

"Of course. Things seemed to be going so well."

"Right. As well as they could be with a married man."

"I thought he was separated?"

"He was."

"Is he still?"

"No." I tore off a piece of bread and stirred it in the thick maroon sauce. "I think when Cabal got bought, he decided he'd better make nice with the almost-ex-wife in case he lost his job and needed her to support him."

"How did he tell you?"

"You're merciless tonight, woman."

She winked. "That's what my boyfriends like to tell me."

"Well, he called me into his office." Images flashed into my mind of the long walk down the sterile white hallways. "My shoulder was still in a sling so I wouldn't move it and open the wound. That arm was hidden under my spare lab coat. He couldn't see it at first. When he did, he didn't react like he normally would have. You know, by jumping up and coming over to take care of me. A look crossed his face... How to describe it? Pain? Regret for having to kick me while I was down? I don't know."

"This was after you'd been told your job was no longer there?"

"You can say fired." I sipped my wine. "It's the reality of it. I was packing up my office one-handed when he called."

"Did you know what was coming?"

"I could hear it in his voice. He asked me to sit down, and he got up and closed the door. I noticed he was limping a little."

"Serves him right."

"No kidding. So then he told me since we didn't have any excuse to see each other regularly, he didn't know if he could deal with that level of deception." The all-too-familiar pressure of tears blurred my vision. "He said he respected me too much to start using cheap motels and made-up business trips."

Lonna rolled her eyes. "Yet he didn't mind the chair in his office."

I smiled a little, and a tear rolled down my cheek into the corner of my mouth. Its warm track turned cold after a second. "So no more boyfriend. That's what I get for seeing a married—separated—man." I again mentally kicked myself for not pushing him for more information about his relationship with his wife, for being that stupid young woman who falls for an older man with a good story and doesn't look for the lies.

"You just had, what is it called? Where the mentee falls for the mentor."

"Maybe."

We each took a sip of our wine, and I wiped my eyes with the napkin.

"*Garcon.*" Lonna signaled our waiter. "This woman needs chocolate mousse."

I looked down at my half-eaten *Coq au Vin*. "But what about this?"

"Take it with you." Lonna swirled the last of the wine in her glass. "You can put it in the fridge and have it for lunch."

That's one of thing I liked about Lonna. She made up any excuse for dessert. It was amazing she kept her model-like figure.

The chocolate mousse came, and we talked about other things over coffee and dessert. Before we knew it, it was nine o'clock, and Lonna raced back to her apartment with me behind her so we could get up early to drive to Crystal Pines in time for her ten o'clock meeting with Matt.

It bothered me a little I hadn't told her the rest of my story. Later, it bothered me a lot. I don't know if it might have saved her—and our friendship—but maybe she would have been more careful. Or maybe I would have.

## 2

_____

It was still dark when Lonna woke me with a shake.

"Morning, sunshine."

"Gads!" I rolled over and turned on the light. We both squinted.

"You were dreaming."

I ignored the invitation to tell her what. It was too frightening. The image of the large black wolf, its eyes blazing red in the fire's reflection, snarled and cornered me behind the shrubbery. I woke up every morning just one step ahead. In my dreams, it never turned back like it had *that* night.

"What time is it?"

"Five thirty. We need to be out of here by six thirty, seven at the latest. It's a good three-hour drive up there."

"Have mercy, woman, and make me some coffee."

"Coming right up." Lonna laughed and left the spare room.

"Good morning, sunshine," I mumbled to myself. I walked into the bathroom and turned to see if I had dark circles under my eyes. I don't know why I bothered. They had become a constant accessory since the dreams started.

"You look gorgeous," Lonna said from the door, and I jumped. She held two cups of steaming coffee.

"God bless you, woman. And no, I don't. You're the only one I know who wakes up as beautiful as she was when she went to sleep."

She cocked her head at my reflection, which made me feel more self-conscious. "You've lost weight, though. And you didn't have any to spare. Your collar bones are sticking out."

I pulled down the collar of my nightshirt. "If I have, I'm surprised. I've been a slug since I got fired."

"You look like you did when you started school. Take a shower, raccoon-eyes. It'll wake you up."

I stuck my tongue out at her and inhaled the aroma of the coffee. Strong, but light and sweet. Perfect. Just how I liked my coffee...and my men.

At seven, we were on the road, I-40 headed west. I followed her green Jeep Cherokee in my little Honda. Luckily, we were going against most of the traffic, the commuters from Conway, and other communities west of Little Rock. I popped U2's *All that You Can't Leave Behind* into the CD player. Once we left the interstate and headed north, it seemed like no time before we traversed narrow mountain roads with hairpin turns.

Finally, we pulled up to a gate, and I looked around. Crystal Pines, the planned community that had eaten the little town of Piney Mountain, was nestled at the base of a hill and surrounded by tall brick walls, or at least that's how it appeared. I later found the walls only extended for about a half mile on each side of the gate to allow for expansion. Lonna pulled up to the gatehouse and spoke with the guard, and the gate swung inward to let us through. I followed her down a tree-lined road to the center of the cute little town, which looked familiar, but not exactly how I remembered it. She parked in front of the diner.

I got out, stretched, and took a deep breath. "This is weird.

Everything looks smaller." Summer in Memphis had been oppressive, and I was grateful I wouldn't have to go back to the sludge that passed for August air. Maybe living up here in lower humidity wouldn't be so bad after all.

I caught up to Lonna as we walked into the diner. Her next words punctured my improving mood. "The guard was more excited about you being here than me. Didn't you see how he craned his neck to see the 'old gentleman's heiress'?"

"No." I wasn't used to people noticing me.

Only a few people, a waitress, cook and a couple of customers, were in the place. At Lonna's words, all activity stopped, and they turned to look at me.

"Shhh," I told her, but it was too late. Luckily the scrutiny didn't last long, but I rubbed my hands over my arms to calm the chill bumps that had covered them.

"Lonna, over here." A tall gentleman waved us over to a booth. I guessed this was the social worker Lonna told me about. As she'd said, he was well into middle age with friendly eyes in a rugged face.

"Matt, it's great to see you." She shook his hand. "This is my friend Joanie Fisher. Doctor Joanie Fisher, actually."

"Oh, a doctor?"

We slid into the booth across from him.

"PhD." I looked at Lonna, who was eating up the attention. She even winked at the man in the next booth over, a tall blond with a narrow, chiseled face whose briefcase contents were spread out in front of him. He curled one side of his mouth in a smile and turned his eyes back to his work. A shiver went down my spine.

"A PhD? In what?" He held up his coffee cup for a refill. The waitress, who could have walked straight off some television show from the fifties, gave him the "one moment" sign with her index finger.

"Behavioral epidemiology."

"That's impressive. You must be in research, then?"

"I was, but I've taken some time off. You know, to handle things up here."

"That makes sense." There was no envy in his tone, only polite interest. Nothing to spark the resentment that rose in my stomach. It's not like I'd asked to inherit my grandfather's fortune.

"Guess not."

"Mind if we have something to eat, Matt?" Lonna broke in. I hadn't realized it, but I was hungry. The cup of coffee and peach had been a long time ago.

"Please." He gestured to the menu. "If I can get Louise over for some coffee, she'll take your order."

"Now Math-yew," the woman drawled as she walked over to the table, her white shoes squeaking on the floor. "You know I can't move that fast with this Arthur-itis."

She refilled Matt's coffee and plunked down a couple more cups, and Lonna and I ordered bacon and eggs with toast. This place seemed a world away from Bistro and chocolate mousse.

Matt leaned in and lowered his voice as Louise shuffled away. "Her grandson is one of the children who's missing."

"Oh," Lonna breathed. "Poor woman."

I never knew what to say in sad situations, so I gazed out the window. The original town of Piney Mountain looked much the same as it had twenty years before when we'd drive through to visit my grandfather. The major differences were that some of the shabby little buildings had been renovated, and expensive cars seemed to have replaced the pickup trucks. Someone had even straightened the leaning World War II memorial statue in the middle of the square. There were also signs at the main intersection pointing to the pool, clubhouse and driving range.

"Your thoughts, Joanie?" Lonna asked.

"I don't understand how somebody can just swallow a whole little town. Wasn't there a protest?"

Matt replied, "Lee Franz, the mayor, convinced everyone it would be for the town's best. He said it would help keep the children in the area if there was more opportunity for them."

Louise appeared with more creamers. "He didn't count on them not being here for the opportunities." She sighed, and her exhalation expressed more than a tirade could.

I turned away to avoid the uncomfortable feeling that somehow this was my fault even though I had no idea what was going on.

A movement outside the window caught my attention, and I spotted a familiar face. The distraught, handsome Leonard Bowman from Lawrence Galbraith's office walked out of the City Hall building across the square. Something about how he moved struck me as odd and familiar beyond our one encounter. The harder I tried to figure out why, the more the answer eluded me. One thing I knew with certainty—I needed more details about him beyond his name. I wanted to know why he was up here.

"Who's that?" I asked.

Lonna followed him with her eyes. "Very nice-looking."

Matthew snorted. "He and his brother Peter, the blond man you winked at, Lonna, are like night and day in more than just coloring."

"Really?"

"Yes. Peter Bowman is a lawyer and the one in charge of the legal aspects of the community planning. He lives in one of the cul-de-sacs with his wife and their son."

"And Leonard?"

"He moved in with them about a year ago, right after the rest of the houses on their street were completed. He was a medical resident at the university and VA hospitals in Little Rock, but then he had some health problems and had to take a break."

"He's a doctor?" He didn't look like any I'd worked with.

Lonna seemed to read my mind. "Research doctors are different, Joanie."

"I guess."

Leonard disappeared into another building—some sort of shop, and the others seemed to forget about him. I watched to see if he would emerge, but the conversation pulled my attention. Still, I glanced back in that direction occasionally.

Lonna curled her fingers around her coffee cup. "Why, exactly, did you want me to come up here, Matt?"

Matt's answer was forestalled by Louise's arrival with our breakfasts. Bacon, cooked crisp but not too stiff, just the way I liked it, lay over a bed of fluffy yellow scrambled eggs beside two pieces of whole wheat toast. My stomach growled in appreciation.

The food momentarily distracted me from the conversation, and when I tuned back in, Matt was saying something about when the strange disappearances had started.

"It was about a year ago. The first phase of Crystal Pines was underway, and some of the families were moving off of their homesteads into new apartments to make room for the larger estates."

"They were relocated?"

Matt stirred more sugar into his coffee. "They were offered huge sums of money for their land that most were too poor to refuse, especially those who wanted better for their kids. Education is expensive."

"Tell me about it," I muttered.

Lonna elbowed me. "So what happened?"

"One of them, a friend of Louise's grandson, was taking a box through the woods on a shortcut the kids all knew from the farmsteads to the apartments. He just disappeared. The search party found the box, but not the child."

Lonna took out her notepad and a pen. "How old was he?"

Matt frowned as he tried to remember. Louise, who had

come by with coffee refills, answered for him. "Eleven, just a year older than Johnny." A tear trickled down her cheek as she poured.

"That's right. It was in August. Then, about every month after that, a new one would go. Well, not every month. People were real careful the next month, then relaxed their guard and let the kids out again. That's when Johnny disappeared. There've been about six or seven in all."

"Any idea what time of the month?"

"Every four weeks."

"What?" I asked. "Are you saying you've got some sort of PMS-ing ghoul out there snatching children?"

The corners of Matt's eyes crinkled. "Not exactly, Doctor. I think it had more to do with the fact it was a full moon."

"Maybe easier to see them, then?" Lonna asked as she jotted down, *full moon*. She had hardly touched her food, which was disturbing because the only time the woman lost her appetite was when she'd fallen in love. Hard. I looked around, and my eyes met the pale blue ones of Peter Bowman, who was looking past me at Lonna. Oh, crap. Lonna's "love at first sight" experiences never ended well. Plus, I didn't know the man, but I instantly disliked him. Maybe I unfairly associated him with his brother's rude behavior.

"Lonna, listen." Matt's voice had an edge, and he leaned in. "I called you because if it were just some crazy person, I could've handled it. But there's something more going on. You're the former private eye."

"Nope, I'm not doing that regularly anymore. And I never did kids."

"But your license is still current."

She looked down into her now-empty coffee cup. "I keep it current for money reasons."

This was news to me. "DFCS pays you more for it?"

"No," she said, the exasperation clear in her voice, "because

DFCS doesn't pay me much, and sometimes I need to take on an easy case on the side for some extra cash."

"Oh. Well, you could stay with me," I offered. "You wouldn't have to pay for lodging or try to get it reimbursed."

"C'mon, Lonna." Matt gestured to Louise, who counted change by the register. The slump of the woman's shoulders and the wet tracks down her cheeks told us she wasn't concentrating on the bills that slipped through her fingers. "These people need us. They need you. There's something big going on here."

"Well, I guess I have no choice then, do I?" She paused, then sighed. "Fine, I'll call the office and transfer my cases until after Labor Day. Luckily none of them are urgent."

"So that gives us, what? Two weeks?" Matt counted it out on his hands. "I know you work fast, Lonna, but are you sure?"

"As sure as I'll ever be. When's the next full moon?"

Matt checked his watch. "Tomorrow night."

"You're sure?"

"Yep. It's something we're all keeping track of nowadays."

"Then we should be able to catch whatever is happening in the act."

The hairs on the back of my neck rose, and I looked out the window, where Leonard Bowman had reappeared in the square.

THE FRONT DOOR to my grandfather's house showed its age like he never had. Pitted and scarred from fifty summers and winters, it had achieved the smoothness common to old wood and cotton. Time seemed to have ignored the gray granite walls, and the manor still loomed over the wide lawn like a castle. The ornate knocker, a smiling lion who held the brass ring in a mouth full of rounded teeth, leered at me as I turned the key in the lock. I shook the key as

I'd always seen my grandfather do on the rare occasion we came in through the front door, and the bolt turned with a grinding noise.

"Is this place haunted?" Lonna asked in a hushed tone as the door creaked inward to reveal the gray marble-tiled foyer. The central staircase curved up into the gloom, its mahogany banister dusty. The open door to the left revealed the fawn-colored leather love seat and sofa that faced the granite fireplace on the opposite wall. Grandfather's old sea chest served as a coffee table, and large wine barrels as end tables. Wan sunlight shone through the front windows and on to the wooden floors.

I realized I still hadn't answered Lonna's question.

"I don't know."

"Don't know what?"

"If it's haunted. I still don't know how or where he died, so I guess it could be."

"It looks like this place hasn't been occupied in a while."

"True."

"Was there a funeral? I would've gone with you."

"Not that I know of. Not that there's anyone to have gone besides my mother and myself, so you would've been welcome."

"A formal reading of the will?"

"Nope. The lawyer just called me in."

"That's suspicious, Joanie."

I also thought so, especially since Leonard Bowman thought he had some grounds to challenge my claim.

Another glance up the staircase and at the gloomy second-story hallway convinced me I really needed to get my leftovers out of the cooler and into the fridge.

When I suggested, "Let's leave the suitcases here and go up later," Lonna didn't argue. We walked through the sitting room and into the breakfast nook. I stopped, dumbstruck.

"What?" asked Lonna.

I gestured to the kitchen. "He completely redid this." A black marble island with a pot-and-pan rack hanging above it dominated the space. New stainless-steel appliances had replaced the old-fashioned fixtures I remembered from my childhood. I couldn't remember my grandfather cooking a day in his life, and I couldn't imagine him giving his kitchen a makeover for some woman he paid from the village.

"Did he know you're a gourmet cook?" Lonna asked.

"Not that I'm aware of." Again, the thought of being watched from afar, even if by a loving family member, made chills dance across the back of my neck.

Lonna walked to the island and tilted up one of the pans to peer at the bottom. "Wow, look at this. A full set of Le Creuset and All-Clad cookware."

I shook my head and put the leftovers in the fridge, one of the super-modern types with the freezer in a drawer at the bottom. I turned to the island, where an envelope with my name on it waited. Lonna picked it up and handed it to me.

"Looks like somebody left you something."

"It's from Galbraith." His long, slanted writing gave it away. I opened it with a knife—Wusthof, of all things—and found a brief note with cash, lots of it, and a spare key. The money was for spending and housekeeping expenses until the rest could be transferred to my accounts.

"I can't even begin to believe this."

"I can't, either." Lonna walked around and opened cabinets and drawers. "This is moving a lot faster than most estate settlements, even if it's simple."

"Really?"

"Isn't your mother a co-beneficiary?"

"Of a small amount, yes."

"And you don't think she'll challenge it?"

"She probably will. She never shared well with others, not even her own children."

Lonna opened and closed cabinet doors. "And would you blame her? I wonder why Galbraith is so eager to have you take possession of the money and property."

"I don't know. I wonder if it has something to do with that Leonard Bowman guy."

She looked up at the name. "Why Leonard Bowman?"

I told her about the encounter at Galbraith's office. "I'd appreciate it if you wouldn't mention it to anyone, especially Peter if you happen to talk to him."

"Not a word," she promised. That she didn't say she wouldn't have a reason to talk to him made anxiety curl in my chest.

I ignored it and asked, "So what's your game plan?"

"For what?"

"The investigation." I gestured to the window over the sink, which showed a wide expanse of lawn sloping toward the woods. "Finding the missing children."

"I don't know. I guess the first step is to call work. Do you think the phones are on?" She held up her cell. "No signal up here, and if there's wireless, it's not on."

After some searching, we found a cordless telephone on its charger in the sitting room. It sounded a dial tone when we clicked it on, so I left Lonna to make her call while I put on some coffee. I had just switched on the coffee maker when the doorbell rang.

I opened the front door to see a middle-aged man whose tan uniform strained over a belly that had probably been fed at the town diner too often. He stood with feet planted shoulder-width apart and thumbs hooked into his black belt. His sheriff badge said he must hold some respect in the community, but I struggled not to snicker.

"May I help you?" I had no reason to be nervous, but there's something about a cop appearing at your door that prompts a quick examination of conscience. Had I gone too fast through the community? Did I roll through a stop? Was I supposed to have a parking permit?

"Miz Fisher?"

"Yes, and you are?"

"Bud Knowles, sheriff." He held out his hand, and I took it. His handshake was firm, if moist. "I wanted to make sure you're rightly welcomed to the community."

"Thanks. Would you like to come in?"

His face lit with a grin. "I'd love to, ma'am."

I suspected the true reason for his visit was to check out the place, but I didn't mind. I had nothing to hide.

"I just made some coffee. Would you like some?"

"Yes, ma'am."

"Call me Joanie, please. How do you take it?"

"Black."

This guy would not be easy to talk to. I led him through the sitting room, where Lonna sat at the card table to the right of the fireplace with an open file. As most men do, Sheriff Bud Knowles took a second look.

"Who is that, Miz Joanie?"

"My friend Lonna. She's a social worker with the state. Her friend Matt called her up here to help with the missing kid problem." Gads, I sounded flippant. I felt like the kid whose teacher has turned up at the door to talk to her parents.

Knowles's only response to my statement was a heavy sigh. I brought him into the kitchen, and after some searching, found a few cobalt blue mugs and poured the coffee—black for him, with cream and sugar for me, and with cream for Lonna. Apparently Galbraith had done a little grocery shopping when he left the note, or had someone else supply the house, and there was at least some creamer in the fridge and sugar in a stainless-steel tin on the counter.

"This seems like a nice community. Crystal Pines, I mean."

The sheriff looked at his coffee so hard I wondered if a bug had landed in it. "It was nice until the kids started disappearing."

"That must be awfully hard on the people here."

"Some of them."

"I'm glad you're here. I'm sure Lonna will want to talk to you."

He winked. "I'd rather deal with her than the Feds."

Ugh. I took a deep breath and prepared to change the subject, but Lonna walked in.

"Coffee's ready," I told her.

"Thanks." She held out her hand to Knowles, who stood up so quickly he bumped the table, and his coffee sloshed. She ignored it and smiled. "Lonna Marconi, it's nice to meet you."

"Bud Knowles, sheriff," the red-faced man mumbled. I hid a smile as I wiped his coffee with a dish towel and poured more.

"It's so nice of you to stop by," Lonna said as she sat and crossed her long, slender legs in full view. "Is this a social visit?"

He swallowed. "More or less. Just wanted Miss Fisher to know she could call on us if she needs anything."

"How kind of you." Lonna smiled at me. "Joanie, isn't that kind?"

"Very."

"Now, Mr. Knowles, you came at a good time. I was just thinking about how to get in touch with you."

She was turning on the deep charm now. I hoped she remembered our earlier conversation and would ask the questions I wanted, too. With a deep breath, I attempted to calm the resentment building in my chest at her usurping the situation. Not that I had been doing spectacularly.

"Yes, ma'am?"

"I'm with DFCS"—as I had, she avoided mentioning she

was also a licensed P.I.—"and I was wondering what you could tell me about the children who have vanished."

Bud had no more information than Matt had given us. When asked about the full-moon connection, he said, "I don't believe in that voodoo witch stuff."

"Now, Mr. Knowles, I have one more question." She studied her coffee as though attempting to divine an answer to a long-standing riddle, then hit him with the full force of her gaze. "Do you know what happened to Joanie's grandfather?"

Bud looked over at me, and I tried not to betray how eager I was for the answer. He leaned back and laced his fingers over his ample gut. "Well now, we don't rightly know."

"There must have been something," Lonna pressed. "Fortunes like this aren't handed over at the mere suspicion of death."

"All I know is we found his canoe, life jacket and shoes a little ways down the river. Something had chewed the jacket and shoes, and there was some blood, but no body."

My breath left me as though someone had punched me in the stomach. Lonna put a hand on my arm.

"Breathe, Joanie. Sheriff, what did the coroner say?"

"Likely the old man'd had a heart attack and drifted down stream 'til he ran aground, and then wild animals got 'im. I'm sorry ma'am," he said to me. "I thought that city lawyer would've told you."

"He didn't." I tried to still the welling tears. I hadn't been close to my grandfather for years, but I had been fond of the eccentric old man. He had been the one steady source of support in my family after my brother died and my parents divorced. Some days I would take comfort in knowing I had a safe haven if I needed it. Now that security had been shattered, doubly so now that I knew he'd been interested in my life and had watched me—watched over me?—from afar.

"If it's okay with Joanie, I'll see you out, Sheriff."

Lonna and the sheriff both got up and walked out of the room. I held tight to the coffee mug, heedless of the heat scalding my palms, so my hands wouldn't shake. The image of a black wolf flashed into my mind.

*Was my grandfather hunted down, too? What have I gotten myself into?*

## 3

After the sheriff's departure, Lonna and I sat in silence and sipped our coffee.

"Somebody wants you to have this place, Joanie."

I resisted the urge to look over my shoulder. "Either that or somebody doesn't want someone else to have it." Like Leonard Bowman. As much as Matt had described him as a loafer living off his brother's generosity, he looked like he worked toward some sinister purpose.

"Regardless, you're the designated heir. I have a mystery to solve, so I need to ponder my strategy," Lonna's eyes focused on a spot on the wall. It was the same look she'd gotten on many previous occasions—some innocent planning, some diabolical plotting. Sometimes they had ended well for me, most often not. I wondered which it would be this time, but I was sure of one thing—I didn't want to be up here alone.

"You can stay here as long as you like," I told her again. "Goodness knows I don't need all this room."

"And you probably need the company. I don't know that you're safe here."

"Thanks." It was nice when we agreed on such things, even if such things weren't nice.

She continued, "The locals probably wouldn't be very forthcoming with me, so how about you talk to them? If nothing else, they may remember the 'old man's little granddaughter.' You're sort of local."

The thought of facing all those curious gazes made my stomach twist. "If spending six weeks for five summers makes you a local."

"It's more credibility than I've got."

Damn, she had a point. "True. Who will you talk to?"

The corners of her lips turned up in a cat's smile. "I'll keep in touch with the charming Sheriff Bud Knowles, of course. And the new families who've moved in."

"Including the Bowmans." I knew it wasn't a question.

Her grin widened. "Including the Bowmans."

LONNA CONVINCED me to revisit the diner since Louise the waitress had seemed nice and nonthreatening, and people like her often had the best intel, but once I arrived, I almost turned around. The after-work rush was more of a swelling of the crowd that had been there earlier, but this time they all looked like locals. Judging from the hard hats and dirty, tanned shoulders huddled at the booths, many of the men were construction workers. I cringed internally when I realized they were essentially forced to build the houses that had displaced their families.

When I pushed through the door, the buzz of conversation lulled, but it picked up again quickly. Maybe Lonna was right—being half a local was better than being an outsider.

"Have you been here all day?" I asked Louise as I slid onto a stool at the counter.

She poured me a cup of coffee without my asking for it. "I took off for the lunch shift and came back to help Terry with dinner. Laurel, the evening girl, is sick. Difficult pregnancy."

I nodded, again not sure what to say.

"You all settled in?" she asked, as though inheriting my grandfather's mansion and fortune was the most natural thing in the world.

"No, Lonna and I weren't brave enough to go upstairs yet. The place looks like no one's been in it for months. Except for the kitchen."

"Now that's a fact. Gorgeous, isn't it? That city lawyer of your granddad's had me bring some stuff up there. Oh, that reminds me." She pulled a key out of her pocket and set it down. "I should'a given this to you earlier. I held on to it for your granddad when I'd do some cleaning for him."

"Thanks. I was wondering who had been helping him keep the house."

"You know men. They need all the help they can get." She grinned wide enough to show the gap between her front teeth, but her sideways glance told me she withheld something.

"That's the truth." I slid the spare key into my jeans pocket.

"So did he tell you about why he redid the kitchen?"

"No, I haven't talked to him. In years, actually." This wasn't exactly Lonna's investigation, but it would help mine. "I was surprised."

"Well, about six months ago..." She broke off as a customer waved her over. "One minute, sweetie."

I watched her as she walked down the length of the counter to where Peter Bowman had just settled in. He glanced at me, so I looked down into my coffee cup for a second. When I looked back up, Louise was nodding at him like he'd just asked her a question.

"You'll notice the local guys are a bit more polite than those city types," she told me when she returned. "They're all about to faint from curiosity about you, but it's Peter Bowman who had the cheek to ask." She wiped at an invisible spot on the counter with a red checkered rag.

"So you were saying something about my grandfather's kitchen," I reminded her.

"Your kitchen, if I recall, young lady." The tenor voice at my shoulder startled me, and I turned to gaze right into the icy blue eyes of Peter Bowman.

"All right, *my* kitchen."

He wedged his briefcase between me and the guy next to me. "'Scuse me, I have some business with this young lady," he told the annoyed construction worker, who glared at him but moved over.

"I'll talk to you later, Miz Fisher. I've got to wait on these gentlemen over here."

Louise topped off my coffee and disappeared, leaving me with Peter Bowman.

I opted for cool and confident. "I don't believe we've met."

He parried with, "Yet each of us knows who the other is."

"True enough. So no formal introduction is necessary."

"Not unless you stand on such ceremony."

"Not usually." I took a breath. Here I was feeling like I needed to keep the conversation going, yet he had barged into my space and my talk with Louise.

"I would appreciate an introduction to your lovely friend, the one you were with earlier."

"Why?" I had to ask, although I suspected his intentions were less than honorable.

"Let me pay for your cup of coffee."

"I've got it, thanks. So, how do you know Lonna?"

"She worked on a case for a friend of mine in Little Rock. Although we never met personally, he pointed her out to me online." He smiled, but only with his thin lips. They reminded me of a reptile's. "I'd like to become acquainted. I may have some work for her here."

"She's busy."

"I'm sure. But I'd like to meet her, regardless."

"I'll think about it."

"Please do. Meanwhile, I'll speak to the sheriff and inform him that we have an esteemed P.I. in our neighborhood."

Threat noted, but I had to try. "She's incognito for now."

"Then we shall definitely have to talk." He reached in his pocket, and for a moment I thought he was going to draw a gun on me, but he pulled out an ivory-colored business card.

"I look forward to seeing her in the morning. My schedule's clear until lunch." He disappeared into the crowd.

"That one's a snake." Louise suddenly reappeared in front of me, coffee pot in hand. "What did he want with you?"

"Not me, my friend."

Louise nodded as if Peter Bowman asking about an attractive woman wasn't at all unusual. "His poor wife. She seems to be such a nice little woman too."

"Any kids?"

"Lance is a cutie pie, but he's difficult. His mother has her hands full with him and his dad."

"How old is Lance?"

"Terrible two. And he is one hundred percent little boy."

Another memory jolted me. My brother had been like that —a challenge for both my parents, although my father had taken pride in Andrew's rough-and-tumble personality. It was a miracle he'd never broken a bone.

Louise glanced over her shoulder, where another new face had joined the crowd. "Look honey, I know you must be real curious about everything that's been going on. Why don't you come by tomorrow morning when it's not so busy, and I'll fill you in on the town gossip about your granddad?"

"That would be great." The tension in my chest that had been there since the sheriff's visit eased a little. "Thanks, Louise."

She waved and moved down the line, refilling coffee cups and greeting newcomers. I left enough money for the coffee plus a generous tip and squeezed out of the diner. As I walked out the door, I realized I had no idea what Lonna and I were going to do for dinner, but there was no way I'd turn around and fight my way back to order something to go from the packed diner. A chill had crept into the air with the setting sun, and I shivered.

"You'll catch your death of cold out here." The voice was deep and familiar, the tone mocking. I turned to see Leonard Bowman leaning against a lamppost. He wore a black leather jacket over an open green polo shirt and khaki trousers, and although he maintained a relaxed posture, he seemed like a compressed spring ready to uncoil at any moment.

I blurted out the first thing that came to mind. "I just had a conversation with your brother."

"Did he try to charm or threaten you?" A smile tugged at his lips. He was the antithesis of his pale brother with his wavy dark brown hair and black eyes. More intense, too. The image of him in Galbraith's office came to mind.

"A little of both, but mostly threaten."

His smile bloomed, and my breath caught at the change from storm cloud demeanor to the warmth of a beach on a hot day. "That's usually how he works."

"Leonard, there you are." His grin disappeared when the staccato clicks of designer heels announced the appearance of a tall woman with emerald eyes. Her milk-white skin glowed in the half-light, and her black hair fell in soft waves to midway down her back. She, too, wore a light leather jacket, but underneath was a ruby red dress that left very little to the imagination. I couldn't really see her purse, but a flash of light off its designer buckle told me it cost more than my car.

"Kyra Ellison, this is Joanie Fisher."

"Doctor Joanie Fisher, actually." I had to get on equal footing with this woman.

"Charmed." She held her hand out for me to shake, but the limpness in her fingers told me she considered it—and me—a waste of time.

"Enjoy your evening." I half-turned to go, but then I made an about-face.

"Do you know where my friend and I could get dinner?"

"Well, we're on our way to Choucroute, a French place here in town." Kyra frowned at my attire as though to suggest I was horridly underdressed.

"Hmm, we just had French for dinner last night."

"Then you might want to try Tabitha's. It's a good casual American place."

"Thanks."

Kyra grabbed Leonard's arm and turned him away.

"Nice to meet you," I called after them. Damn, I was feeling insecure. Lonna, with her Italian beauty, never had that effect on me. But then, no one would describe her as a "snob". Kyra Ellison definitely qualified as one. And a bitch to boot.

TABITHA'S PROVED to be a pub-style restaurant with a full bar against the back wall. The dark wood paneling gave the place a snug feel despite the large mirrors that hung behind the bar and on the top half of the walls behind the booths. Candles in Mason jars flickered on the tables and provided most of the low light that suffused the restaurant.

"We've got to find a grocery store," I remarked to Lonna after we gave the hostess my name and the other diners in the restaurant—all six of them—looked up with curiosity. After Robert had dumped me, I'd wished to be more noticeable. The notoriety had now worn thin, and part of me wished I could just go back to my apartment in Memphis, crawl in bed and wake up to find all of it from the fire onward had been a bad dream.

The hostess reappeared with menus and a smile and seated us in a booth near the front of the restaurant. No sooner had we opened the menus than a young man appeared. His name tag said, "Ted, Manager".

"Welcome to Tabitha's, Miz Fisher."

"Doctor Fisher, actually," Lonna broke in. I kicked her under the table.

The young man wasn't fazed. "Doctor Fisher and Miss..."

"Marconi, Lonna Marconi."

"A friend," I explained.

"Of course." He winked. "I just wanted to come over and say hello and I hope we'll be seeing much more of you. Please accept this complimentary appetizer."

Another server placed a plate of stuffed mushrooms and two little plates on the table along with a bottle of wine and two glasses.

"Your grandfather appeared in town only rarely, but these were his favorites."

Lonna smiled up at him. "And how much is the wine?"

I cringed. I didn't want any more attention, and Lonna's directness was getting plenty of stares.

"Compliments of an admirer." The corner of Ted's mouth twitched as he opened the wine, a red blend from California. "I'll give you ladies a moment to look over the menu and be back to take your order."

"An admirer?" I asked as soon as Ted was out of earshot. "Must be for you."

"You're too hard on yourself, Joanie." Lonna sipped her wine. "It's very good, by the way, very smooth."

I lifted a couple of mushrooms to my plate. They smelled of some sharp, salty cheese—gruyere, I thought—a savory blend of herbs, and fresh sourdough breadcrumbs. The tops were perfectly browned, and when I cut one in half, real lump crab-meat that smelled sweet instead of fishy spilled out. While buttery, it was by no means greasy, and the mushrooms them-selves were cooked to the perfect texture.

"They know how to do food here." I thought back to the breakfast we'd had at the diner. I considered myself a pretty discriminating eater, and it was rare for me to have two meals in a day that bowled me over.

Lonna nodded, her mouth full. I studied her as I blew on a bite of mushroom. While she and Kyra Ellison may be similar in build and coloring, Lonna had kindness and genuineness, which made her much more attractive than the arrogant Kyra. To me, anyway. It figured Leonard Bowman would go for someone like that.

As I snagged another mushroom, I admitted I was torturing myself by comparing the two women. I would never be as tall, attractive or curvy as either. No one would give me a second glance if they saw me next to either of them. And as much as the thought of a secret admirer thrilled me, I had to admit it was probably Lonna who had one. Either that, or someone decided my grandfather's fortune made me attractive.

"Two cents for your thoughts?" Lonna grinned at me. She resembled a vampire with the red wine on her lips and teeth.

"I thought it was just a penny?"

She waved her hand. "Inflation."

"They're PhD thoughts. They should be worth at least a dime."

"You're evading the question."

I sighed. "Lucky in life, unlucky in love?"

"Yeah, that's self-pity." She leaned forward. "You've had a hard day. Hard month, actually."

"That's one way of putting it."

Lonna reached over to cover my hand with hers. "You're not in it alone."

At that moment, Ted reappeared with an "Aha, I thought so!" smirk. Lonna leaned back, and laughter danced in her eyes with the candlelight. As she gave her order, I glanced over the menu and picked out the first thing that sounded good: blue-cheese-stuffed beef tenderloin with port wine and mushroom sauce. It came with a salad and rolls, and my stomach growled in appreciation when my eyes landed on the dessert selection.

"Doctor Fisher?" he asked.

"I'll have the tenderloin, house salad with balsamic vinaigrette, and mashed potatoes for the side."

"Very good. I'll get these in and check on you in a little bit."

"He's cute." Lonna followed him with her eyes. "I'm a sucker for a guy with dark hair and a dimple. By the way, how are the locals treating you? Any hostility?"

"Only from the Bowman brothers. And by the way, Peter Bowman is a creep." I filled Lonna in on the almost-conversation I'd had with Louise about the kitchen. I lowered my voice. "And then he basically said he'd out you as a P.I. if you didn't go by to see him tomorrow."

She pursed her lips. "It may be a good idea. I'm sure he has a different perspective on the child disappearances."

"It sounds like he wants to get a different perspective on you. Like with your clothes off."

"Possibly."

"Now you're being evasive."

She shrugged. "Jerks are my type."

"And married men who lied about being married were mine, but I've sworn them off."

"Probably a good thing. Wives'll have you killed if you're not careful."

"Stick to the cute waiter." I looked over at Ted, who opened a bottle of wine at another table.

"I don't think he'd be into me."

Our food, carried by Ted himself as well as a regular waiter, arrived, and we didn't speak for a few minutes.

"How is yours?" I asked.

"Excellent. I'm jealous."

"Of what?"

"That you get to live up here among the rich and culinarily spoiled. And you get a kick-ass kitchen. All you need is a butler and you're all set."

I laughed. "What would I do with a butler. And 'culinarily?' Is that even a word?"

"It is now."

Before I could reply, the door opened and let in a draught. I shivered and turned to see Kyra Ellison and Leonard Bowman. Although he wore a carefully neutral expression, something about the set of his jaw and the tightness around her lips said they disagreed about something.

"Isn't that Peter's brother?" Lonna craned her neck to follow their progress to the bar. Leonard's eyes scanned the room. Kyra frowned, almost pouted.

"Yep, that's Leonard."

"Who's the sulky woman?"

"Her name is Kyra Ellison. She's the one I told you about."

"Ah, yes, the snob." Lonna studied her with narrowed eyes, then tossed her hair. Threat dismissed. I wished I felt the same.

The couple took seats at the bar, and Leonard held up two fingers. I hadn't noticed before how slender and graceful his hands were. I pictured him running them through his thick, dark hair while thinking or gripping a steering wheel as he maneuvered winding mountain roads in his rugged four-wheel drive, or running them over my—

*Stop it*, I told myself. The last thing I needed was to become attracted to another attached man. And Kyra Ellison had definitely attached herself to Leonard.

"I know that look," Lonna murmured. She held up her wineglass. "Here's to the Bowman men, unattainable yet irresistible."

"I don't know about that," I grumbled but clinked her glass with mine anyway.

"How about some chocolate? It'll cure a broken heart."

"Two nights in a row?"

"Is that what you tell your lovers?"

I couldn't help but smirk. "Depends on the lover."

"Touché."

Ted came over and took our dessert and coffee orders. I ordered a Chocolate Insanity, which proved to be a chocolate mousse filling in a cookie crust. Lonna opted for crème brûlée.

I had deliberately averted my eyes from the bar, so when I glanced up after dessert, I was surprised to see Leonard and Kyra still there. Whatever disagreement they'd had seemed to have been resolved, and they laughed as he tucked a stray ebony curl behind her ear. I tried to ignore the finger of pain that poked my heart. Robert had loved to do just that as we talked over after-dinner drinks. On the nights his wife had been out of town—they still lived together because of financial reasons even though separated, or that's what he'd told me. I'd been so gullible. I envied Leonard and Kyra their freedom. They looked like lovers who didn't care that others knew they were together.

Ted's voice startled me out of my observations. "Your check has been taken care of."

"By whom?" I asked.

"Your admirer."

"*My* admirer?" He was definitely looking at me.

"He said to tell you he hoped you enjoyed your dinner."

"Wow," Lonna said. "I wonder who it could be."

As we left, I glanced toward the bar. Leonard's eyes flicked our way, and when they met mine, my heart skipped a beat. Was that what enchantment felt like? The giddiness lasted the moment it took to walk out of Tabitha's and into the cool night air, which dissipated it like the smoke from a snuffed candle.

"Where to now?" I asked.

Lonna pulled her keys from her non-designer purse. "We have to go back to your grandfather's house sometime."

"I know." I sighed and wished we had explored the place during daylight. Who knew what might lurk there after dark?

LONNA HAD DRIVEN to the restaurant. I was concerned her Grand Cherokee would roll down the mountain after a too-fast curve, but she might as well have been behind the wheel of a sports car the way the large vehicle responded to her touch. It was a good thing she drove because her first question would have startled me into a tree.

"Have you ever thought of suing Robert?"

My heart skipped a beat. "For what?"

"Sexual harassment. He was your boss."

"Nope. It was consensual. I could never perjure myself."

"That's too bad. He deserves something for what he did to you."

"I don't know." I smiled and imagined him tucking my hair behind my ear. "I usually enjoyed what he did to me."

"That's not what I meant."

We reached the front gate, and I clicked the remote Galbraith had given me. The squat brick gatehouse stood lonely and forlorn just behind the gate on the left, and I wondered how much staff my grandfather had kept while he was alive. I remembered not being completely alone in the house with him, but I couldn't remember who exactly was there or why, which made me feel worse.

As we rounded the first curve, I caught my breath. I thought we had turned everything off, but light blazed from the windows.

## 4

"Is there a timer?" Lonna asked.

"I don't know." I was glad I didn't have to go upstairs in the dark, but I was wary of the house itself. It seemed to have a mind of its own.

"Well, I guess we'll find out." She rolled to a stop in the drive between the fountain and the front steps. "This place was built for parties," she commented as I hopped down from the passenger seat.

"That's the funny thing about it. I don't remember him ever having any."

"You said there was a ballroom?"

"Yep." I turned the key in the lock. "It's in the back on the lower level."

"That's strange."

We walked into the empty foyer. "Everything about this is strange. Did you move our suitcases?"

"No, I left them right here."

"*Bon soir, mademoiselles.*" A hearty male voice greeted us from the top of the stairs, and I jumped. When the stranger passed through the shadows, he looked like Galbraith, but the light revealed someone younger and with a lot more personality.

I challenged with as much authority as I could muster, "Who are you and what are you doing in my grandfather's house?"

"My name is Gabriel, and I am your butler."

"Butler?"

Lonna attempted to hide her laugh with a cough.

Gabriel's eyes widened. "Lawrence Galbraith didn't tell you?"

"He left that bit out."

The surprise butler shrugged, his tailored suit coat moving perfectly across his broad shoulders. I guessed him to be about forty with a wild mane of light brown hair and a twinkle in his eye. He seemed to have more of a sense of humor than most butlers—at least the ones I'd seen on television.

"I only flew in from vacation this afternoon. Otherwise, I would have met you on your arrival."

Lonna and I looked at each other, and he seemed to take our surprise as hesitation.

"Would you like my references?"

He handed me an envelope, and I gave it to Lonna. She slit it open with one long thumbnail and pulled the papers out. Gabriel lounged against the end of the banister, his arms crossed.

"It looks in order. According to this, he was contracted by your grandfather six months ago."

"Yes, that's right. Do you know when he'll be home?"

I looked up from the papers. "Never. He's dead." Saying it finally drove the words home, and my knees went weak. Until then, I'd fooled part of myself into believing he was away some-where and would return soon, and I would hear his confident step in the front hall before bolting down the stairs to meet him. A wave of dizziness washed over me, and I reached out with numb fingers to grab on to some sort of support. In an instant, Gabriel was there, his hand under my elbow, and helped me into the sitting room, where a fire blazed merrily.

"I'm sorry to hear that, Doctor Fisher. He was a very kind man."

Lonna followed us. "When was the last time you spoke with Galbraith?"

Gabriel shrugged again, his favorite gesture, I was to learn. "A month ago, perhaps two. He only wanted to confirm I was happy with the position and to let me know he'd renewed my green card. He told me there was no need to worry about anything and I was to arrive today."

"If you'll excuse me, I need to make a phone call." Lonna went into the kitchen.

"Your grandfather spoke very highly of you." Gabriel walked to the bar, which faced the fireplace on the inside wall of the room, and began to sort through bottles. "I went into the wine cellar and found some of the reds he said you favored."

"How..." All this was making my head spin. I took a deep breath and began again. "I haven't seen my grandfather since I was a teenager. How could he know what I drink?"

"Ask your friend." Gabriel inclined his head in the direction of the kitchen.

"My grandfather hired a private eye?"

Another shrug. "Perhaps. Or maybe he knew one of your colleagues."

"If he did, why didn't he tell me?"

"He was a smart, enigmatic man. He had his secrets."

I recognized the evasion and decided on a different strategy. "How did you know him?"

"I did some work for him in Europe. He liked me and invited me over."

"Your accent isn't quite British?"

"Scottish." He glanced back at me with a grin.

"I should've recognized it."

"It's become a bit muddled, I fear. I had to fake an English accent for a while to gain entry into the butler academy."

I couldn't help it—I giggled. He handed me a glass of Australian shiraz on a tray. I sipped it and studied him. He gazed into the fire, apparently lost for a moment in memory.

"Well, he's legit," Lonna said as she came through the door. She took the glass of wine he offered from the same silver tray.

"How do you know?"

"Called Galbraith. The poor man was asleep. I also checked with the National Registry of Domestic Help, and they were kind enough to verify that yes, he is a real butler with impeccable history."

"Thank you, mademoiselle."

"This just keeps getting weirder and weirder." I yawned.

"Are you ready to retire, Madame?"

"I think so." I rose with my half-finished glass of wine and headed toward the kitchen to put it in the sink. That was odd; I'd never been unable to finish a glass of wine before, but I was so exhausted I didn't care. Maybe it was the half-bottle I'd had with dinner.

"I'll take that, Doctor Fisher."

"Oh, thanks."

"I made up the bed in your old room and put your friend across the hall. Miss..."

"Marconi. Lonna Marconi."

"Thanks." I placed the glass on the tray. "I'm glad we didn't have to go upstairs in the dark."

Lonna and I climbed the stairs together. The first rooms were guest rooms. Mine was at the very end of the hall on the left. Fresh flowers stood in a vase on the bedside table, which was covered in a lacy cloth. My grandfather had decorated the room for a young girl, and it hadn't changed since my first visit twenty-something years before except the twin bed had been replaced by a queen-sized one. Stenciled pastel carousel horses careened across the top of the cream-colored walls. Each horse was different and at a different place on its pole to mimic the motion of the carousel. I picked out my favorites—a blue unicorn above the bed and a green stallion with peach-colored mane, tail and hooves over one of the French windows that opened onto the upper back balcony.

"Wow." Lonna turned in a circle, taking it all in. "Someone spent a lot of time in here decorating."

"I think he had one of the local artists do them."

We walked across the hall into the room that had once been my brother's. The jewel-toned colors were more compatible with the tastes of little boys. The walls were painted cream, but instead of carousel horses, the top border was of vines and tree branches the clever artist had intertwined with berries and pinecones so it was impossible to tell where the pattern started or repeated.

"This is incredible." Lonna was wide-eyed. The furniture, all of darkly stained wood, had brass fixtures. The bed was situated on the wall to the left facing the two windows that looked over the front lawn. No balcony. In between the windows was a large painting of a mother wolf with two cubs reclining in the brush.

"Your brother's room?"

"Yes." Andrew had loved wolves—the larger, gray kind—so my grandfather had decorated his room to be forest-like. Andrew had never seen it.

A heaviness hit my eyelids, and I bade goodnight to Lonna. I could see fresh towels in the bathroom off my room to the left, but I decided to wait until the morning to take a shower. I washed my face, brushed my teeth and crawled into the larger bed, grateful for the extra space. Part of me had been dreading sleeping in a twin bed again. My head hit the pillow, and I was asleep.

~

AT THREE O'CLOCK I was wide awake. Sure, my head ached like someone had hit me with a wine bottle, but something had awakened me, and for once it wasn't the usual nightmare. Although at that time of night, bad dreams couldn't be too far away. No, it had to be something else, something external. I listened and discerned voices coming from outside. For a moment, I dismissed it as the usual hubbub outside my apartment, but then I jerked fully awake. I was at my grandfather's manor in the middle of nowhere, Arkansas. The only people in five miles' radius were me, Lonna and the butler.

I put on my robe and slippers and tiptoed down the hall and stairs. My feet remembered the location of the creaky boards and avoided them. Instead of going through the front door, I crept through the kitchen and out the side door to the small kitchen garden.

The almost full moon illuminated the lawn and surrounding trees with weird shadows. I paused and crouched behind a hedge and tried to still the beating of my heart so my ears could pick up the voices again.

"Let Ronan make the kill," one of them, a female argued. The voice sounded familiar, and I peeked through the shrubs. A pack of wolves too large to be Arkansas red wolves or coyotes circled a deer, the animal's eyes wide with fear. Two of wolves, the largest and smallest, were black, and they were accompanied by a silver wolf and a golden one.

"He's messy."

"He's young," another replied.

Talking wolves? Was I dreaming? I shut my eyes and opened them after a few seconds. *Nope, still there.*

"I don't know, guys. We shouldn't be here."

"The old man always let us hunt here. Why should now be different?"

"His granddaughter—"

"Is a flat-chested, elf-faced ivory-tower academic who won't even know we've been here." It was the female's voice again. "If you're careful, Ronan."

The golden wolf lunged at the deer but misjudged its angle, and two of the others leapt aside as the animal crashed through their circle, hooves flying.

"We've got to figure out how real wolves do this," panted the silver one as they took chase.

Real wolves? I shook my head. It was too incredible. What were these things? And what did my grandfather have to do with them?

I waited five or ten minutes to make sure they wouldn't come back and staggered to my feet, my head still reeling from what I'd just witnessed. Especially the last comment by the gray wolf. If they weren't real wolves, what were they?

"Amazing night, isn't it?"

The voice shocked me, and I wheeled around. For a moment, it sounded like my grandfather, and I was transported back in time to my childhood as he and I stood on the balcony and found constellations. I was never good at it, my brain already bent to the reality of math and science rather than fanciful creatures in the stars.

A flicker of flame and then the smoldering ash of the end of a cigarette brought me back to the present. I coughed.

"Thought I'd light up while you thought about your answer."

Leonard Bowman stood there, leaves stuck to his sweater and jeans. The light of his cigarette and the moon flickered in his dark eyes.

"What are you doing here?"

He raised an eyebrow. "I could ask you the same question."

"It's my grandfather's house."

No answer, just a long stream of smoke.

"It's my house." The words felt awkward on my tongue, and I became aware I stood there in my nightshirt and boxers in a flimsy robe on a cool night. I shivered.

"So your lawyer says."

I tried my best imitation of a Gabriel shrug. Leonard smiled and dropped the cigarette, which extinguished with a hiss in the dew-damp grass.

"So do you always lurk in the bushes of your own house?"

My cheeks burned with the flush that crept up my neck. "Not always. Sometimes I lurk in the trees."

"I'd be careful if I were you, then." A smile flickered across his lips, but his eyes remained serious. "You never know what might be in the woods around here."

*Why am I putting up with this stupid questioning?* I took a deep breath. *Because he might know about the talking wolves.* "As long as it speaks, I can handle it."

When he moved, the moon flashed in his eyes that looked more yellow than his previous dark brown, and the rumble of a snarl vibrated the air between us. I stepped back, but stumbled, and I put my hands back to break my fall. Bad move. A sharp pain stabbed through my left wrist and up to my elbow.

"What did you say?" he growled as he loomed over me.

I tried to crawl away, but I couldn't put weight on my hand. I hissed.

"What did you hear?"

The pain clouded my awareness. I cradled my wrist to my chest, and a bright throbbing squeezed the pain up through my bicep and to my shoulder and collarbone.

Something large and covered in flannel rushed by me.

The pain eased, and I found myself curled in the fetal position on the lawn as two men wrestled not far from me. It was Leonard and Gabriel.

"Get off of me, you overgrown poodle," Leonard grunted.

"Take your filthy hide somewhere else, Lothan." Gabriel

was on top of him, hands around his throat. Both men grimaced in a feral way, and my heart beat in staccato as teeth and yellow-irised eyes flashed in the silvery light. Gabriel had tossed his flannel robe aside and wore only his white T-shirt and boxers. He had the arms of a basketball player—lean and muscular. Leonard was built more like a football player, all knotted muscle, but neither man had an ounce of fat on him. I knew I should run, but my fascination held me rooted to the spot.

"I believe the Lady of the Manor would like you to leave," Gabriel snarled.

"I'm sure she would."

Gabriel sprang away, and Leonard got up and slowly brushed his clothes off.

"Until later, milady." That last word was an insult, I knew, but I was just happy to see him walk away. The shadows of the trees swallowed him, and I turned to Gabriel, who still managed to look the distinguished butler in spite of disheveled hair and grass stains on his T-shirt.

I rolled to my feet, still holding my left wrist with my right hand.

Gabriel's expression hardened. "What happened? Did he do that to you?"

"No, no, I fell on it."

The tension on his face melted into sympathy. "Let's get some ice on that. Even so, it will probably leave a nasty bruise."

He let me lead the way inside, and I sat on the couch in the study as he fixed an ice pack out of some towels and a zip-top bag of ice.

"Thanks." Somehow sitting on the couch was soothing, a bit of normality in an otherwise bizarre night. The ice pack stung, but it quieted the throbbing.

"I wouldn't be too terribly upset with Loth—Leonard,"

Gabriel told me as he set down a cup of herbal tea and a bottle of honey.

"Why?"

"He was not entirely in control of his actions."

"What?"

"How much honey?"

"A teaspoon. But what do you mean, he wasn't entirely in control of his actions?"

"He was in a state of impaired impulse control."

"Why?" But part of me knew the answer, and it was in a place I wasn't ready to go yet.

"Can I get you anything else?"

The frustration finally kicked in. "Gabriel, sit."

He surprised me by sitting in the armchair, but he did not settle in.

"Look, it's obvious you know what's going on better than I do. Can we just chat like two normal people and forget you're the butler for a little bit?"

"I can try." He eyed me warily. I think he was surprised he had been so obedient.

"Okay, let's back up. How did you know what was going on out there?"

"I heard you cry out."

"I never cried out."

Another shrug.

"I wasn't supposed to see them, was I? And don't you dare shrug."

He sighed instead. "In time, you would have been introduced properly to them. But no, your grandfather wanted you to be sheltered at first."

"So you drugged me?"

"No, I just picked out the wine with the highest alcohol content in the cellar and hoped it would work. It did."

"Obviously. Why did he want to shelter me?"

"He knew how your brain works. He thought that, after the fire, you may not be ready to see what your mind would classify as impossible."

"But now he's dead, and I'm in the middle of something I need to be able to understand."

"You may be able to understand it better than anyone."

"What do you mean?"

"Your research."

"My research?" The cold sweat slicked the back of my neck, and I closed my eyes. *Glowing eyes in a black face. Fangs.* I shook my head to clear the images of the last night at the lab. "What does my research have to do with all this?"

"CLS." He rose from the chair. "Excuse me a moment. I have something for you."

I sipped the tea, which may have been drugged, but at that point I didn't care. Before I had been let go from Cabal Industries, I had been studying a pattern of breakouts of Chronic Lycanthropy Syndrome, a new psychological disorder of impulsivity. With the help of a historian, I had been tracing family trees and gathering family medical histories on the victims. The raw data was in the lab, and I had been running analyses that night to see if there were any patterns in the variables.

Gabriel returned with a box streaked with smoke but still intact. He set it on the coffee table by my tea.

"What are those?"

"Some of the records you were working with."

"How did you get them?"

"A friend. I cannot say any more."

I cradled my left wrist against my chest and leaned over to the box. It smelled of smoke.

"Did any of the others..." I couldn't believe anything had made it through the fire. The image of the lab as it had been the day after, all my data smoldering ash, flashed through my mind. For some reason, whatever had been entered in the computer hadn't been backed up yet, so I had lost all of it. Or at least I thought I had.

"This was the only one that survived."

I could barely make out the filing code on the side of the box. It was the most recent batch of Arkansas and Tennessee files, copies of medical records from pediatricians' offices.

"It was still on a hand truck in the hallway. My assistant hadn't entered the data yet."

"Do you feel like looking at it?"

I put my head in my hands to stop the wave of dizziness and the memories that rode it. "Not tonight. Do you have any painkillers?"

"I may. Something that will dull the pain but not upset your stomach?"

"Perfect."

He returned with a little orange pharmacy bottle and spilled out a pill. "This should help."

"Thanks."

WHEN I ROLLED over the next morning, I wasn't so sure I should've accepted the pill from Gabriel. The wine must have dulled my judgment. What was I thinking, accepting medication from a stranger, especially one who had deliberately tried to intoxicate me to sleep?

The clock said ten o'clock. Drat, I was going to miss Louise.

"Ready, sleepyhead?" Lonna poked her head around the door, which I'd left ajar. If it hadn't been for the grass stains on my feet, I would've thought the whole talking-wolf thing had been a dream. Actually, I was hoping the butler thing wasn't a dream, aside from the illegal sharing of prescriptions. The sheets needed washing.

"Gimme a few." I brushed my teeth and splashed cold water

on my face, then grabbed a T-shirt and jeans out of my suitcase. When I looked at myself in the mirror, I couldn't smirked at the resemblance to the first-year graduate student I'd been seven years before down to the "what have I gotten myself into?" look. A purple-black bruise spread almost all the way around my throbbing wrist. No watch for me today.

Damn. What *had* I gotten myself into?

# 5

---

"**B**reakfast, Doctor Fisher?" Gabriel set a bed tray on the gold-colored brass and glass table at the foot of the bed. "You dressed quickly."

He showed none of the disheveled look of the previous night. Instead of a butler's suit, he wore khaki pants and a crisp white Oxford shirt. I approved of the look. Anything more would be too formal for every day.

"How's the wrist?"

I turned the joint in question, and it protested with pain that traveled to my elbow. "Sore."

He held out his hand, and I extended my left wrist. He held it like a fragile glass, and I appreciated his cool, gentle fingers.

"Nothing broken, just bruised," was his assessment. "Good thing we got ice on it right away."

"Damn, girl, what happened?" Lonna walked into the room. She sniffed the air. "I smell bacon."

"Which I'm sure you've already had copious amounts of," I teased.

I made the quick decision not to tell her about the talking wolves or Leonard. It would make me sound nuts, and I didn't want to test my own credibility in the eyes of my friend, who thought I was close to going off the deep end anyway.

"I had a wacky dream and bruised my wrist on the night table."

She looked at it more closely. "What were you dreaming?"

"Don't remember."

"Just bruised," Gabriel repeated. "I shall set your breakfast on the table downstairs, Doctor Fisher."

"Actually, I promised to meet someone for breakfast this morning," I told him. The clock said ten fifteen. I didn't want to miss Louise.

"Should I expect you for lunch?"

Lonna shook her head. "Dinner, probably."

"Around seven, then?"

"That will be fine."

As we wound our way down the mountain in the Jeep, Lonna asked me, "So, what's up with you and the butler?"

"What do you mean?"

"He was looking at more than your wrist. And he's a cutie. Got that Sean Connery accent going on."

"Nothing."

"It just seemed like you and he had some secret."

I leaned over and put my right hand on her shoulder. "He's not going to take over your job of protecting me, if that's what you're worried about. As if I need another guardian angel."

Lonna didn't take her eyes off the road. "Just tell me if it's too much. I'll go back to Little Rock."

"Yeah, right you will."

But from the line between her perfectly arched brows and the slight pout to her lips, I could tell she was worried.

"I need you here. At least until we know whether this Gabriel guy is legit." I didn't tell her the foundation of my suspicions.

The line cleared. "Good. Then I'll drop you off at the diner, and I'll go see the charming Peter Bowman."

"Good luck. You may be the one who needs protecting."

"I've not met a man yet I needed protecting from. Usually it's the other way around."

"You've been lucky." As much as I tried not to think about Robert, there were times like now when I missed our conversations.

"You've got that look again."

"Will you just keep your eyes on the road?"

"And snappish. You were thinking about Robert."

Luckily we had reached the diner, and I didn't have to say exactly what my thoughts had been.

Instead of being greeted by Louise, I was ignored by a teenage boy with acne across his cheeks. He wiped the counter with sullen slowness.

"Where's Louise?" I sat down and picked up a laminated menu. A sticky brown coffee ring obscured the weekly list of blue-plate specials.

The boy didn't even look up. "Dunno. Got the call to come in this morning because the old lady didn't show up or call or anything."

"Oh." My heart fell into my stomach. Louise had been the only one who had spoken with my grandfather and knew what he intended. Besides Gabriel, whom I still didn't quite trust, but even he hadn't been completely informed.

The bell above the door jangled, and Sheriff Bud Knowles strode in. In spite of my disappointment over Louise, I had to hide a smile. He had the air of an old Western sheriff walking into the saloon and scanning the counter and booths for troublemakers. The change jingling in his pockets could have been spurs.

"Coffee, Terrence Junior."

The poor kid fumbled the pad he'd held poised to take my order and scrambled to pour the sheriff a cup of coffee.

"Mornin' Doctor Fisher." He tipped his hat. I hoped he mistook my smile as friendly rather than mocking. Could he not see how ridiculous he was?

"Mornin', Sheriff. How's your day going?"

"Well, aside from Miz Louise's disappearing." He cocked his head and narrowed his eyes. "You wouldn't happen to have seen anything strange on your way into town, would you?"

"Nope."

"Hear anything last night?"

My cheeks warmed, and I hoped he didn't see the flush that must have been there. "Nope. Slept straight through."

Terrence Junior set a mug of coffee by the sheriff and one for me. I gave him my breakfast order—a biscuit with jam—and fixed my coffee. When I looked up, my gaze met the sheriff's, who still studied me with suspicious creases under his eyes.

"Hear you have a butler now."

I decided to treat this as I had my dissertation defense— only answer the question, and don't volunteer anything that might get you in trouble. "Yep."

"Did you hire him?"

"Nope."

"Who did, then?"

"My grandfather."

Breakfast appeared, which allowed me to chew as I pondered how to answer the sheriff's forthcoming questions.

"Where's he from?"

"England." Okay, Scotland, but I wagered the sheriff wouldn't know the difference.

"Is he permanent?"

"Don't know yet."

Sheriff Knowles appeared to become impatient with my

lack of elaboration. "Got to find these things out, you know," he said, switching to a friendly, persuasive tone. "With all that's been going on around here, we can't be too careful."

"I agree. What do you think happened to Louise?"

The level of background noise plummeted as people paused to hear the sheriff's answer. I realized no one asked him questions—they just answered his and tried to get out of his way.

He put his coffee cup down a little too firmly, and I winced at the sharp sound. "Under investigation, young lady. Not that it's any of your business."

"Have a good day, Sheriff. Oh, and thanks for buying my breakfast." I slid the fiver he put down on the counter over to Terrence Junior. With a wink, I got up and stalked outside, my heart pounding with elation and terror, like the kid who had just gotten away with putting a whoopee cushion on the teacher's chair.

"Doctor Fisher?" The deep voice prompted a rush of adrenaline, the kind that precedes panic. I turned slowly to see Leonard Bowman.

"Mr. Bowman?"

"Doctor as well, actually."

"Oh?"

Dark circles ringed his eyes, and his hair hung in waves, still damp from his morning shower.

"Sleep in this morning?"

He blinked like he didn't understand the question. He had nothing of the angry attitude from the night before or two days previously, and now—in the full sunlight—our encounter began to feel more like a dream. Except for my wrist, which throbbed after I had thoughtlessly used that hand to open the diner door.

His sheepish demeanor didn't stop me from putting my hands on my hips and giving him my best glare. "Look, do you have something to say to me? Because, quite frankly, I have things to do, and I still need one good hand."

Instead of becoming angry, he raised his right hand to his face, placed his thumb and forefinger on his temples and massaged them. "Would you believe I don't remember much of our encounter last night?"

"What? Were you drunk? Drunk and trespassing? Or were you high?"

He put his hand down and looked around. "I have a lot to explain. Can we go somewhere?"

"What do you mean?"

"Can I buy you lunch?"

"Can you buy me lunch?" I knew it was stupid, repeating what he said, but this was a different Leonard Bowman than either the cocky young man or the rage-filled one I'd seen early that morning, and I wasn't sure what to expect.

"Please?" he begged. "I just put together who you are and what you do for a living. I'll take a look at your wrist."

"What do you mean?"

He held out his hand, and I slowly put mine in his. Like Gabriel, Leonard's fingers were cool, but roughened like he had worked hard with them. But when he turned my hand over, it was with the fingers of an expert.

"I was doing my residency in orthopedics," he explained, "when I got CLS."

My heart skipped a beat. All my better instincts told me to say no, but I couldn't resist. Plus, that biscuit hadn't been enough to satisfy my appetite.

"How about Tabitha's?"

～

THE WORLD WASN'T ready for the new breed of genetic disorders. Normally Nature seeks to advance the development of organisms. But Nature is a true lady and can admit her mistakes, one of which is that too much intelligence, opposable thumbs, and a self-centered outlook is a dangerous combination. Where Leonard Bowman fit into all this, I had no idea. But by accepting his lunch invitation, I stepped right back into that world of questions.

The walk from the town square to the restaurant gave me time to think about the first time I'd heard of CLS. And when I first met Robert. It seemed his memory would haunt me as much as my former life as a researcher. I had been twenty-seven, just out of graduate school, and was looking forward to starting my first real job. Robert, the first man I'd seen at Cabal, had been similar to Leo with dark hair, but old enough for his wry sense of humor to trace lines at the corners of his eyes.

"You the new intern?" He'd come up behind me and startled me so I almost dropped the box of books I carried. He took the load from me without asking, and all I could do was follow, openmouthed, as he led the way.

"Ah, no, it looks like you're the new epidemiologist." The lines crinkled, and I caught my breath at his smile.

"And you are..."

"I'm Robert Cannon, a geneticist, and your new boss. I'd shake your hand, but I'm carrying this ridiculously heavy load of books."

"Right. I'm Joanna."

"Fisher, as I recall. Chuck Landover's granddaughter."

"Yes." The mention of my grandfather had startled me at the time, but I forgot about it with the rush of information I'd gotten from Robert.

"So here's the deal, Fisher..." He indicated I was to precede him into a laboratory with computers on one side and a host of genetics equipment—most of which I couldn't identify yet—on the other. I held the door open and he set my box down on the table next to a computer.

"Is this my desk?"

"This is our lab. I'll show you the office later, but I thought you might like to keep your books at hand, not that you'll need them much."

"Why?"

"Because we're dealing with something new here. It's something we need your help tracing in the population so we can localize the genetic mutation."

"What does it do?" I tried to keep my excitement in check. This was just what I'd hoped for—to be on the leading edge of researching new disorders.

He leaned back and crossed his arms. "Lots of fun stuff. It causes a host of behaviors like fierce loyalty to friends, inability to understand or buy into the culture's materialistic messages, for starters."

"And physically?"

"Early appearance of secondary sex characteristics, particularly body hair on the males. But it's the psych stuff that's the most fascinating. Basic drives such as hunger, lust and sleep are assessed as extraordinarily high. Somehow these adolescents find each other, bond, and disappear for days at a time, particularly around the full moon."

"Around the what? Now I know you're kidding me."

"Ever hear of lycanthropy?"

I had, but it had been a long time ago and in a different context. "You mean, like in werewolves? Are you serious?"

"It's a true disorder. I'll have to introduce you to Iain McPherson in Scotland; he's made it his life's work. But yes, by adulthood, most of the afflicted isolate themselves from their families and all but disappear. Those who stay in society are described as wild loners."

"But isn't that rare?"

"It was. Until a few years ago."

He'd gone on to explain this lycanthropic disorder was relatively rare until the very end of the twentieth century. Previously, one case might occur in a generation and spawn a local legend of werewolves. However, we lived in the era of impulsivity, and disorders such as ADHD skyrocketed.

CLS, or Chronic Lycanthropy Syndrome, seemed to be the latest step in the evolution of impulsivity disorders, and it soon became the new diagnostic darling of the pediatrician and child psychiatrists' offices. Children displayed the full range of symptoms by early adolescence, and often those that couldn't be cured or drugged into submission would just disappear or end up in the correctional system.

My research centered on finding a common thread. I'd investigated familial patterns, but there was something missing. Why were these rare genes expressing now? An environmental toxin? A virus? Just before the lab had burned, I had acquired boxes of these children's medical records, particularly from western Tennessee and the Ozark region of Arkansas, where families of Germanic and Scandinavian descent abounded. The Scandinavian culture had the most sophisticated spiritual explanation for werewolves...and the highest incidence of CLS.

And now, here in the Ozarks, I was face-to-face with an adult CLS sufferer. I sat across from him in the booth pretending to study my menu and bit my lip to keep the questions from flooding off my tongue. *How long have you had it? When were you diagnosed? Were you a hyper kid? What illnesses did you have? Do you know anyone else with CLS?*

Instead he asked me, "What are you having for lunch?"

Luckily I'd digested the biscuit quickly. "I think I'm going to have the Turkey Cobb salad."

He raised an eyebrow.

"What?"

"Why can't you women ever eat?"

I looked up from my menu. "'Scuse me?"

"Just a salad?"

"Well, what are you going to have?"

"The steak you had for dinner last night looks good. Someone tiny and delicate like you needs to eat to keep up her strength."

Not sure if he was teasing or insulting, I returned my eyes to the menu, and my cheeks warmed again. "How do you know what I had for dinner?"

"I was here, remember?"

How could I forget? He and that witch, Kyra. Unbidden, the image came into my head of him tucking a stray curl behind her ear. And then of him standing over me as I was obviously injured. I took a deep breath to loosen the tightness in my chest, and it released a flare of anger.

"Did you want to talk to me about something, or did you just trick me into coming here to mock me?"

He sighed and rubbed his temples again, but the gesture didn't inspire the sympathy I thought he was going for. Instead, frustration curled beneath my sternum and reach into my throat. This man could have murdered me the night before. Could have but didn't. I took another deep breath and blew out slowly to calm myself.

"Look, if this isn't a good time, I can catch you later." His expression reminded me of a begging puppy.

"No, no, I'm fine. What did you want to talk to me about?"

"You're Doctor Joanna Fisher?"

"Yes. I thought we'd already established that."

"Of Cabal Laboratories?"

"*Formerly* of Cabal Laboratories."

"What happened?"

"A fire. An affair. All my data was burned, and so was I."

"I read your work on cultural patterns and CLS when I was in medical school. At that point, it was all theory, not something I planned on dealing with."

The waiter arrived. Ted, Manager, was nowhere in sight. "Are you ready, Doctor Bowman, Doctor Fisher?"

Leonard raised his eyebrow. "Word gets around."

"Apparently."

We ordered, and after the waiter brought our drinks—sweet tea for me—I asked, "Wait a second, so you didn't have CLS from childhood?"

"No. I would be much better able to control it if I had." The bitterness in his tone startled me.

"When did you get it?"

"The second year of residency at UAMS."

The door opened, and a shadow flickered over Leonard's face. I turned to face the door, but at first I couldn't make out the features of the couple who had just entered. The host greeted them, and once the door closed against the bright light of outside, I saw Lonna and Peter Bowman. He had his hand on her elbow. Leonard sank down in his seat.

"What's wrong?"

"I'm supposed to be at home watching Peter's wife. He thinks she's having an affair."

"Looks like projection to me." Already there was too much eye contact, too many casual touches.

Leonard smiled his half smile again. "She's too busy with their kid to think about an affair. He's two."

"And a terror from what I hear."

"He's not that bad, just a lot of energy."

"Not that you're biased."

Leonard's face lit with a true smile. "When I come home in the evening, he'll run full tilt down the hall and jump into my arms." He frowned and lowered his voice. "He doesn't care about what happens after he goes to bed."

"What does happen?" I leaned forward on my arms.

"You should know." Leonard's black eyes met mine. "But then again, you can't. I don't even know if I do."

"Why not?"

"It's a different state of mind. And what happens feels like dreams." A line appeared between his eyebrows as he frowned. "I try to remember them in the morning."

"But you can't." I let my breath out slowly. I had read interviews of CLS kids who had originally been diagnosed with sleepwalking, but their EEG tracings had indicated a state closer to Rapid Eye Movement sleep than to the slow wave sleep associated with sleepwalking. When questioned the next morning, they claimed to have no idea how they got where they did or why. It was a different state of mind.

So those creatures I had seen on the lawn last night had been CLS sufferers hunting—true werewolves. Gabriel had hinted, but now it made sense. Or didn't. I couldn't grasp the idea of humans turning into actual wolves.

Our food came, and I continued to glance over Leonard's shoulder at the table where Peter sat with Lonna. They had their drinks, and it seemed as though Peter liked a civilized cocktail at lunch. There was also one in front of Lonna, which surprised me because she never mixed business and alcohol. Apparently this was more than business.

"What are they doing?" Leonard still slouched in the booth so as to be out of sight.

"Talking. Drinking. Why?"

"I can't leave until they do. He might see me."

I tried not to smile at the irony of the situation. "What are you so worried about? What will he do to you if you're not there?"

"Peter is mercurial. I think that's the right word. He likes to hold our dependence on him, especially our financial dependence, over our heads."

"Wait a second, 'our'?"

"My cousin Ron also has CLS and lives with Peter."

"Both of you?"

"And we both got it last winter while we were in residency at UAMS."

"Before that, nothing?"

"Nothing. We were both always incredibly healthy."

*Incredibly healthy...* My stomach gave a lurch and I put down my fork. *Joanna, I don't know why you always get sick, and your brother doesn't,* my mother would say. *Andrew is the most incredibly healthy boy.*

*That's because he's a tough kid,* my father would add, pride in his voice. That conversation had occurred when I was six. Three years later, my "incredibly healthy" twin brother had died.

"Doctor Fisher? Joanie?"

My name snapped me back to the present. I shook my head to clear the fog of old grief. "Sorry, memories." It disturbed me that they had snuck up on me. Since the fire, only recent unhappy memories intruded on my days. Was I now to be tortured by old ones, too?

"Did you know someone with this?" Leonard frowned.

"Beyond my research subjects? I...I don't know."

*Have you ever heard of the Landover curse?* Now it was Galbraith's voice in my head. *It supposedly skips a generation. If it popped up, you'd know.*

Or would I? An incredibly healthy child who had died mysteriously of complications after an elective tonsillectomy, Andrew had always had too much energy for his own good. He wasn't dissimilar to the CLS victims I'd studied, but his problems had occurred long before the diagnosis had emerged. I filed that away in the back of my head to look into later.

"Dessert, Doctors?" the waiter asked. It was a different one with blond hair, blue eyes the color of the ocean on a clear day, and a smile that invited a response. He winked at us, his pad poised. His nametag said, "Ronald".

"Sure, Doctor." Leonard smiled. "I think that would be an excellent idea."

"Avoiding big brother, are we, Leo?"

"Always."

"No worries. I can get you out the back if needed. Who's the babe?"

Leonard looked at me. "Do you know who she is?"

"Yeah, she's a social worker from Little Rock."

"No, doofus." Ron tapped Leo on the top of his head with the pencil. "The one who's sitting with you."

Again, heat spread across my face and chest.

"Ron, this is Doctor Joanna Fisher, formerly of Cabal Laboratories and one of the world's leading researchers of CLS."

"Nice to meet you." I held out my hand and Ron shook it. His hand was warm, but also rough.

"Ah, that's who I was hoping you'd be. I've read your work and told Leo he needed to try to meet you. I'm Doctor Ronald Bowman, formerly a surgical resident at UAMS."

"And now waiting tables?" I asked, then bit my tongue. "Sorry, that was rude."

Ron's mouth twisted into a bitter smile. "That's all right. The CLS was interfering. Wouldn't do to lose it in the operating room."

I put my fork down. "Why don't you both come up to my place? I have a lot more to ask you."

Ron smiled. "Sure, when?"

"When do you get off work?"

"I've just been cut, so half an hour. Just enough time to fetch you some dessert and coffee. What would you like?"

"Chocolate. But I had that dessert last night."

"The chef does an awesome chocolate cream pie the regulars know to ask for. It's not on the menu."

"That sounds perfect. And a latté, please."

"Leo?"

"Apple pie. Plain coffee."

"Coming up."

When Ron left, the room seemed to get a little darker.

"Do you know how to get to Wolfsbane Manor?" I asked, then remembered, "Oh, yes, you do."

Leonard smiled, but with bitterness. "Will your butler be there?"

"Oh, Gabriel, I forgot." I thought for a moment. "Why should it matter?"

"Well, there was last night."

I remembered the two men locked in their wrestling match, their faces intent. "He'll have to be okay with it. We're all trying to solve the same puzzle."

"Fair enough. I knew you'd need more than a salad."

"Leonard, are you teasing me?"

He smiled without bitterness this time. "I can't let my charming cousin have all the fun. And call me Leo."

I smiled back. This could end up being a fun afternoon.

## 6

The caffeine and sugar from the chocolate pie and latté buzzed happily through my bloodstream as I rode up the mountain in the back of Ron's compact car. Lonna still had the car keys with her, so I left a note on her Jeep, and the guys brought me home. Leo had originally offered me the front seat, but I was the shortest, so it made sense for me to take the back. After about ten minutes, the guys seemed to forget I was there.

The situation made me think back to graduate school. Most of my friends had been men, and I'd learned to fade into the background and listen to them tease. The differences between the thought processes and communication styles of men and women had always fascinated me. Now I had to learn a whole new vocabulary—that of the werewolves.

Leo and Ron bantered about women of their past, but when they slipped into a debate about a certain reconstructive surgical procedure in the most recent issue of JAMA, I became bored and watched the world out the window.

"It's been a long time since I've used the road to get up here," Ron commented as we pulled up to the gate, which was closed. Lonna had the remote, too, so I hopped out and pushed the buzzer.

"Wolfsbane Manor." Gabriel's clipped accent came through with some static. "State your business."

"It's me, Gabriel, and I have guests."

"Very good, Madam."

I hopped back in the car as the gate swung open. Ron maneuvered the car up the long drive to the circle in front of the house. Gabriel had cleaned out and turned on the fountain, and the water droplets sparkled in the sunlight. For a moment, all felt right with the world, but then Ron's comment about not having used the road to approach the manor jolted me back to the present sticky situation.

"How long have you been coming up here?"

"Months." Gabriel appeared in the door, which opened without a creak. He'd been busy.

"Gabriel," Ron said with no trace of his former joviality.

"Ronald. Good to see you again."

But it obviously wasn't.

Leo frowned. "Gabriel? When did you get back in town?"

"Yesterday. Apparently you don't remember our conversation last night."

"What conversation is that?"

"The one during which I taught you a lesson about threatening ladies."

"I don't remember."

"You were fresh off the hunt."

Now I was the one rubbing my temples. It seemed impossible the violent, angry Leo of the night before could be the same affable chap who had just bought me lunch. The conflict had slipped my mind even though my wrist throbbed when I moved it in the wrong direction, and most directions were wrong. It seemed like everywhere I turned today there would be some sort of surprise waiting. I just didn't want to end up with a fight on my hands, but Leo didn't look like he wanted one. His frown was of concentration and frustration.

"Would you care for a drink?" Gabriel asked.

"I'd love one." Ron bounded up the stairs.

"I need one," Leo added and followed. Gabriel held the door open for them but moved to block me.

"A moment, Madam."

"Okay."

"The drinks are on the bar in the den," he called over his shoulder, then shut the door.

"What is it?"

"As you can tell, there is some, ah, tension between us."

"No shit." I crossed my arms and tried to look as stern as I could even though I barely reached his shoulder. "Tell me why?"

"We were part of the same pack. There was a falling out. I became a solitary hunter."

Gabriel's revelation jolted me.

"You're one of them, too?" I whispered.

He looked at his feet. "I thought you might have guessed after last night. My case was from childhood. Your grandfather had hired me for research, and as domestic help as a cover-up."

"So why are you still here?"

He inclined his head toward the inside of the house. "The same reason they are, I suspect. I know of your research. And you need the help around here. It's a big house."

"Fine, you can stay." I put a finger on his chest and tried to look intimidating. "But no more funny stuff. At the first sign of something suspicious, you're out of here. Got it?"

Gabriel nodded solemnly. "Yes, Madam."

"Why was my grandfather interested in werewolves?" I asked. "Don't tell me he was one, too."

"He had the lycanthropic energy about him, and he under-stood the condition, but he never changed. He told me he was working on a cure, and I became a willing subject. It was soon after that he disappeared."

"What do you know about that?"

"The same facts you do: he went on an ill-fated canoe trip. I was out of town working out immigration issues, so I wasn't here."

I glanced toward the windows to the den. "Do you think they had something to do with it?"

"Perhaps we should question these two and see what we can learn."

"Sure, why not? Although... You haven't put anything in the drinks, have you?"

He smiled, and wrinkles appeared around his eyes. I realized he had seen and done a lot more than he'd let on, and I mentally added about five years to his estimated age. "No, Madam. I am counting on the truth being in the bottle, as they say."

We entered the den. Ron and Leo sat on the sofa and sipped beers.

"Done with your conference?" Leo asked.

"Yes, he was just filling me in."

"Must've been quite a fill-in. Ron's already on his second beer."

Gabriel took the first bottle—which Ron had put on the sea chest without a coaster—into the kitchen. I poured a glass of white wine from the bottle that chilled in the ice bucket along with the beers.

"So you guys are doctors?"

"*Were* doctors." Ron waved his beer in a dismissive gesture. "We could be saving lives, but we're stuck here, in the middle of the backside of nowhere."

Gabriel came in with a plate of assorted cheeses and crackers. "Doctor Fisher doesn't need to hear a reprise of this old conversation. She has some questions for you."

As much as I appreciated his interrupting the rant, I resented him taking the lead just as Lonna had earlier. Did I really seem so incapable of gathering my own information?

I took a deep breath. "Ron, when were you diagnosed with CLS?"

The lycanthrope in question sat back and sipped his beer. "I don't remember exactly when I was diagnosed, but I knew when I had it."

Leo sat forward and laced his fingers over his bottle, his head down. Dark brown curls obscured his face. "The night of Temmerson's dinner."

Ron looked sick to his stomach. "The chief surgeon Alfred Temmerson had us residents over to his house. I didn't have a date, so I brought Leo."

I listened, fascinated. No one had ever told me the story from the first-person adult's perspective.

Leo had been out sick that day, as he mistook the early signs of CLS infection for the flu, which he assumed he acquired from the flu shot he'd gotten earlier that week. Ron also wasn't feeling great, so the cousins decided to go to Fred Temmerson's dinner together in case Ron needed Leo as moral support and chauffeur. When the cousins arrived, they were greeted by the very attractive Lisa Temmerson, who was home from college and helping her father host the dinner. Her mother had died from breast cancer the year before. The moon was waxing, only a day away from full, and as it rose, Ron and Leo felt its charm —and those of the young Lisa.

Lisa took their coats and told the young men to loosen their ties.

"We're being casual here tonight," she told them with a wink of her green eyes. For an irrational moment, Ron wanted to punch Leo. He shook the feeling off and accepted the glass of red wine another resident offered him.

By this point, both Ron and Leo felt as though they were

floating in a dream with events happening in illogical sequences. Dinner—catered barbecue—was served from the kitchen, and the residents ate on paper plates on their laps and pretended not to wonder who would screw up first. Lisa struck up a conversation with Leo, who was quite glad to entertain the pretty girl, particularly as he was the only non-surgeon physician there. The other surgery residents had brought girlfriends, boyfriends or spouses—none of whom had doctorates in anything with the exception of a psychologist who dated one of the female surgery residents.

"Nice place," Leo commented to Lisa. He remembered a few more details than Ron but wasn't sure how their conversation went, only that she made a comment about her mother and left in tears. The rest of the memory spun out in slow motion as he watched his cousin's career crash and burn.

Ron glared at Leo. "What did you say to her?"

"Nothing." Leo, hurt and surprised, became defensive. "She's still upset about her mother."

"I'm going to find her. No reason for you to make her cry."

"I didn't make her cry." Leo grabbed Ron's arm. "What's gotten into you?"

"Nothing. I wouldn't have brought you along if I'd known you'd be hitting on Fred's daughter."

"I'm not hitting on her."

Ron jerked his arm out of Leo's grasp. "You're going to take advantage of her, and I'm not going to let you."

By this time, their voices were raised so the other residents could hear them, and the hum of conversation halted.

"Ron, calm down."

But Ron, drunk on the combination of the CLS virus coursing through his veins, alcohol, and the innocent beauty of a young woman, didn't heed him. He balled his hands into fists.

Somehow they ended up in the kitchen with the psychologist, who had been trying to get Leo's attention.

Ron's pupils dilated and contracted, and his breaths came in ragged gasps. "He needs to go to the hospital," the psychologist said. "And I think you need to go, too."

"Why?" Leo's head spun and spots swam in front of his eyes. "I've only got the flu."

"I think he's got something more." The young man's intense gaze anchored Leo's. "I think he has CLS."

"What?" Leo vaguely remembered something in his pediatrics class, but he couldn't pull it into conscious thought. He leaned on the kitchen table for support, and the painful spot where the edge bit into his palm became his center of focus.

"Chronic Lycanthropy Syndrome. He's displaying the classic symptoms. The adult version."

"CLS?"

"Too fast, too fast," Ron moaned. At that moment, Lisa walked in. Leo, hyper-aware of her, shot a nervous glance at Ron.

"My father wants to know if everything's okay."

"I think you'd better go, Lisa." There was steel in the psychologist's voice, and she took a step back, her eyes wide.

"Is he okay?" She pointed to Ron, then looked at Leo. "You're a doctor, too. Can't you do something for him?"

"Not right now," Leo said with a sigh. "The best I can do is get him home. Please thank your father for a lovely evening."

Lisa smiled, and her left cheek dimpled. "I will. Would you like my number?"

"No!" Ron lunged at Leo, who jumped out of the way. Ron missed and tumbled into Lisa, and they ended up on the floor. Ron pressed his lips on hers and mumbled through the kiss, "No, won't let him take you, won't let him have you! Mine."

Lisa screamed.

Before the psychologist and Leo could pull Ron off the girl, her father and the other residents ran into the kitchen. The male residents managed to get Ron into Leo's car, but it took all four of them plus Leo and two male significant others. By that time, Ron was delirious, ranting about women and the moon and the sweet, hot blood in her kiss. Leo took him to the hospital, where he stayed under observation in the psych ward. The ER doctor took one look at Leo and confined him too, just in case it was something catching. Both cousins were put under respiratory contagion restriction, and all Leo could remember about that week was people in "space suits" coming to check on him.

All Ron could remember was a sense of burning shame as he recalled making a fool of himself in front of his residency director and his beautiful daughter.

I sat there, the wineglass forgotten in my hand, after the cousins told their story and tried to make sense of what it could mean. One of the frustrating things about research is finding data contradictory to your hypotheses.

People weren't supposed to be diagnosed with CLS as adults.

CLS sufferers weren't supposed to turn into werewolves and go hunting on one's lawn at night, and they weren't supposed to sit in one's den and tell you about embarrassing dinner parties while sipping their beers.

"So you lost your residency position?" I asked.

Ron hung his head. "They allowed me to resign. For medical reasons."

"And you, Leo?"

"I stuck around for another month, but it was too hard." His black eyes flashed under heavy brows. "The impulses got to the point where I had a hard time controlling them around patients, especially female patients."

"So we came up here," Ron added. "Peter took us in. I got a job in town as a waiter. Leo helps around the house."

"It's big enough, and Marguerite's no housekeeper."

"No, she's a French princess."

"With a cad for a husband," I added.

Instead of jumping to the defense of their benefactor or agreeing with me, Ron and Leo sat in awkward silence.

"They may agree, but they won't bite the hand that feeds them," Gabriel pointed out.

"Better that than living as a servant for pay," Leo snarled. "Lab rat."

"Charles wished it."

Again, my grandfather's name.

"Do you guys know what happened to him?" I asked.

Ron shook his head, but it was Leo who spoke. "We know as much as the sheriff. I can show you where they found his canoe."

"Really?" The thought of being out in the woods with no telling what was watching me sent a shiver down my spine, but I didn't want to show them I was frightened.

Ron leaned forward. "You don't have to if you don't want to."

"Maybe you'll see something we missed," Leo added.

"You looked?" I pictured the animals circling the canoe, sniffing the blood, and this time, I shuddered.

"He was good to us," Leo said. "He let us hunt here, and he would have us over for dinner when we were bored with Peter's domestic drama."

"But if you'd rather not go, we understand," Ron broke in. "I can see you're a city girl."

I met his eyes in a challenge. "I was running through these woods before Crystal Pines was even dreamt of. Take me to the crime scene."

"Aye, there was a crime," Gabriel murmured. "We just don't know what, exactly, it was."

LEO AND RON led the way down the steep path to the river. Wolfsbane Manor stood at the crest of the hill. On one side, the estate sloped gently toward the subdivision. On the other, the much steeper grade prevented development without major blasting. My grandfather had built a boathouse on the river when I was little, and he kept his kayaks and canoe in it. That way he didn't have to haul them down the path, although he was in good-enough shape to do so.

We could have driven the long way around back through town, but Ron and Leo assured me the trail would be quicker, if steep. As we walked along, I remembered skipping down this path with my grandfather, who never admonished me to hurry up, slow down, or do all those other things the adults in my life lived to fuss at me for doing or not doing. He let me go at my own pace, slower with my little legs, and we would explore the woods together. He had infinite patience with my questions about bugs or leaves or clouds. From what Galbraith had told me, he later enjoyed reading my own answers to the puzzles of what CLS is and where it comes from. At that moment, past and present merged, and it was almost as though I could turn around and see him, his craggy face bent in a smile he only showed to me.

"Never be afraid to ask questions, Joanna," he told me. "Just realize some of them take more work to answer than others."

We walked in silence through the dappled sunlight, and I searched for anything that might be familiar. Kids notice all kinds of things: rocks, trees, logs. Everything had changed. And nothing had. Instead of being dumped off for the summer by my mother so she could jet off to Europe with the other doctors' ex-wives for Parisian shopping trips and get her nails done by the pool without a kid underfoot, I had been dumped by my boss and fled out here for lack of anything else to do.

Rather than missing Andy—which I still did, but he was more a shadow of the past than a real person to me now—I ached for my grandfather's calm and wisdom. I especially wanted to ask him about his studies, how close he'd gotten to a cure, and how we could get it to the people who needed it like Leo, Ron and the others. And why he had never told me of his interest. That hurt most of all.

*But you were the one to cut off contact with him*, the little guilt voice told me.

*I didn't cut it off. It faded away.* But I knew the voice was right. Maybe he had waited for me to contact him again, or maybe we were both so busy with our work that reestablishing contact became a task for some undetermined "later," a time that would never come now.

The path leveled out, and we had to be careful not to trip in the grooves that mountain water runoff had created in the soil. I could hear the river more clearly now and knew we must be close to the boathouse. I rubbed a tear off my cheek before the guys could see it.

"We know he started out here," Leo said as he held a tree branch aside. The boathouse, a ramshackle wooden box with a tin roof, stood over a calm spot out of the way of the main flow of the river. The only way in was to use a rope that hung on the outside to open the garage-door-type mechanism.

The boathouse still held two kayaks, both molded and with chipping orange plastic. Their oars dangled on fraying rope beside their shelves. I noticed someone had put the canoe back, and it looked like it had been recently painted. The shiny metal oar sat in the seat where someone had tossed it after they brought it back.

"That's all they found?"

"That and some clothes," Ron replied. "It had rained, so any footprints had been washed away."

"And scents," Leo added.

Something didn't add up. "It wasn't like him to go out if the weather was going to be bad. Let's go to where the canoe was found."

We closed the boathouse back up. Sure, it wasn't exactly secure, but no one had ever bothered it before.

We walked along the bank of the river, where the path had been partially eaten away by the landscape's natural shifting as well as trees that had been uprooted. We sometimes had to climb over or under logs and jump over puddles. My legs ached by the time we reached a spot about a mile downstream from the boathouse. I had tried to keep up a regular exercise regimen while at Cabal, but the past four weeks of self-pity and isolation had taken their toll on my muscle tone. The two men showed no sign the trip was anything but a nice afternoon stroll.

Leo pointed to a large, pitted, dark gray boulder that jutted into the river on the other bank. "It was about here. They found the canoe wedged against that rock. The clothes were farther downstream on this side."

Ron continued, "The theory was that whoever did this had tried to push the canoe off so it would float downstream, but it got stuck. Why anyone would want to harm Charles is beyond me. Did you know him well, Joanie?"

"No. I wish I had known him better." I wished he had told me we were working on the same problem.

We circled the spot in wider and wider arcs until we found ourselves at the edge of the woods. I sat on a log, looked around, and tried to see it as my grandfather would have. The guys continued to search, and I wished for a moment that I could see the world through their eyes and noses.

My mind drifted back to lunch at Tabitha's. I couldn't understand how Ron worked in a restaurant with his extra sharp senses. The trash cans must've tortured him. I shook my head. That train of thought wouldn't get me anywhere, and I doubted Ron wanted me to try to empathize with him. His resentment kept him going. Leo had what? His nephew?

I brought my mind back to the present. I studied each tree and shrub and took in the texture of the bark, the spread of the branches. The water rippled and ruffled against the riverbank, and I noticed a tree that tipped out—a drunken sailor looking for a quick drink of water, my grandfather would have said. Its roots pulled from the bank, and tan mud clung to them. Lichens had sprouted along the trunk. Fairy steps.

I smiled and walked over to the tree. Grandfather had always loved to turn our walks in the woods into a magical journey, and when I was here year after year, we'd visit old haunts with whimsical names like Fairyland and Smurf Hollow. I could imagine lithe sprites tiptoeing up the stairs and pausing in the hollow that gaped toward the sky. The jagged edges of the branches had pulled away like large wooden spikes, and something green and silver winked at me from inside. I checked for snakes and biting insects, then reached for it. It took a moment to work my fingers down into the hollow and tease out the pendant on a tarnished chain. A silver cat with emerald eyes sparkled in the sunlight.

"Miskha?" I whispered.

## 7

The silver and emerald cat charm lay heavy in my hand, but I didn't know if its weight came from the metal itself or the memories it carried. I couldn't help but remember the first time I'd seen it—also during a time of loss and grief.

Grandfather and I had gone walking in town one Sunday morning. I was still dressed in black, the dress Mother had gotten me for Andy's funeral, and even though it had a full skirt —my favorite kind to twirl in—I wasn't feeling up for a good twirl or laugh. Grandfather had been very patient with me that summer. I didn't know, but my parents were working through divorce proceedings while I played in the Ozarks, and my grandfather had a sense things may even be worse when I got back.

"You're walking slow today, Joanna," he said.

"These shoes pinch."

"The way you're walking reminds me of a cat. They always pad on their toes, you know."

"I know." I wasn't in the mood to discuss cats since my mother would never let me have a kitten.

"And if you're lucky, they wink at you."

"Cats don't wink." I had read all about cats and knew their facial expressions weren't the same as people's.

"That's what the books say, but they never asked a cat."

"How would you ask a cat?" The thought of talking felines tugged me away from my sorrow for a moment.

"Sometimes you just need to sit down with them and let them tell you in their own time."

"Cats don't talk."

"They usually don't want to. They find people dull and boring."

That coaxed a smile from me. I tended to find people dull and boring too. Books were much better companions.

"Now look at this little lady." We stopped at a jewelry store window. The shop was closed, but in one of the display cases, a silver cat charm with slanted oval emerald eyes winked at us in flashes of green light. "Would you say she doesn't wink?"

"I guess not."

"When the store is open on Tuesday, I'll come back and get her, and you can keep her here."

"Why can't I take her home?"

His brows bent as he pondered how to tell a nine-year-old her mother would always try to take away whatever she valued. "Because she's an Ozark cat. She'll get lonely in the city. She needs to be up here where there are red wolves and other wild things."

"How do you know?"

"Because she told me. But she'd be happy to be your friend and protector while you're here."

"Oh. Okay."

The following Tuesday, Mishka the silver cat came home, and whenever I visited, she would always be there around my neck on a silver chain. I hadn't seen her in years.

~

"HELLO, MISHKA." As I turned her, she winked at me with her emerald eyes. Other than being a little tarnished, she looked the same, like she'd been polished just before being left outside.

Ron came over. "What did you find, Joanie?"

I stuffed the charm in my pocket. "Nothing." I knew this was a message from my grandfather, and I didn't want to talk about it until I could figure out what it meant.

"Still nothing." Ron's scowl reminded me of my grandfather's. "Happy now?"

"Yes, thank you. I have a much better idea of what happened."

~

LONNA RETURNED JUST before we sat down to dinner. While Gabriel cooked, I asked the guys about my grandfather. I was careful to refer to him as Charles Landover to put some distance between me and their memory of him so they'd feel comfortable sharing with me. I really wanted to know if he'd ever mentioned a family curse or his research on it. They repeated conversations, and we analyzed them until nothing made sense anymore. I had the feeling there was something they weren't telling me, but I couldn't tease it out of them. Occasionally Leo's gaze would catch mine, and our eyes would lock for a moment longer than necessary. Ron always looked away immediately. I figured he must still feel shame over his behavior when he came down with CLS and wondered if I should apologize for having him talk about it.

A timid knock on the front door broke our concentration. There was Lonna, and I didn't need to have a werewolf's nose to tell what she'd been up to.

Ron wrinkled his nose. "Sir Peter's peter strikes again. I guess he won't be making any more babies with Marguerite tonight."

Lonna shot a scared look into the den and raced up the stairs to her bedroom.

I called up after her, "Don't be too long. Dinner's about ready."

"I'm not hungry." I could hear tears in her voice. What the hell could she be crying about? Had they already broken up? I'd tried to warn her about the perils of messing with a married man.

"Suit yourself." With a shrug, I walked back into the formal dining room, which could also be reached through the front hall. It had a view through French doors of the mountain vista, and I took a deep breath and basked in the twilight scenery. Green waves of mountains faded to purple in the distance and broke under a pink and orange sky. I took another breath, slowly, in through the nose and out through my mouth and tried to block the memory of Lonna in the café with Peter. Involved with a married man. Had she not paid attention at all? At the end of the day, they always go back to their wives and tots and leave you in the cold. Even if they do lie and tell you they're separated.

"Is everything all right, Madam?" Gabriel carried a silver tureen redolent with the smells of savory herbs, onions, garlic and red wine into the room. He put it on the table, which was set with fine cream-colored porcelain plates on burgundy table linens.

He gestured to the tureen. "Rabbit stew. It's one of your grandfather's recipes."

"I'm fine, I guess." I tried to calm my roiling emotions, which bubbled like the stew. I had to admit some of the conflict came from the unfulfilled sexual tension bursting between me and the werewolf men. Something about them was so primal and untamed, and the fact they hated it made it even more alluring. I didn't think I'd be able to feel those impulses again since Robert had broken my heart.

Gabriel opened his mouth, then shook his head and went back into the kitchen.

I turned back to the mountain vista and tried to imagine standing there with a husband or lover. Maybe that was it—jealousy. All Lonna needed was a glance, and any man was hers. I could risk career, sanity, everything, and it was never enough. I'm sure Kyra had the same talent, but at least Lonna wasn't a bitch about it.

I closed my eyes and breathed deeply again. That line of thought wasn't getting me anywhere. In the scientific world, solving a puzzle might take years, but at least it had a solution somewhere that could be found by breaking the problem into little manageable bits. In the world of emotions and people, things were never simple.

"Full moon tonight," Gabriel commented as he returned and poured the wine. I jumped and opened my eyes. The sky had darkened, and the first few stars—planets, I guess—shone forth.

"I guess the boys will have to run." I had known that, but my memory wouldn't tell me why it was important beyond the significance to the werewolves.

"They already have."

"Oh." A pang of disappointment stabbed my chest. "I'll see if Lonna wants to join us."

The upstairs hallway was dark, but the light in Andy's—*I mean Lonna's*—room was on, the door cracked.

"Knock knock," I called.

"Come in."

Steam from Lonna's recent shower made the air warm and humid, and the citrus-coconut scent of her shampoo hung in the air. I walked through the room to the bathroom door, which was ajar. She stood by the sink and toweled off her long, luxurious dark brown hair.

"The guys—Ron and Leo—left."

"Good. I can come down to eat."

"Why didn't you want to before?"

"New people. I've had enough of strange men today."

I raised my eyebrows but resisted the retort that came to mind. Instead I asked, "Was Peter able to give you any insight into the missing children?"

"No, but he did fill me in on the families that were here, specifically which ones fought the development."

"Does he think the two are connected?"

"He doesn't know. But at this point, everyone is a suspect."

"Even him?"

She ran a comb through her hair. "Even him. You know the saying, keep your friends close and your enemies closer."

I bit my tongue over the reply that she seemed to have kept him close enough that afternoon. Instead I said, "I'll let you get dressed."

I made my way down the stairs and paused by the front door. I don't know what I was hoping to hear, but I could only make out the typical night sounds. I imagined what it would be like to shed human responsibilities for a few hours, to run under the moon and stars through the wild hills with the pack.

I shivered. Would it all fall away, the grief over my grandfather's strange disappearance, the guilt that blossomed at the thought of Louise going missing that morning, and the bitterness and anger over Robert's betrayal? All those things whirled around in my head, a miserable fog that weighed heavily on my heart. Ah, to be rid of that for even a few moments. A tear slid down my cheek, and I took a deep breath so sadness wouldn't overwhelm me. Even with two guardians in the house, loneliness crushed my heart.

I SWIRLED the red wine around in my glass as Lonna recounted what she'd learned from Peter. The alcohol warmed me from the center out and loosened some of the tension in my chest. A good fruity Merlot, it paired well with the rabbit-leek stew and the crusty French bread, which Gabriel had somehow found out I loved and which he had picked up at the bakery in town that afternoon.

Most of the settlers of Piney Mountain were of German and Scandinavian stock, and not much had changed due to the community's isolation until the weekend commuters had discovered the joys of clean air and mountain living. The town's resistance to being incorporated into Crystal Pines had been led by three families: the Van Dorens, the Schmidts and the Jorgens. Honey Jorgen was Louise's daughter, and her son— Louise's grandson Johnny—had been the second to disappear. Eleven-year-old Simon Van Doren had been the first.

"How did the developers explain that one?" I asked. "It seems the connection is obvious."

Gabriel used tongs to refill the bread basket with fresh, hot bread slices. "It snuffed the resistance, that's certain. Suddenly the families who'd been here for generations were more willing to sell their land and get out. Your grandfather talked about it often."

"And the ones who moved in haven't lost any kids?"

Lonna took a piece of bread. "I pressed Peter for more information..."

The angry little voice in my head broke in, *Into the couch in his office?*

I shushed it. "And?"

"He said they just took it as a sign they were meant to be here, and the land was supposed to change hands now for a new era."

"How pompous!" Wine sloshed in the glass as I set it down. "He'd be great in politics."

Gabriel looked up from the bread. "Worse arguments have been made for relieving people of their birthrights. This used to be Native American country before the settlers came through."

"Good point. So he couldn't come up with any good explanation either?"

"No, only a strange one. The Piney Mountain residents seem to feel the developers have brought an evil spirit upon them. Did you have any luck with Louise?"

"No." I lowered my eyes. "I didn't get to talk to her."

"What happened?"

"She didn't show up for work today. The sheriff didn't know anything, either."

"He wouldn't," Gabriel muttered.

"Why didn't you say something before now?" Lonna's tone accused me of a grave sin of omission, so I decided to commit one and not tell her about the CLS victims in our midst.

"I got a little distracted, okay? Leo and Ron knew my grandfather, and they'd seen the spot where he disappeared. They took me there."

"Did you find anything?"

I lied. "No. But at least I got a mental picture of the crime."

"Some of us can do our jobs without getting distracted by a cute piece of ass."

"And some of us can do our jobs without sleeping with one."

We locked eyes. Gabriel cleared the bowls and beat a hasty retreat to the kitchen.

Lonna broke the silence. "I come up here to protect you, and this is the thanks I get?"

"Oh, that's rich." I threw my napkin down. "Since when

does protecting me entail getting into the first pair of trousers you come across?"

"I wouldn't have if I'd known about Louise."

"Not like we could do anything anyway. The sheriff has his eyes on us. He's not the only one."

"Your job was to get information from the locals." She pitched her voice low and dangerous. "I wouldn't have spent so much time with Peter if I'd known you couldn't even manage that today. I was going to interview Ron and Leo tomorrow."

"What is my job, Lonna? I. Have. No. Job. I have no boyfriend. I have no ability to find either right now, not until I figure out what happened to my grandfather."

"Ladies, would you like dessert?" Gabriel came in with three dishes of chocolate mousse on a silver tray. His eyes begged for us to be finished.

"I'm done." Lonna slowly folded her napkin and placed it on the table. "I'll be upstairs reviewing my notes on the missing-children case if anyone needs me."

I put my head in my hands as I listened to the angry click of her heels on the hardwood floor. "I think I need something stronger, Gabriel."

"Yes, Madam. An Irish coffee, perhaps?"

"Decaf. I'll be on the balcony."

The motion-sensor light clicked on as I opened one of the French doors and slipped outside. The house was built on the mountainside, so the ballroom sat on the lower level in the back with a patio under the balcony that could be used even in the rain. The night was quiet as though the hills slumbered, and the river murmured. An owl hooted somewhere in the woods, and then a howl broke the stillness.

The bone-piercing cry chilled me to my marrow, and I didn't see the wolves in my mind's eye, but rather another presence, this one infinitely menacing and ready to snatch up victims without notice. I wondered at this and at the fight Lonna and I had just had. It wasn't like either of us to confront the other. Something about this place was unsettling. Too many had gone missing. What could be out there?

"Your coffee, Doctor Fisher."

"Thank you." Before he could step away, I asked, "Gabriel?"

"Yes, Madam?"

"What's out there? The wolves, I know, but I heard something else."

"These hills are full of tales, Madam. Perhaps it was the evil spirit of which Ms. Lonna spoke."

I shivered as the realization of what we'd planned to do that night hit me. "Lonna had wanted to go and see if she could catch whatever's taking the children in action. After hearing that cry, I'm glad we fought. Maybe she's forgotten."

"I wouldn't recommend going out clothed only in human flesh, not on the night of a full moon." Gabriel took a sip of his coffee, and I wondered what he could see out there in the gloom, what he could smell with his ultra-sensitive nose. "There is old energy in these hills. And old creatures."

"And the boys are out there hunting?"

"They are with their pack and are therefore protected."

"I hope so. Why don't you go?"

"I don't feel the need. Not tonight. Being near them helps me to stifle my own desires."

"Why?"

"I have no pack."

"That makes two of us." I noticed he held a glass mug of Irish coffee as well. I didn't care. "Cheers. To us lone wolves."

"Cheers, Doctor Fisher."

I grinned up at him over the rim of my glass mug. "Perhaps that's not such a bad thing."

His elegant lips curled into a smile. "Perhaps not."

⁓

I LEANED AGAINST THE DOORFRAME. In spite of my quivering rage, it didn't rattle, so I had to satisfy myself with glaring into the gloom instead.

"Well?"

"Well, what?" came from the lump on the bed.

"Did you find out anything else that was useful?"

"Bug off."

"You're supposed to be a P.I.," I reminded her.

"Remember the Oliver case?"

"The one where you found out it was the teacher abusing the child, not the father?"

"Yes. Peter knows it. One of his law firm partners defended the guy."

I snorted "You're not convincing me he's a worthy person if he was with a firm that defends perverts."

"He said my work was brilliant, that he couldn't have built a case against it." The lump rolled over. Her eyes glowed in the darkness, and I stepped back. "I just wanted the appreciation not to end. Do you know what it's like when your purpose, your career, is affirmed like that?"

"Can't say that I do."

"Oh, Joanie, I'm so sorry." She burst into tears.

"Sleep it off, Lonna." I sighed and closed the door behind me.

⁓

AND WOKE UP.

Dream analysts say every character in one's dreams symbolizes some aspect of the self. The Lonna in the dream was the part of me that had sold out, that had turned tail and run before I could discover the truth. I'd felt too ashamed to protest my termination because they'd all suspect I had been having an affair with my boss. Instead, I'd left the appeal to him...and he'd failed me.

"Nothing like the honesty of the mind at three a.m." I strained to hear the sounds of the night. Nothing. No voices, no wolves. Not even the bone-shuddering cry.

I rolled over to go back to sleep, but my eyes wouldn't close. I only stared into the darkness, curled into a ball against a sense of *wrongness*. Then grunts and the swish of something being dragged from the bottom of the driveway paralyzed my stomach while my heart thudded against my ribs. Now I recognized the emotion. It was the same feeling I'd had the night of the fire, the one that urged me to hurry, to find something meaningful in the data as *something* closed in on me.

The same feeling I'd had the night Andrew died.

Footsteps, a muffled exclamation, then the front door opened and closed. I rose, splashed some water on my face, and put on a robe.

"Doctor Fisher?" Gabriel stood at the door. At first it looked like his shirt was stained black, but the smell told me it was blood, and he was soaked with it.

"Gabriel, are you hurt?"

"No, Doctor, but she is, and she's asking for you."

"Lonna?"

"No." He took a deep breath. "Louise."

I shoved past him, heedless of the smear it would leave on my robe and ran downstairs.

Louise lay on the sofa. I couldn't see her wounds, but I could smell the burns, the blood. Her immaculate coffee-shop uniform had been torn and stained with grass, with the rust of old blood and the crimson of new, and with smoke. Her face, pinched and white, strained with every rasping breath.

"Louise!" I wanted to hold her hand but I was afraid to hurt her. She grabbed mine and struggled to articulate something. It re-started the throbbing pain in my wrist, but I didn't care.

"Lay still," I told her. "Gabriel, have you called 911?"

"Yes, Madam. The paramedics are on the way."

Louise squeezed my hand. "The black wolf..."

My heart hammered and skipped more than one beat as adrenaline poured through me. "What black wolf?"

"It. It."

"Hush now, you've got to save your strength."

She shook her head. "It knows."

Gabriel took her other hand. "She shouldn't be speaking. Her pulse is faint."

She still struggled to speak. "Beware. It knows."

A knock at the door. Gabriel ran to answer it.

Louise convulsed one, two, three times, then shuddered and lay still.

"No, Louise, *no!*" I didn't want to believe it. The tears came then, racking sobs. Strong hands separated mine from hers and guided me to the armchair. I couldn't stop as the guilt welled up. I should have searched for her. Should have done something.

"She's expired," Gabriel told the paramedics. They started CPR anyway and brought out the paddles. I couldn't see what they did—I only heard the noises as they tried to revive her. And then the muffled curses and uncomfortable silence as they failed.

Gabriel held my shoulders, his strong grasp two points that anchored me to reality as sobs subsided into hiccoughs, but the tears still flowed. I couldn't see the paramedics, merely blurs of blue uniforms. They parted for a figure in khaki.

"Well, Doctor Fisher," drawled Sheriff Bud Knowles. "It looks like Miz Louise's disappearance yesterday mornin' has become your business after all."

"Doctor Fisher is in no condition to be questioned, Sheriff,"

Gabriel said. Damn, I just couldn't manage to speak for myself this week.

"Well, then, I'll start with you, seeing as you're the one covered in blood. Don't move her," he barked at the paramedics, who prepared to lift Louise's body on to a stretcher. "This here is now a crime scene."

Gabriel's frustration came through in his tone. "What is the crime, Sheriff? We merely brought in a friend who was hurt and appeared at our door this morning."

"You must be the butler." Knowles deliberately reached into his back pocket, brought out a pad, licked his thumb, and flipped the little notebook open to an empty page. "I've heard of you. Could I have your name, sir?"

"Excuse me. I'm going to get some water." I pushed by Gabriel and staggered into the kitchen.

I turned on the water and waited for it to warm. I needed to wash my hands both of the sticky blood and the impossible situation. The icy-cold water gave me an anchor to reality, and I watched blood swirl off my hands and down the drain. Blood! I tasted acid in the back of my throat, swallowed hard. Tried to concentrate on the water, on the cold tile beneath my sock feet. *Wouldn't do to puke in front of the sheriff.* Focused on the cold water splashing on my face, thinking of the stinging on my cheeks, the drip as it crawled down my neck to my collarbone, chest, right breast, nipple... I raised my head and looked out the window.

The motion-sensor light turned on and illuminated something big and black. Yellow eyes flashed at me, and I staggered back, found the sharp edge of the island with my lower back. *Yellow eyes, white teeth, fire!* I sank to the floor and curled up. *No, no, no. Away, go away, go away!*

I must have screamed because footsteps pounded into the kitchen.

"Miss? Doctor Fisher?" An unfamiliar voice, one of the paramedics. "In here. She's in here."

"Did she faint?"

"Bring her out here. Lay her down."

"Not on the sofa. Put her in the chair."

Strong arms. No good. All went black.

## 8

I came to in the armchair with something acrid wafting into my nose: smelling salts.

"Are you all right, miss?" The young paramedic's eyes told his concern.

"I'm fine." But I couldn't focus on anything, and a rushing sound filled my ears.

"Here's some water."

"Thank you." The cool liquid helped to dispel the grogginess.

Gabriel stood by the fireplace with the sheriff. His feet were square to Knowles, but he kept glancing over his shoulder at me. I raised my glass to show him I was okay. He inclined his head, but his back remained tense.

"Well, if that's all, Sheriff, perhaps you can come take Doctor Fisher's statement tomorrow. I will be here all day as well if you think of anything else you'd like to ask me."

Surprisingly, Knowles took the hint. "I'll be by in the morning."

Louise was gone, but the couch showed stains where she'd

lain. Also gravel and grass. What had happened to the poor woman?

Gabriel didn't sit down until he had locked the door behind the last of Knowles' crew.

"I guess there's no way to salvage the couch, is there?" Even before he said so, I knew the soft fawn suede had been ruined.

"The sheriff asked me to keep it here until forensics can come and collect it. I can't even try to clean it."

"What else did he say?"

"That none of us are to leave tomorrow until he and the forensics team return. The driveway and grounds are also considered a crime scene. It seems as though Louise was dragged up the driveway."

I remembered the sickening sounds. "I heard it, but I didn't know what it was."

"Me too. When I went out to investigate, I found Louise lying in the grass. That's when I brought her in."

"Poor woman." I blinked to keep the tears from falling again and to not relive the whole encounter. *The black wolf. How did it get here? How did it find me?* I shuddered.

In an instant Gabriel was by my side searching my face. "Are you all right, Madam?"

"I am. Did you see it?"

"See what?"

"The black wolf."

"No, but I could smell it on her."

"Was it…" I couldn't bear to say it.

"No." He leaned closer. "Don't worry, it wasn't Ron or Leo."

"Phew." Some of the tension drained from my chest, although the other possibility was just as disturbing. "Where's Lonna? I'm surprised she wasn't woken up by all the commotion."

Gabriel smiled. "She was very upset last night and asked for something to help her sleep."

"Ah. Are you going to turn us all into addicts? Because I may need something."

"In your case, I'm going to say no. Warm milk, that's it. You need to be alert when Sheriff Knowles comes to question you in a few hours."

"Oh, that's right." I rubbed my eyes. Dealing with Knowles was the last thing I wanted to do. "Warm milk it is, then."

"With a cookie?"

"If you're offering."

He rose, but I stopped him with a hand on his arm. "Gabriel?"

"Yes, Doctor?"

"Thank you. I'm glad you're here."

"I am, too."

It was too quick to tell, but I thought I saw an extra sparkle in his eye.

IF I SLEPT at all the rest of the night, I didn't know it. My wrist throbbed from Louise's twisting of the injury, and I couldn't get comfortable. The absence of city noise magnified every small sound against the backdrop of silence. Not even the insects sang. Every time I was just about to drift off to sleep, some noise startled me awake. One time it was Lonna crying out in her sleep, and then Gabriel got up and walked outside. I supposed he was as restless as I was. Or maybe he had other reasons to be out.

Finally I gave up, put a different robe on, and walked to the balcony. Dawn tinged the sky in the east faint blue, then golden, and then a blaze of pink and orange as the sun strained to rise above the trees. I had to look away from the searing brightness when it emerged, and a large brown wolfhound on the lawn caught my attention. Its tongue lolled out at me, then it rolled on its back and stretched in the grass. In spite of myself, I laughed. It became blurry around the edges, rolled on its stomach, and gave a great heave. Instead of a wolf, I found myself looking at the fuzzy backside of a man.

That was it. No going back now. I'd seen one of them change, and the fire inside me was lit.

"How did you do that?"

"I wish I knew." With a grunt, Gabriel straightened up from his hands and knees, rolled up one vertebrae at a time, and stretched, his back still to me. Bones and joints popped back into place under the smooth muscles.

"Madam, would you mind?" He made a circular motion with his hand, and I obediently turned around. "All right, then."

He stood below the balcony in a plaid flannel robe.

"What was that all about? I thought you weren't going hunting?"

"I needed to wash the scent of blood off. A mountain stream seemed preferable to a shower."

I shivered at the thought of bathing in a torrent of icy water. "Suit yourself."

"Coffee?"

I blinked at the thought of such a mundane substance after the magic I'd just witnessed, but.... "Would love some. Be right down."

I didn't know much about werewolf etiquette at the time, but I later learned allowing a human to watch the transformation was one of the most intimate things a werewolf could do because of the moment of complete vulnerability mid-change.

I ran down the stairs to the kitchen, where I found a full pot of warm, steaming, fragrant coffee. Thank God for coffeemakers with timers. I poured two cups and waited for Gabriel to come in.

The Gabriel that walked through the door was not the same

man I had become accustomed to. Rather than glance at me, then immediately away, his eyes raked me, like he took in every inch of flesh under my robe and pajamas.

"Um, coffee?"

He came to stand by me, but he didn't take a cup. His eyes still held a golden cast.

"Gabriel, something's different about you." I held my coffee in front of me. Its scent mingled with that of crisp mountain air and the dampness of his clothes, and electricity crackled between us. Standing so close to his energy, his raw wildness, made my nipples tighten.

"I don't want any coffee, Madam." The look in his brown eyes told me exactly what he did want.

"I don't think I do either." I put my cup down and held my breath.

I could sense Gabriel's usual self-control at war with the wildness and passion born with a dawn run and transformation. Envy blistered my heart. I wanted to run, to shed the responsibilities of convention, the grief and trauma of life as a human.

I wasn't a werewolf, but by God, I could get as close as possible to this one.

I grabbed his robe and let my nails rake through the soft hair and along his chest as I pulled him to me. His head tilted toward my neck, and for one exhilarating instant, I thought he would bite me and invite me into that world, but he merely nibbled without breaking the skin and kissed along the side of my neck to my earlobe. I wrapped my arms around his neck, and he pulled me to him.

Lonna's voice, low and icy, broke us apart. "Well, isn't this interesting? I get lectured for sleeping with the married lawyer, and here innocent little Joanie is dallying with the butler. How juicy."

I crossed my arms. "Nothing happened."

Gabriel tied his robe back and looked at her with disdain-ful, hooded eyes.

Guilt blossomed in my chest. Caught with my hand in the werewolf cookie jar. "At least he's not married."

"This time."

Gabriel raised his eyebrows. My cheeks warmed.

"Didn't she tell you? She was having an affair with her boss. Her *married* boss."

"He told me he was separated." But the excuse sounded flimsy.

"I can see how the man would be tempted." Now he was back to the old Gabriel, guarded and careful. "Pardon me, I think I shall dress unless you need me to fix breakfast for you."

"No thanks, we're fine."

"Very good, Madam." In spite of the awkward situation, he kept his back erect as he walked out of the kitchen.

I slammed my coffee cup on the counter and tried to ignore the hot liquid that sloshed on my hand. "What the hell has gotten into you? I thought you were up here to help me, not judge and get in my way."

She sucked her breath in like I'd hit her. "You judged me first. Peter—"

"Is our number one suspect for now."

"Which you've pegged him without even talking to him."

I wiped the coffee off my hand with a dish towel. "I did talk to him. And it took him less than a minute to threaten and try to bully me."

"He was only trying to talk to me. Some men don't know how to do that with finesse."

"He's a lawyer. He should know better."

"He's a damn good lawyer. Remember the Oliver case?"

The room spun. Déjà vu. My dream.

With shaking hands, I poured more coffee into the cup. "Yes."

"Yes. Peter knows it. One of his law firm partners represented the parents."

"What?"

"I didn't know it, but his senior partner took on the case as a pro bono one. Cleared the father and pegged the teacher. With my help."

I sat down at the table. My head hurt. "So he's one of the good guys?"

Lonna laughed. "Good at some things. Don't worry, I won't let him fool me."

"Like Robert fooled me."

"This isn't about you. Look," she said as she sat beside me and put a hand on my arm. "There's something about being up here that's creeping me out."

"I feel the same way."

"By the way, why is the den such a mess? There's blood on the sofa."

I filled her in on Louise's mysterious appearance. And death. But I didn't tell her about the black wolf. In the light of day, I doubted my own perceptions.

Rather than showing any sympathy for my part of the ordeal, she only asked, "Why didn't you wake me? Why didn't you *tell* me?"

"You were drugged asleep. Anyone else would've woken on their own."

"Joanie, how the hell am I supposed to do my job with you withholding information like that? With you not letting me be involved?"

"Shit happens, Lonna. You can either be involved or not. If you're going to keep yelling at me for seeing and hearing different things than you, it's going to be not."

"Fine, be that way."

What could I do? I offered her the only thing I could think

of. "Hey, you've got the first shot at the crime scene. The sheriff didn't do much to it last night."

She bit the corner of her lip and narrowed her eyes. "All right. Just don't get in my way."

"Oh, yeah," I told her back as she went out the door. "He also said none of us could leave today until he comes back with the forensics team and gives us the all clear."

She mumbled something I chose not to hear. I fixed another cup of coffee and went through the other door into the dining room and out on the back porch. The Adirondack chairs were still damp with morning dew, but I sat anyway, the chill against my back and legs helping me ground myself in reality. This reality.

Most of the back lawn was still in shadow, but nothing out of the ordinary moved. My heart still thudded against my chest, anger warring with unfulfilled sexual tension. *Deep breath, Joanie.* Cool morning air. Waves of green trees. I had always loved the mountains in the summer but hadn't seen them in the fall. I wondered if I would be up here for autumn this year to finally see the leaves change. My mother hadn't allowed visits during the school year, and then in college and graduate school, I hadn't had the time.

I wished for my grandfather to be there. He had never looked upon me with judgment, had never given unsolicited advice. If he'd been there, he would've drawn my attention to the interesting aspects of the morning. Like the black wolf. And Gabriel's transformation.

It hit me, a lightning bolt of insight. *The transformation. CLS intensified.* I needed to talk to all the werewolves. And I needed to revisit that poor charred box. And see what data my grandfather had hidden in the house. Even though I hadn't seen him in years, I knew he must have been looking into it from what Ron, Leo and Gabriel had said. Not that he'd made much headway, but maybe a fresh set of eyes—and more data—would help.

I could go through the information without leaving the property, and something told me Ron and Leo would reappear today. With a plan in mind, I went back into the kitchen for a third cup of coffee.

Gabriel was there eating a bowl of cereal while standing at the island. He had showered, and his hair hung in damp ringlets. Nothing like a shower to make one feel civilized. Had it been a cold one even after his morning dip in the stream?

He looked up when I entered, his gaze cautious, and my heart sank. It would be a while before this awkwardness subsided.

"Breakfast, Madam?"

"Just more coffee for now. I'll be working in my bedroom if anyone needs me."

"If you would prefer, your grandfather left his study ready for you."

"Oh, okay. Thanks. I'll get dressed and be in there. Just let me know when the sheriff arrives."

"Yes, Madam."

Happy with my plans, I walked up to him and quickly stood on tiptoe and kissed his cheek.

"Madam, about this morning..."

"I'm still figuring it out, Gabriel. We can talk later."

He nodded. "I look forward to it." The frown that turned his lips contradicted his reply

THE STUDY, the second room on the right after the library, was locked. I tried the smaller key that had been left by Galbraith, and it worked. The shades filtered the dim light, but even with such limited visibility, I could tell the room had not been opened in weeks. A stale smell hung in the air, and dust frosted every available surface.

I opened my mouth to call Gabriel, but then decided not to. It was obvious my grandfather hadn't even trusted his supposed confidant with access to this room, so I decided to respect his wishes. First things first, though. I opened the blinds.

Dust motes swirled in the early morning light. An antique desk clock of polished wood and brass told me the time was seven twenty-five. I hadn't been up that early since I'd gotten fired except for when Lonna woke me at the crack of dawn to come up here. If I'd known the trip would put such a strain on our friendship, I might have just slept in that day.

I put my cup of coffee on a cork coaster and looked around. The large mahogany desk sat in the middle of the room. Behind it, two windows framed a fireplace. That might be a nice start—the air was chilly. The desk was flanked by two small file cabinets, but I knew what I sought would not be in such an obvious place.

Bookshelves lined the two walls. My grandfather had been an avid collector of rare, antique books and artifacts. One section caught my eye immediately. He'd collected books on werewolves, and along with more modern tomes was an early printing of Sabine Baring-Gould's *The Book of Werewolves*, considered by many to be one of the definitive works on lycanthropy as far as the 1800s. The shelf also held works on related topics including doppelgangers, witches, and vampires. In front of the books sat a small wooden figurine of a cat with emerald eyes. It winked at me in the morning light, but when I pulled out the books that sat behind it, there was nothing.

Puzzled, I replaced the book and the cat. The figurines my eyes had passed over previously stood out now, the books fading into the background. I had the silver cat on a chain, and then there was the wooden cat on the shelf. I thought back to how my grandfather and I would talk about the elements. Wood was an Earth material; silver could be Earth but could also represent air. So that meant I needed fire and water.

The scientist in me laughed at such a silly game. Elements? I hadn't inhabited the world of fairies, elementals, and magic since childhood. Nonetheless, I started at the window on the left and studied the contents of the shelves one by one. Although the next room was a large library, it was obvious my grandfather had kept many of his most beloved volumes here. There were books on herbs and plants, gardening, trees, and other flora. The next shelf held the journals that had published my articles. It appeared as though my grandfather had found my work and subscribed to the journals hoping to read more. Galbraith had told me that he followed my career closely, and that he'd done his own research as well, but this was concrete proof of his interest. It was almost better than a hug. Almost.

The third shelf was the one with the wooden cat and werewolf books. Some of the volumes were in different languages including French, German, and some sort of Scandinavian language. He had done his homework on werewolf history and legends. The fourth and final shelf before the door held legal briefs and medical and psychological texts. On this shelf I found a glass cat candle holder, again with emerald eyes. I made note of it and didn't touch it.

The shelves on the right side of the room held yet more books. Statistics, research methods... Even more than I'd gathered in my graduate school and research careers. There I found a cat statuette made completely of tiny seashells. It even held a miniature plastic fish in its mouth.

So those were my four... Mishka in the hollow of the tree. The wooden cat by the werewolf books. The candleholder cat with the psychology texts. The seashell cat with the research texts.

I found a spool of tape and put a piece on the shelves where I'd found the three cats. Then I pulled the book or books if the cat had been positioned at the border of two texts off the shelves and put them on the desk. I reached with my fingers but didn't find anything behind them, just the smooth wood of the shelves themselves.

I sat in the large leather chair, dwarfed by its huge size. Charles Landover had been a tall man, about six and a half feet. Standing next to him, I'd always looked and felt younger than I was. Now, standing in his footsteps in the study, I had that feeling again, of missing something important because of being too short or not smart enough.

"But you are smart enough, Joanie-cat," he'd told me. "You just need to see what's right in front of you."

I looked at the books I'd pulled off the shelves. Claude Lecouteaux's *Witches, Werewolves, and Fairies: Shapeshifters and Astral Doubles in the Middle Ages*. *Lycanthropy Case Studies* and *The Mysterious Disappearance of Hillary Baehr* by a colleague of mine, Iain McPherson. Iain was a Scottish researcher who had devoted his life to seeking out and studying lycanthropes who developed CLS as children. We had met at an international conference, had immediately made kindred spirit connection, and had kept in regular contact until I had lost my job. We had an agreement to share what we knew. I wondered what he would think about what I had discovered here at Crystal Pines: not just lycanthropes, but actual werewolves. The final books behind the seashell cat were *Herbology* by someone unfamiliar to me and *The Genetics of Lycanthropy and other Rare Psychological Disorders* by—and it hurt to read his name—Robert Cannon.

The first book made sense, as it presented a fascinating summary of the possible origin of werewolf legends in the Middle Ages. The ancient Scandinavian people had a different understanding of the soul. The spiritual part of a human had three parts: the *fylgia*, or psychic double, often seen as a female representation of the self that can act prophetically; the *hamr*, an aspect of the soul under the control of some people, which can take on a different form and travel when the individual is asleep; and the *hugr*, which can motivate the *hamr* or can represent universal principles of behavior. Some believed werewolves were actually the peoples' *hamrs*, their spirits taking on another form after they left the body to carry on works that may or may not be diabolical.

I had seen physical transformations, not just behavioral. The books on the table indicated my grandfather was also looking into the old legends that a person didn't physically transform, but rather their spirit did. Once in animal form, the person could then effect physical change on the environment such as carrying objects and wounding others. The problem was that whatever happened to them in that form also happened to their human body. Hence the stories of someone cutting off a werewolf's paw and the person, usually a witch, waking with a severed hand.

Iain's books detailed modern cases. In one, a woman named Hillary Baehr had displayed lycanthropic symptoms but then had completely vanished from a locked padded cell in 1956. No sign of struggle or forced exit were evident, and investigators could never get any of the staff to admit to aiding her. It was one of the earliest cases of a psychic, in this case Hillary's sister Bethany, being brought in to aid police. All Bethany could tell them was that Hillary's energy had changed. The case so fascinated the psychiatric community that it was still used as an example of poor facility management. Iain had studied it from a different angle and put it in a context similar to that of Lecouteaux's book. I had no idea how *Herbology* fit in.

Robert's book had posited the premise that certain ethnic histories predisposed individuals to psychological disorders, and he used lycanthropy as being present in people descended from the Scandinavians as his primary example. His argument was that, due to immigration and emigration and a host of other factors, these disorders were becoming rarer because they were dependent on a certain combination of genes: one to make them susceptible to the disorder, and another to make that first gene express. If both genes were recessive, it would take a multigenerational process for them to activate the syndrome. So far all he had was theoretical family charts and formulas. I had been working on a similar project to map out the factors associated with CLS when the lab had caught fire.

I still needed to figure out how all this fit together with Charles Landover's disappearance. However, before I could begin to make notes, there was a beep. I hadn't noticed the intercom on the desk.

"Doctor Fisher?" Gabriel sounded like he was miles away.

"Yes." My exasperation and having been knocked out of my focus was evident in my voice. It wasn't so much as a "yes" as a "leave me alone."

"The sheriff is here."

## 9

I took a deep breath through my nose and let it out through my mouth to ease my frustration. "I'll be right out."

I put the books in the desk drawer to my right. Not that anyone would be able to tell with a glance what I had been working on, but one never knew how nosy the cops would get. I reminded myself that the sheriff had a legitimate reason for being there: a woman who had gone missing had died in my home. I couldn't hide amongst my books if I was going to prove my innocence.

I walked through the den and surprised a forensic team member in the act of wrapping the leather couch to be transported to their lab in Little Rock. I hated to lose it—it had been my grandfather's, after all—but I decided I'd rather not be reminded someone had died on it. I made a mental note to talk to Gabriel about whether we should replace it with a different style of furnishing. When I walked into the kitchen, Lonna was pouring the sheriff a fresh cup of coffee.

"Nice of you to join us, Doctor Fisher."

"Thank you for stopping back by, Sheriff." Gads, I hated

being fake, but it wouldn't do to get the man riled up at this point.

"Ms. Marconi was telling me she slept through all the excitement last night."

"She'd had a long day."

"She also can't account for your whereabouts after approximately nine p.m."

"I had my coffee on the balcony with Gabriel and went to bed."

He took notes as I talked. "When did you wake up?"

"I don't have a clock visible from the bed, but it was probably about two a.m., maybe a little later."

"What woke you up?"

"I'd been sleeping fitfully, so it was one more awakening."

"Any idea what disturbed your sleep?"

I couldn't help it, I laughed. "My life has just been turned upside down, Sheriff. Isn't that enough?"

His ears turned pink. "Yes, right. Did you hear anything?"

"Yes, something moving the gravel on the driveway. Then footsteps downstairs, an exclamation, and then the front-door bolt being unlocked."

"Anything else?"

"I wanted to see what was going on, so I went to the bathroom, splashed some water on my face, and put on a robe. The running water kept me from hearing anything else."

"And then what happened?"

I filled him in from that point, but instead of mentioning the black wolf, I just told him Louise had been trying to warn me about something, but she'd not been able to articulate anything. He took notes. Finally, he asked me, "And what made you pass out in the kitchen?"

"I'm not an M.D., Sheriff. I get squeamish at the sight of blood."

He shook his head with a superior smirk. "And you're a doctor?"

"A different kind."

"Is there anything else you'd like to tell me?"

"Not that I can think of."

"The boys'll take the couch. Just in case, you know."

Before I could ask, *"Just in case of what?"* Gabriel interrupted. "It's obvious what happened, Sheriff. She appeared here on the lawn and died on the sofa."

Lonna chimed in, "I don't really think it's necessary to take the furniture. If you need to see it again, you can come back."

He hooked his thumbs in his belt and planted his feet. "These orders come from above me, people. I'm just doing my job."

"I'll send you a bill," I muttered.

"I'll, ah, also need those clothes you were wearing last night, Mr. Gabriel."

"My clothes?"

"Evidence."

"They're bloodstained from me carrying the woman in. I didn't do anything to her."

"No one's sayin' you did. Just give me the clothes."

Gabriel raised one eyebrow but complied and left to fetch them. I could tell he was exasperated. We all were. At last, Knowles dismissed us, but with a command to call if we were going to leave the area.

Gabriel appeared with the clothes, and we watched, helpless, as the forensics guys finished wrapping the couch in moving plastic and took it away. They also took the rug it sat on. A pang of grief surprised me, like they took a part of my grandfather's memory with them.

"Look at this," Lonna called. She had walked to the front window, and I joined her. More men were outside gathering up clumps of grass and gravel. First they photographed them, and then they gathered everything that could have been touched by Louise and placed whatever it was in a bucket.

"Is this standard procedure?" I asked.

"The photographing, yes," Lonna told me. "The gravel and grass theft, no. I just don't understand this." Her arm brushed mine, her skin clammy.

"Are you okay?"

"Just feeling a little washed out. Too much going on right now. And that sleeping pill was strong."

"Why don't you go lay down? Sleep off the hangover."

"Can't. I've got to go interview some more residents. And the mayor."

"Are you sure? You look like hell." The pale tint under her olive skin made her look slightly green.

"I'm fine."

"All right. But at least let me come with you."

"Sure. It might help to have a second set of ears."

The wobbly way she walked up the stairs to change shoes made me wonder if she needed an extra set of legs, too.

THE MAYOR OF PINEY MOUNTAIN, now Crystal Pines, lived in one of the newer houses of the subdivision. We arrived just after ten a.m.

"His standard of living didn't suffer." I looked around after we rang the doorbell. The house had been built to look like a large 1920s-style bungalow. I remembered that before Crystal Pines, this neighborhood had been a park.

"No doubt." Lonna gave a low whistle as a uniformed maid answered the door. "You don't even have one of those."

"Yet," I whispered as we were shown into the living room. She smirked.

"Gabriel might have some competition."

"I doubt that. I'm not into maids."

For a moment, everything felt like it was right between us again. Then Peter Bowman walked in.

Lonna took a quick breath, and I knew that what my grandfather used to call the "Stony Joanie" look cross my face. He said when I got uncomfortable, I would retreat behind a mask, and it was impossible to tell what I was feeling or thinking. When I grew into adulthood, others found the expression to be intimidating. Now I hoped it covered the rage burning in the center of my chest at the memory of Peter's threats from two very long days ago. Plus I blamed him for the erosion of my friendship with Lonna.

Peter, meanwhile, nodded to both of us but smiled only at Lonna. "Ms. Marconi, Doctor Fisher, please have a seat. Mayor Franz will be with you shortly."

"And why does he feel the need to have a lawyer present?" I settled into a plush armchair and crossed my legs. "Is he feeling guilty today?"

A sneer curled the left corner of Peter's patrician mouth. "I was here working with the mayor on some paperwork for the new town hall."

"What's wrong with the one you've got?"

"It has termites, mold, and structural issues. Some of the documents currently stored there are irreplaceable, so we're working on building a new place for them before we tear that old wreck down."

My heart skipped a beat. Tear down the Town Hall? I remembered walking by it with my grandfather and eating picnic lunches on the front steps. How could they take away another one of my memories?

I blinked to keep the tears from forming in my eyes and asked, "What kind of documents?"

"The birth, death and marriage records for the town, for

one thing. Some of them are so old they can't be moved too often."

"What about bringing in trained document restoration experts?" Lonna studied her nails. "Surely the town would be invested enough in its history to pay someone to come out and take care of its records, especially since genealogy is such a popular hobby."

"It would cost too much to do it right now, and the town council doesn't want to send the records away."

"Yet they can afford a whole new building?"

"They can justify the expense if it's for more than one purpose. It will be Crystal Pines' first multi-use facility with the Town Hall, Library and administrative offices." Peter shrugged. "That's how government works, ladies."

I almost choked on my shock. "So you're tearing down the library, too?"

"It's been closed for a few years now due to moisture and mold problems, and the books are in storage."

"It doesn't seem that Mayor Franz is hurting too much." I couldn't keep the bitterness out of my voice.

"I was well-compensated for my land when Crystal Pines." A tall man with sandy red hair and freckles and wearing an impeccably tailored white shirt and gray trousers entered from the front hall. "I'm Lee Franz." He held out his hand and shook mine with a firm, confident grip. He looked to be in his fifties, and his blue eyes sparkled like those of someone who shared an inside joke with the world.

"Joanie Fisher," I introduced myself, my cheeks hot.

"Ah, yes, the town heiress. We sorely miss your grandfather. He kept up with a lot of the town history for us."

"This is my friend Lonna, a social worker from Little Rock."

"I assume you weren't here to talk to Mayor Franz about family records?" Peter, now in full lawyer mode, asked. Lee

Franz sat on the leather sofa, and Lonna and I reclaimed our seats in the armchairs.

Lonna took the lead, as usual. "Yes, er, no. We're here to talk about the missing children."

Lee shook his head. "It's such a shame. I get telephone calls every day about that from worried townspeople. I wish I knew something that could help them. And you."

"Natives of Piney Mountain, right?" I asked. "Not the Crystal Pines newcomers."

He rubbed his temples. "They think the new development has stirred up an evil mountain spirit that wants to take revenge for being disturbed."

"An evil mountain spirit?" The hair on the back of my neck pricked with the memory of the cry the night before.

"The Ozarks have several legendary monsters. One of them, the Gowrow, was supposedly common up here in the 1800s."

That was new to me. "What's a Gowrow?"

"A twenty-foot-long lizard with tusks. It liked riverbeds and caves."

Lonna and I exchanged a skeptical glance. She asked the next question. "And what do you think about this monster, or at least the possibility that it's the one snatching your children?"

He spread his hands. "We can't seem to find any other explanation."

"What about wolves?" I asked, my heart beating fast.

"The Arkansas red wolf and the coyote are probably too small to carry off a child of nine or ten. Besides, we'd at least have something left to find. They wouldn't just vanish."

I shivered at the gruesome thought, and the memory of Louise, battered and burned, came into my head.

"So no one has reported a large black wolf roaming around?"

"Why?" Alarm bled through Peter's condescension. "Have you seen one?"

Didn't he know about his brother and cousin? His reaction said not. Neither did the mayor, and now that I thought about it, I hadn't had the chance to tell Lonna yet. Gabriel and I were the only ones who knew there were real, honest-to-God werewolves running around.

I decided to evade the question. "It was something that someone told me."

"There are a lot of, shall we say, eccentric people in these parts, Doctor Fisher." The mayor dismissed them with a wave of his hand. "I would take what they say with a large grain of salt."

"I see."

"If you don't have any more questions for the mayor..." Peter stood, and his cell phone rang. He frowned at the screen, then answered it. "Marguerite, I told you not to call me this morning. I'm in a meeting with the mayor."

He walked into the hallway, but even from there, we could hear hysterical crying on the other end. "What? That's impossible! From his room? Okay, I'll be right there."

Peter came back in, his face pale. "Lance is missing."

"Your son?" Lonna asked.

"Taken from his room. Last night. Marguerite thought he woke up early and might have wandered off, but she can't find him anywhere, and the front door was unlocked."

"Go," the mayor told him. "I can handle things from here."

We all stood, and Lonna said, "We'll come with you." I looked at her, speechless. "If they have to search the woods, they need as many feet as they can find."

"Fine. We can follow you," I told Peter.

"Thank you." He clasped Lonna's hand. "That means the world to me."

I bit my tongue over my sharp retort and followed them out.

～

PETER and his family lived in a large Tudor-style brick house at the end of a cul-de-sac. Their front yard was small, as with most modern subdivisions, and their back lawn sloped gently to the woods. Right now both front lawn and back teemed with uniformed men who inspected every blade of grass and every inch of driveway.

Peter drove in immediately before us, and he was greeted by a petite woman with blonde curls and a cute snub nose. He took her into his arms and held her stiffly as she sobbed into his tailored suit jacket.

"That must be Marguerite."

Lonna just watched the scene, her expression shuttered. I sympathized. I'd met Robert's wife the first time at a company party. He'd told me she was there because she'd formerly worked for the company, and he didn't want it to look like we were together, but still, the situation had been extremely awkward. I remembered doing the point-by-point comparison —my hair was not as stylish, but I was thinner; her breasts were bigger, but mine didn't sag; she'd obviously had some work done, and I was in the bloom of youth. But in the end, it didn't matter. He'd gone back to her. Not that I blamed him, at least not in my rational moments. He'd built a life with her. I was just a pleasant diversion to make work more interesting.

And Lonna was just a pleasant diversion for a man who had a weakness for beautiful women.

"It's not easy to realize you're an attractive distraction," I said softly as I put my hand on her shoulder.

"Let's go." Her voice broke, but she smiled slightly.

We turned to go, but he called after us, "Lonna, Joanie, this is my wife, Marguerite. Lonna is a pr— I mean, she has some useful skills that could help."

"You've got to be kidding me," I muttered.

We turned to meet the woman's suspicious gaze. I couldn't blame her. She must know what kind of man her husband was.

She immediately turned her brown eyes on Lonna, and I could see the point-by-point occurring in both their heads. I couldn't tell who won. Well, Marguerite, obviously—she was married to the cad, after all.

"What time did you notice Lance was missing?" Lonna straightened her spine. I could see by the angle of her chin that she wouldn't back out of the situation.

Marguerite looked at Peter, who said, "The police don't know it, but Lonna is a private investigator who's also working on the missing-children case. She may be able to help."

Marguerite's shoulders slumped. "At seven." She spoke with a French accent. "I went to wake him for his breakfast, and he was gone."

"What did you do?"

"I thought he was playing a joke on his Mama." She accented the second syllable of Mama. "So I looked for him everywhere in the house. Then I saw the front door open."

"What time was that?" I admired Lonna for her gentle tone. She did very well hiding the emotions that must have been roiling beneath her professional demeanor.

"About eight. We have a big house with many places for a little boy to hide."

I counted the windows. They did have a mansion. Lance would never have gotten lost in the small houses that had originally stood on the land.

"Then what did you do?"

Tears trickled down her cheeks. "I have already told the police this. Why do I have to live it again?"

"Marguerite, honey, it's okay. Just tell Lonna what you did then."

"I went outside and yelled for Lance. I looked in the pool. In the woods, but the brush is too thick. Then I called the police and Peter."

"Where are Ron and Leo?" I asked. "They live with you, right?"

"They were out all night. I haven't seen them."

Peter's jaw tightened. "They never came in?"

"No. For all I know, they went to the city to party."

I remembered Leo talking about his nephew and knew he couldn't have had anything to do with the boy's disappearance. I hoped.

A police car drove up, lights flashing and siren blaring. For the third time that day, Sheriff Bud Knowles and I glared at each other.

"Well, Doctor, you've just got your finger in all sorts of pies today, don't ya?"

"Sheriff Knowles, how good to see you again." Lonna turned up the charm and held out her hand. "We were meeting with Counselor Bowman and the mayor when he got the telephone call about his son."

"It's amazing how y'all always end up in just the right place at the right time."

"Amazing or unlucky." I didn't care to stand there breathing in Knowles's bacon breath or hearing the poor woman have to talk about her missing son in front of her husband's newest girlfriend, so I wandered around to the side of the house. The ground was slightly damp, the grass struggling to grow in the shade of an oak tree. Something in the mud caught my eye: a large animal footprint.

I looked over my shoulder, and sure that all the others were either engrossed in the conversation with Knowles or searching other parts of the yard, I knelt down. It was a wolf print. I hadn't ever seen one, but I could tell. It must have come through the side yard before snatching the child.

I shivered. Did I think the black wolf had something to do with it? Louise had warned me about it, but I didn't know what it all meant—just that now one of the "aristocrats" had disappeared, and my newfound research subjects were in that much more danger. Or were they the danger? Either way, I needed to know where they were.

"Can you believe this? That poor woman." Lonna's voice startled me out of my mental calculations as to where Ron and Leo were and how far they could have gone. I hastily straightened up and stepped on the paw print with my left foot, which obliterated it. The last thing the guys needed was a mob of wolf hunters to descend on the woods.

"I thought she was the enemy?"

"C'mon, Joanie, she's just misplaced her son. We must take care of her bruised ego and coddle her."

"Sarcasm doesn't become you. Neither does jealousy. But she probably could use some tea. Or something a little stronger."

"If Peter actually invites us in, I'll offer."

"How big of you."

"Now who's sarcastic?"

As we walked toward the door, Marguerite looked up, and her eyes met mine. Guilt stabbed through me again even though I hadn't done anything. This time. Still, the whole situation had a sense of déjà vu. I could feel Lonna squirm under Marguerite's gaze. I knew from painful experience that it would be best for Lonna not to set foot in the Bowman house. Marguerite. may be distressed about her missing son, but she wouldn't be distracted for long from what had been going on.

In spite of the warmth of the morning, a foreboding chill spread through me.

## 10

Marguerite's anger, disappointment and hurt showed on her face when she looked at Peter. Her expression said she needed his comfort, not that of two strangers, one of whom may have slept with her husband.

Sheriff Knowles and the other policemen conferred, then put their equipment away. "We'll be in touch, Mrs. Bowman," he said. He didn't—couldn't?—meet her eyes. I wondered if he'd done this so many times by now he couldn't face one more parent in pain.

A tear trickled down her cheek. Peter waved to them and snapped his cell phone shut.

"I just tried Ron's and Leo's cell phones. Neither of them are answering. Dammit, they should have been here! They should be out there earning their keep and searching for Lance."

Marguerite turned to him and crumpled into his arms. He had to drop his cell phone to catch her.

"Here, let us help you," I said, and together we got Marguerite inside to the sitting room. Peter held her somewhat stiffly.

"I'll make some tea," Lonna offered.

"No. I mean, that is not necessary, Ms. Marconi." Marguerite raised her tear-stained face. "I would rather go lay down. It has been an exhausting morning."

"We understand, and we'll leave you alone now." I tugged on Lonna's arm and led her to the car.

She glared at me as she got into the passenger seat. "Why did you do that?"

"Are you insane?" I turned the key in the ignition, perhaps a little too hard because the engine protested. "That woman has just lost her son, and she probably wants to kill you. Jealousy and loss don't make a good combination."

"You're probably right." She drummed her fingers on one leg. "But I want to be there to comfort him."

"That's his wife's job. If he lets her."

"He'll comfort her, but there's not much coming the other way. He told me yesterday the marriage has been cold since the son was born. Two years, and hardly any sex. I think that's why he was so quick to jump into bed with me."

I bit my tongue over any words concerning her motives. It would be a lesson she'd have to learn on her own: married men didn't need to be rescued from bad marriages, only from themselves.

"What now?" Whereas she'd seemed almost lethargic when we left Wolfsbane Manor, she practically quivered with energy.

"Are you feeling okay?"

"Better now that I've been moving around. I think I just have some sort of bug. Maybe this mountain air isn't really that healthy for me."

"We need to find Ron and Leo and tell them. I have a bad feeling about what Peter might do."

We drove into town. Tabitha's was open for lunch, so we inquired as to whether Ron was working that day. He wasn't. Leo was also nowhere to be seen.

I had the horrible feeling that whatever it was, it had gotten them. The bollywog or whatever it was the mayor had told us about. That it had slithered out of its cave and had snatched the guys, maybe one, and then the other had jumped in to defend his pack-mate and had gotten swallowed as well. And then the hideous creature, which grew in my imagination, had gone to Peter Bowman's house. With a whistle or croon, it enticed the child down the stairs, out the front door, and into its massive, fang-lined craw.

"Joanie? Joanna? Attention Doctor Fisher?" Lonna shook me by the shoulder. "You were off in your head again."

"I just wish we could find them."

"Let's go back to the house. It's lunchtime anyway. Then maybe we can look more this afternoon."

"Are you sure? Don't you have an investigation to follow up on?"

"I need to review my notes and see where to go next. Which parents to interview first and so on. Besides," she added with a grin. "It's good to see you on the hunt again."

"What?"

"You've got that look in your eyes."

"I have no idea what you're talking about."

Or did I? As much as I didn't like to admit it, I was fascinated by these werewolf-men and their primal charm. The question was, which one could I possibly be falling for? Did I have to pick just one?

I hummed along with the radio as I drove out of the town and turned the car toward Wolfsbane Manor. If anyone could help find a werewolf, it would be Gabriel.

❧

HE'D FOUND THEM, or they'd found him, and they were all sipping beers on the back balcony when we arrived. Gabriel leapt up when we walked out, but the concern on his face quickly melted into a smile. The tension of the previous day wasn't there, and I wondered what could have reconciled the werewolves.

"Madam, these gentlemen have some news about a strange wolf, perhaps even about your friend who died this morning."

Leo grinned for a second when our eyes met, but then his expression returned to its habitual almost-scowl. "We followed it through the woods until we reached a stream near Highway 14. Then we lost the scent."

Ron picked up the thread with, "So we traced it the other direction to see where it had come from and ended up here."

The chill from earlier returned and settled at the back of my neck.

Lonna looked from one to the other, her brows drawn together in a perplexed line. "What are you talking about? And what do you mean, 'lost the scent?' Do you have a dog?"

Gabriel saved them—us—from having to explain by opening the door and saying, "They were tracking an unfamiliar wolf. I have lunch ready for you, ladies, if you'd like to move into the dining room."

Introductions were quickly made since they'd gotten a glimpse of Lonna the night before, but when she shook hands with Leo, he and Ron shared a look. It was fleeting, but I was watching their eyes to see how they reacted to her, so I caught it. They spoke to her with interest, but it was more polite than lustful.

"Did you see anything last night?" Leo asked me, and I tried not to preen under his attention. What was wrong with me? I glanced at Gabriel, who put a finger to his lips. He hadn't told them. He went into the kitchen.

"I. Maybe. I don't know."

"What do you mean?"

"I thought I saw something outside the kitchen window, but

I'm not sure. I fainted." It pained me to show that weakness to them. Part of me screamed that they were predators and I shouldn't give them any opportunity to attack me. But we were all in it together now.

Gabriel brought out plates of cut fruit with crackers and chicken salad. "Did you ladies find anything interesting out from the Mayor?"

Lonna speared a pineapple slice with her fork. "Just the same old line. But Peter Bowman was there."

"I'm not surprised." Leo helped himself to chicken salad. "He's the town lawyer."

I took a deep breath. It seemed as good a time to tell him as any. "Leo, Lance is missing."

"What?" He dropped the spoon, which landed in the chicken salad bowl with a plop. His expression, so genuinely panic-stricken, proved his innocence more than any protestations. I filled the guys in on the events of the morning.

"And Peter's looking for you with thunder in his eyes," Lonna finished.

Leo shook his head. "I'm sure he is. I'll bet he's ready to blame his little brother for this."

"Why?"

Ron explained, "Because then Marguerite can't blame him. Things are rocky between them, as you well know."

Lonna blushed.

"It's not your fault, Ms. Marconi," Ron told her. "I know how charming he can be. And how deceitful."

"Really?" She didn't sound surprised.

"Oh, yes. When I first came to Little Rock for residency, he invited me into his home. I later found out he had done it, not out of cousinly love, but in order to gain access to the hospital."

"For what?"

"Fertility drugs. And the female residents. To get Marguerite pregnant and keep himself entertained."

That was worse than I expected. "Did you ever report him?"

"No. By the time I figured out what had happened, my credibility was shot, and the girls were too intimidated by that time to say anything about him."

"Excuse me." Lonna pushed back from the table. "I don't feel well."

"That's usually how those relationships go," Leo said as she ran from the room. "Better she find out now."

"Since she's gone..." I told them about the wolf paw print in the side yard. "I stepped on it to hide it. I didn't want either of you to get blamed."

"Thanks." Ron held up his beer bottle. "Although I don't think Peter knows about the true nature of CLS. He just thinks it makes us impulsive and crazy."

"I don't think anyone in the outside world realizes what it does."

"But you do." Ron looked at me with his piercing blue eyes. "And your grandfather did. I think he found something out."

"I don't know, honestly."

"Do you think you could pick up where he left off?" Leo asked. "You're the only one who can."

I met his eyes. I had vowed not to enter the research world again, but this was the perfect opportunity to regain my status and credibility. And maybe Robert.

My heart skipped a beat. Robert was the only one who had ever understood me. If I could figure out a cure for CLS, or at least a way to control it, I could re-enter the field in triumph, and then he would have to respect me. But when the thought of him taking me back crossed my mind, I found it had lost some of its appeal. Some, but not all.

Lonna had been right. I was back on the hunt, but was it for the same old quarry?

I needed to be immersed in data, not people problems. I

pushed back my chair and stood. "Gentlemen, feel free to stay here this afternoon if you like, but I have work to do."

Leo and Ron exchanged glances, and Leo sighed and said, "We should probably head back to Peter's house. I'm sure he has a few things he'd like to say to us, so we might as well get it over with." He made a rude noise. "Like we could go out partying even if we wanted to. We'll go back through the woods and see if we can find any clues as to what happened to Lance."

"Good luck." I meant it.

I went up the stairs to Lonna's room, my heart pounding with the thrill of my resolution to pick up where my grandfather had left off, but when I got there, she was asleep, snoring softly. I didn't know Lonna to be a napper, but maybe it was the after-effects of the previous night's sleeping pills. Or the shame of being taken in by Peter Bowman's charm and manipulation. With a sigh, I returned to the office, ready to start working again.

I LOOKED AT THE BOX. The charred edges curled slightly, water stains blotched the outer layer, and it still smelled faintly of smoke. Even so, I had never seen a more beautiful sight. With shaking fingers, I lifted the top and was comforted by the neat row of charts. I didn't know how this box had escaped unscathed, but there it was. I only hoped it had enough data in it for me to find my answer.

I sat at my grandfather's desk in the study. The drawer to my right still held the books he had earmarked. He had figured out something and had possibly been killed for it. For the first time, my mind made the leap and wondered whether his disappearance and the fire at my lab were connected. I hoped whoever had set the fire hadn't realized some of the data had been saved.

I also wondered who had saved it. That went on the list of questions to ask Gabriel.

The charts held the notes I had seen countless times before. There had to be something beyond what I had been looking for. Rather than the usual columns in my database, I decided to go the brute-force route and document everything, even down to the minutest detail of objective evidence. That way my mind could look for patterns as my fingers typed, and then I could run some exploratory correlations to see if anything matched up.

A knock on my door startled me when I was halfway through my second chart.

"Yes?"

"Teatime, Doctor." Gabriel came in with a laden tray. "Your grandfather mentioned you like to have tea and biscotti at four o'clock."

"It's four already?" I stretched my shoulders. The first two charts had been particularly thick, and my database stretched to over a hundred columns.

"You must be working hard." He poured the tea out of an antique silver pot into my favorite childhood mug, white with the picture of a black cat, its tail the handle.

"Where did you find that?"

"There's a storeroom downstairs off the ballroom. Your grandfather mentioned he had saved several things for you down there."

"Why didn't you say so?"

"I only found exactly where it was this afternoon, and I didn't want to disturb you. Every time I thought to ask you previously, you were out of the house. And chaos seems to follow you home."

"I wonder what else is down there."

"The room gets the afternoon sun, so it would be a good

time to look. If you're not making progress?" He inclined his head toward my computer screen.

"I am, but it's slow. It's progress by brute force, not finesse. I'd rather see if he left me anything of his own research to help give me a jump-start."

"I understand."

"Help me drink this tea, then, and we'll see what we can find."

THE MAIN ENTRANCE to the ballroom was down the steps that curved to the left of the front hall stairs. I had almost forgotten it existed, but when I was a child, my grandfather and I would go down there and have teatime—or he would have tea, and I would have milk and cookies. We'd sit in the middle of the big, dusty floor and look at the murals illuminated by the afternoon light as dust motes danced around us like sparks. It made sense that his laboratory and whatever he left for me would be down there.

Gabriel had opened the heavy red velvet drapes, faded on the window side from years of sun exposure, and I caught my breath as I descended the stairs. The butler's footsteps marked a trail through the dust on the familiar floor, as mine soon would, but the room held its old magic. The marble had been cut and laid so as to mimic the pattern of light on the forest floor. Above me the domed ceiling with its chandelier that tinkled as I walked also displayed years of neglect, the paint and gold leaf from the night sky replete with stars starting to flake. Even so, it showed no evidence of moisture or mold. The walls of the ballroom by the stairs were covered in paintings of trees to give the impression of a forest. My grandfather had wanted to put new creatures in every year. He had done all the painting work himself and contracted the gold-leaf labor, and he had only made one addition. A black wolf peered at me from behind an oak tree, its golden eyes glowing in the afternoon light. It was so lifelike I caught my breath.

"Amazing, isn't it?" Gabriel's voice made me jump even though I knew he was right behind me. "I found the room by following your grandfather's footprints."

"He never let it get this dusty. He'd always have someone from the village come in and clean it once a year."

"It sounds like he was distracted."

"It wouldn't surprise me. When he was on the hunt, especially for knowledge, there was no turning him back." Perhaps we were more alike than I thought.

"What of your grandmother?"

"Died before I was born."

"Ah."

The door to the supposed storeroom was by the wolf, its handle concealed as a tree knot. The only time the outline of the door itself would be visible was now, in the late afternoon, as the sun shone directly into the room. By candlelight or chandelier it would blend into the forest painting. I turned the handle, my heartbeat loud in my ears.

The storeroom was lined with metal shelves like one would find in a lab, but no table stood in the middle. It was illuminated by a single bulb on a chain. The shelves were lined with a few boxes, but mostly with objects I fondly remembered from my childhood, toys and cups and even some of the old kitchen equipment like the cast-iron skillets he had taught me to make cornbread in. The boxes held old letters from me to my grandfather from during my school years. I would write to him and give him news about me and Andrew since my brother didn't like to write as much as I did. Something tickled at the back of my brain, but I decided not to chase it and just let it lie dormant until I could tease it out.

In spite of the dustiness of the ballroom, this room seemed

less dirty. Even the old toys showed no evidence of the dust and dinginess that should have accumulated over the course of twenty or so years. My grandfather must have moved them down here recently.

"Find anything?" This time Gabriel's voice seemed an intrusion.

"Lots of things, but I'm not sure you'd find it interesting. Old toys and stuff, mostly. Did you take anything else out?"

"Only a cat statuette I thought would look charming on the kitchen windowsill."

"A cat statuette? What did it look like?"

"It was a little angel cat with your name on it. I was going to show it to you this evening."

A little angel cat? I didn't remember one, but my grandfather had pointed my way to important volumes upstairs with statuettes like it. "Do you remember where it was?"

"I believe it was on the pile of boxes in the back, on top of the box with letters."

Indeed, the back wall held only one set of shelves, the rest of it file boxes piled high. An angel cat. I had found the four terrestrial elements, but to balance them, one needed the fifth element of spirit. And I needed to be alone.

"Whatever I'm doing down here will bore you, Gabriel. Why don't you go upstairs and continue doing what you were doing? And maybe Lonna would like some tea or coffee."

"Yes, Madam." Resentment tinged his tone, but I wanted to handle this on my own. I opened the storeroom door all the way back on its hinges to let the light into the little room. Indeed, the back wall held a door set into the wall so closely that again, it required the sun to see it. I moved the boxes away from it, careful to keep them together in case they, too, held clues to this path my grandfather wanted me to follow. I also had to feel around for the handle—the metal type that needed to be pulled out, then turned—but it moved easily and silently once I found it, and the heavy door opened back and into the laboratory I had only dreamed of.

The room took up the entire rest of the first floor of the house. It had formerly been the entertaining kitchen with two sinks, a long wooden prep table with marble top, and marble counters along all the walls. The basic equipment was still there, but now every surface was littered with different paraphernalia. I could only guess at the purpose of some of it. Row after row of long wooden test-tube racks with various substances, burners, and even a large piece of equipment that looked like something from a genetics lab crowded the room. I knew my grandfather had been very intelligent and had almost unlimited financial resources, but this was beyond anything I had ever expected to find at Wolfsbane Manor.

I searched for notes to see if he had written what he'd done, as most scientists would. Nothing. The directions must be in that pile of boxes in the storeroom. I looked around the lab one more time and promised I would be back. My fingers itched to play with the fancy toys all around me. But before I played, or even cleaned, I needed to know what he had done. The question was, where were his notes?

I returned to the storeroom and sifted through the boxes that had been directly in front of the door. I opened one to find letters in childish handwriting, the ones I remembered sending to my grandfather. Instead of being organized by date, they were tied in little bundles with ribbon. I put that box aside and moved on to the next one.

My breath caught when I found more pediatric charts. A note in scrawled handwriting lay across the top of them: *"Charles, this was all I could get. The H. rep and the head nurse are getting suspicious. H.J."*

The third and fourth boxes held more charts, these very old, including mine and my brother's. There were also some other papers, yellowed and faded, that appeared to be birth and marriage certificates. I brought these up to the office first, then returned for the other two. I had no idea what the significance of any of it could be, only that my grandfather seemed to have been on the same track. Then there had been a fire, a mysterious disappearance, and now a likely murder. What were we so close to finding that we posed a threat to someone? What kind of threat could be so big it was worth killing for?

I shuddered as I remembered Louise, her last breaths, her warning about the black wolf. It was out there somewhere, and it may have snatched Lance Bowman after its escapades at the Manor. Another strand in the web, but I was no closer to finding the spider. And if I did find the spider, what would it do to me?

## 11

I sat with the boxes in the study. Now I had five of them, one from my own destroyed laboratory and four from the storeroom downstairs. Television portrays research scientists with a certain glamour, as though the profession is all about sexy underwear under white lab coats, which are ready to come off at the end of a long day of making life-altering discoveries. In reality, there's a lot of paper and late hours involved. That's why most of us wear comfortable clothes and geeky glasses.

The door opened, and Lonna poked her head around.

"Can I come in?"

"Sure." We looked at each other. I let her speak first.

"I don't really know how to say this."

"Okay." I'd never known her to be at a loss for words. "What's up?"

"This place is giving me nightmares. The first night I was fine, but I don't know, I guess it's all the talk of missing children and those awful screams in the woods."

"Would you rather stay in town?"

She shivered. "No, because even though I'm not sleeping

well here, I feel like I shouldn't leave, like there's something here I have to find."

"A husband? Or someone else's husband?"

"No, there's something else."

Dark circles showed under her eyes, and a wisp of guilt curled from my stomach to my chest. "I'm sorry, that was out of turn."

"I'm sorry too. I've been a bitch. It's just that I came here to help you, and it seems you're keeping me out of the loop."

"Everything's been happening really fast."

"I understand. But would you please try to do better with including me?"

The weight of others' secrets pressed on me. "I will if I can."

She sat in one of the overstuffed leather armchairs by the reading table. "What's all that stuff?"

"Things I found in the storeroom off the ballroom. I'm hoping they'll give me some clue as to what my grandfather found and the direction his research was going in."

"And the smoky one?"

"From the lab in Memphis. Somehow it got sent here. There must have been a mistake, but I'm keeping it."

She raised an eyebrow. "What's in it?"

"Medical records from kids with CLS. I'm looking to see if there's something I missed. Hopefully there's enough for my database to sift through."

She came to stand by the computer and looked over my shoulder at my database. "Research through brute force, huh?"

"You got it, baby."

"I was thinking about going to interview Louise's family. They've lost a child and now a grandmother, so they may be more tied into this than anyone else. How about some research by charm and sympathy?"

"I could do that, but let's wait 'til tomorrow. It's already dinnertime, and I feel like I'm really, really close to figuring out something important."

Lonna laughed. "I know that look. And that feeling. I'll have Gabriel bring something in for you for dinner."

"Thanks." I squeezed her arm. "You're a good friend."

"You are too. Even if you're a stubborn little thing."

"You have no room to talk."

But stubborn as I was, I couldn't figure out what, exactly, I searched for in the data. Finally, a little after midnight, I gave up. The numbers and notations swam before my eyes, and I decided to go to sleep and let my brain work on the puzzle.

I woke to the sound of male voices in the front hallway. The clock said 6:05, so I rolled out of bed and threw on my robe. Leo and Ron stood in the door, duffel bags in hand, both of them unshaven and with bags under their eyes. Gabriel physically blocked them from entering the house.

"What's going on here?"

"Doctor Fisher. I didn't intend for them to wake you."

"That's not what I asked, Gabriel."

"We have a couple of strays." He pitched his voice low, almost a growl, all the amicability of the day before gone. "And they want to stay here. I knew if we fed them, they'd keep coming back."

"At least be civilized and give them a cup of coffee, Gabriel, so we can find out what's going on."

He shot me a look but backed down and went through the den into the kitchen.

Ron rubbed his face. "Thanks, Joanie. It's been a rough night."

"What happened?" I gestured for them to put their bags to

the left of the door by the umbrella stand, not a promise to let them stay, but a possibility.

Leo plopped down on the new sofa and ran his hands through his hair. "Well, we looked for clues in the woods between here and town, but we couldn't find anything."

"Why would you expect to find anything between here and there? What about the other side of the subdivision?"

"Because whatever's happening seems to center around this place." Leo looked up at me. "I know you probably don't want to hear that, but it's true."

He was right. I didn't. "Fine. Then what did you do?"

"We hung out in town for a while and asked people if they'd seen anything unusual the night before last."

"They hadn't," Ron added.

"So we went back to Peter's place. Marguerite was in bed with the help of a sedative, and Peter sat in the drawing room with a glass of Scotch. He looked like hell, I'll give him that."

"I bet."

Gabriel came in with three steaming mugs of coffee and set them down on the table with cream, sugar and spoons. "Would you like anything to eat?" He only addressed me.

"Do you have any muffins ready?"

"Baked them this morning."

"Would you bring those out, please? And three, no, four plates."

Lonna came down the stairs, beautiful as always in her morning dishevelment. When the guys saw her, their nostrils flared for a moment. Her womanly scent, perhaps? She had showered. They exchanged a look, but Leo shook his head.

"What was all that about?" I asked. Leo gave me a "tell you later" look, and my traitorous heart thrilled at the thought of being alone with him.

"Morning, guys," Lonna chirped. "The muffins smell good, Gabriel."

"I'll bring out some in a moment, Madam. Would you like coffee?"

"Yes, thank you."

Ron smiled shyly at Lonna. "How are you today, Ms. Marconi?"

"So anyway." Leo picked the story up. "He told us, 'I guess the two of you don't know anything about what happened last night?' We didn't want to tell him about the strange wolf, not yet, in case the townspeople decided to hit the woods and hunt down all of them, maybe even us."

Lonna raised an eyebrow at me, and it was my turn to give her an "I'll explain later" look. Leo must be tired to be so careless.

"He accused us of sneaking down to Mountain View and living it up there or at the club at the time-share resort at night and neglecting our duties to watch over Lance. Can you believe that?" Ron spread his hands and gave us a rueful grin. "As if we have the energy to do that after working all day."

"It was a full moon that night, so it was time for our change," added Leo. "We couldn't go party if we wanted to."

"So he kicked us out. Said if we wanted to run around all night, we wouldn't be doing it on his dime. He has enough on his plate, and now his kid's missing."

"Something about all of this doesn't make sense." Lonna had wrapped her hands around her cobalt coffee mug. Her nails were ragged, something she never allowed to happen, as though she had been chewing them. I held my breath, hoping she wouldn't ask about "the change" or why the townspeople would hunt the two young doctors along with the wolves.

"What do you mean?"

"You don't just kick people out unless there's another compelling reason."

"Such as..."

"You want them to be away from whatever you're doing."

I watched Leo drink his coffee, the muscles in his forearm tensing as he held the cup. He took his time with it, almost like he knew I watched him, and shot me a flirtatious look.

Lonna took a deep breath. "So, is someone going to tell me what's going on here? You've mentioned a strange wolf twice, and you just said something about a 'change'?"

I looked down at my coffee as though something in the light brown liquid would guide me to the right answer.

"I'm not stupid, you know." She fixed Ron with her gaze, and he turned away. "I need to know what you boys have been up to. There are children missing."

Leo's nostrils flared. "I'm well aware of that, Ms. Marconi. One of them is my nephew, remember?"

"I do remember. And I also remember there was something about a strange wolf. Since when do two former medical residents track large predators?"

Ron looked up. "How did you know about our jobs?"

"I know people who know people. You're evading my question." She sat back and crossed her legs. "And no one is going anywhere until I have an answer."

I decided to take the plunge. "Ron and Leo have CLS, but their CLS is different from anything I've ever seen or read about."

"Oh?"

"Right," agreed Leo. "You see, we actually turn into wolves."

"You turn into wolves?" The astonishment on her face almost made me laugh.

"We're werewolves. So is Gabriel."

For a moment, Lonna was speechless. Then she burst out laughing.

"Oh, Joanie, I cannot believe you. How did you get them to play along?"

"What do you mean?"

"Werewolves? Come on, you knew about the full-moon connection. Now you're just playing me."

"She's doing nothing of the sort, Ms. Marconi." Gabriel set the muffins in their basket on the table. "She's serious." He kept his facial expression neutral as he turned and walked back into the kitchen.

The color drained from Lonna's face. "Oh my God. You're not kidding, are you? You're all insane."

"No." I spoke as gently as I could, not sure of her reaction. "I didn't tell you before now. I didn't know how you'd take it. It's hard to believe, and I've seen them."

"You've seen them..." She made a hand motion. "Change?"

"Only Gabriel."

Now it was Leo's turn to raise an eyebrow. "Oh, have you, now?"

I lifted my chin. "Yesterday morning."

"And now you're here," Lonna said, her eyes wide. "And there are children missing. And there was a strange wolf. How do you know?"

"His scent was different. He wasn't part of our pack."

"How many are in the pack?"

Ron bit his lip, but Leo answered. "Four."

"Can you tell me who they are? For my investigation, of course."

"Well, you already know two of us, and I'm sure you've guessed the third."

I thought about the only other person I'd seen Leo hanging out with. "Kyra?"

Ron nodded. "Correct, and the fourth may come as a surprise."

"Who is it?" Lonna asked. "Peter?"

Leo laughed. "No, even if he had CLS, he wouldn't deign to hunt with us. No, the fourth is someone from in town, one of the original Piney Mountain residents."

"Who?"

"Matthew Grunden, the social worker."

Lonna coughed. "Impossible."

"Matt?" I took another sip of coffee. "That puts a new spin on things."

Lonna, meanwhile, appeared as though she'd just had the rug pulled out from under her, which I guessed she had. It's not easy to find out the shadows that haunt your dreams are real, and besides, who had ever heard of a werewolf social worker? She stared into her coffee cup.

"He lied to me," she said in a small voice. "He told me that he called me up here for the kids."

"The kid disappearances aren't the only thing, apparently." My mind worked, drawing connections from thread to thread of this twisted web. Matt to the kids. The kids to the new development. The subdivision to the lawyer. The lawyer to the two recently infected doctors. The doctors to the social worker. And Matt to Lonna and to me.

"It's all connected through CLS, but there's something I'm still missing. Like, what happened to Louise? If it wasn't an accident, then why did someone kill her?"

"We need to figure out what happened the day of the accident." Lonna stood, her expression determined, and she smoothed her hands on her skirt. "And I need to talk to Matt."

"Louise had a daughter, right?" I asked. "Mom of one of the missing kids."

"Yep, and she's more likely to talk to you than to me."

"It sounds like we have our tasks cut out for us, then." I looked at the guys. "And what are you going to do?"

Leo yawned. "Sleep."

"Good hunting last night?" Lonna gave himh a wry grin. She almost sounded sarcastic. I knew that look and guessed she was still trying to puzzle out if we were playing a joke on her.

"So-so." Leo popped the last bit of his muffin in his mouth.

"The prey has been driven away lately by the screams. They were just once a month or so. Now they happen every week. It sets everyone on edge and makes the prey skittish."

The memory of the noise made my hands shake. "I can imagine. I've heard it."

"Do you know what it is?"

"No. Do you?"

Leo shook his head, his dark eyes serious. "No. But it scares the shit out of me every time."

Ron yawned. "Can't we talk about this after we get some sleep?"

"You can bum a couple of the rooms upstairs. I'll tell Gabriel not to disturb you."

After they left, I looked at Lonna, who stared into the hall after them with a frown.

"You're taking this better than I expected."

She shook her head. "I'm still not sure whether to believe you, but I'll acknowledge something strange is going on. Whatever the case, if it's connected to the missing kids, I have to work around it."

She went upstairs to get her purse and left me standing openmouthed. *Well, at least she's not freaking out. Maybe she just needs to see one change to believe it.* But I had to admit part of me didn't want to share them.

HONEY JORGENS LIVED in an apartment in the new buildings on the other side of town. That little wisp of guilt curled in my stomach again as I knocked on the door. I was sure I was the last person she wanted to see.

The door opened, and a woman who looked like a younger version of Louise peered at me from behind the chain.

"Who're you?"

"I'm Joanie Fisher. My grandfather—" I choked on the words, the woman's grief tugging my own out. I turned my head so she wouldn't see my tears.

"You're the old man's granddaughter. He'd've come with condolences, too." The door closed, and the chain scraped as she unbolted it. "Please come in."

She let me in to the apartment, which was furnished cheaply but neat. "I'm Honey. My boyfriend is at work today. He's upset about my mama too, but the foreman won't let him off 'til the funeral."

"That's not very understanding. Do you know when the funeral will be?"

"No, not yet. The sheriff says since she died under 'suspicious circumstances', it may be a while."

"Are you here all by yourself?"

"Nope. My youngest..." She shook her head. "My daughter is asleep in the bedroom. She's three."

"You've been hit hard this year."

She smeared a tear back up her cheek with the heel of her hand. "First Johnny and now Mama. I told Rich it was because he sold out and is helping to build the new houses, the ones on the land they kicked us off of. We were gonna use the money for Johnny's and Julie's college so they can get out of here. I just hope Julie's smart enough to want to go to a good school."

"I bet she is."

The woman rewarded me with a small smile. "I'm surprised you came on your own." She wiped her hands on her jeans and motioned for me to sit on the corduroy sofa. "I'd heard you brought a friend with you."

"Lonna came up here with me to help me get settled and also because her colleague Matt wanted her help investigating the children's disappearances. She's in town talking to him right now."

"Matt's a right good man. He's done more for us than that sheriff has."

*More than you could know.* "Is Sheriff Knowles a native of Piney Mountain?"

Disdain twisted her features. "Oh, no. He came with the developers. He mighta grown up nearby, but he spent a lot of time in the city before coming back."

"Which city?"

"Little Rock. He was a cop down there while it was bad."

I had a hard time picturing Bud Knowles battling gangs in mall parking lots. Maybe he came up here like so many did for less money but more peace. Until now, of course.

"What has he told you about the kids?"

"That they're running away, upset at their houses getting torn down, and they're headin' for the city or upstate toward Missouri to work in the tourist towns." The frustration built in her voice like gathering thunderheads. "But they're too young for that. And I know my son. He's a good boy and wouldn't run off. He wouldn't've left his sister!"

I noted Honey's use of the present tense. "So you believe your son is still alive?"

She set her jaw. "A mother knows. All of us who's lost kids in the past year, we know they're still alive, it's just gonna take the right person to find them."

"What do you think happened to him?"

"I think there's an evil spirit out there. I've heard it screaming in the night. I think it's taken them and hidden them. Men won't be able to find them—it's gonna take somethin' more."

"Like what?"

This time she met my eyes. "Someone with a connection to the land like your granddad had."

My heart flip-flopped in my chest. Did she mean me? "And

what about Lou—er, your mother? Can you tell us anything about her last day?"

Honey's eyes welled with tears. "She left that morning to go to her job at the café. I didn't know anything had happened 'til they called looking for her a couple hours later."

"Did she say anything before she left? Was there anything different about her?"

Her eyes met mine with a directness that made me squirm. "She was all excited because she was going to be seeing you, Doctor Fisher. She and your grandfather had become kind of close before he disappeared. She was awful upset when he went missing. She wanted to talk to you to see if you might know what happened to him. And she'd helped him redo the kitchen because he'd told her you might be visiting soon."

Again, a hint he had known I would come. He hadn't contacted me in years, and I hadn't been planning a visit. It seemed the more I learned about the eccentric old man, the more the mystery deepened.

"What did you mean about my grandfather having a connection to the land?"

"I know he didn't grow up here—we all did—but he and that house, it's like they just belonged here, like they grew there." She leaned forward and lowered her voice. "There's some who say he's responsible for all that's gone bad here, but I know better. Mama said he'd even offered some of his money to keep the developers out of the town, to give scholarships to kids, but Mayor Franz didn't want to hear him. I think he wanted a big, shiny house of his own, and then that lawyer appeared."

"Which lawyer?"

"Peter Bowman." Her mouth puckered like the name itself tasted foul. "He came whispering in the mayor's ear. There's lots of places they coulda gone, but they came here."

"Did you hear Peter's son was kidnapped the night before last?"

Honey's mouth opened in an oval. "That little blond boy? Don't get me wrong, I got no use for the father, but the mother and son are precious. And his brother and cousin are right nice, too. You know they're doctors?"

"Yep."

She seemed to want to say something more but kept her mouth firmly closed. The phone rang. She got up and took it in the little galley kitchen.

As she talked, I looked around the apartment. Pictures of the whole family in wooden frames lined the walls and crowded the coffee tables. Johnny Jorgens figured prominently in them—a smiling baby, then a happy young boy, then as a pre-adolescent, his smile a little cocky but also sad in the photo of him, his mother and Louise in front of a small, old wood-frame house. I searched his face. Nothing hinted that he would have run away. I wondered what had happened to his father. Honey's voice startled me.

"That one was taken right after we moved from our old place. We wanted a picture of it before it was torn down so the kids would always remember where they came from."

"I see."

She turned away and rubbed her palms on her jeans again.

"Are you okay?"

"That was Ricky down at the junkyard. He said the tow truck brought Mom's car in, and it's messed up real bad." She wiped a tear with the heel of her hand. "He asked me what I wanted done with it. I told him to just keep it and sell it for parts if he wants. I don't ever want to see it again."

"Where did they find it?"

"On the road between town and your house." She frowned. "Was she supposed to be seeing you that morning at your house?"

"We were going to meet at the diner."

"That's what she'd told me."

An idea struck me. "Would you mind if I took a look at it?"

"If you think it will help..." My original feeling that she resented me and the part I played in her mother's death reasserted itself. "Do whatever you want with it."

I stood. "Thank you for your time, Ms. Jorgens."

"If you can figure out why..." She bit off the rest of the sentence, her mouth a straight line.

"I'll do my best."

"That's all anyone can do. But sometimes it's not enough."

LONNA MET me at the diner, where we grabbed another cup of coffee and compared notes.

"How'd it go with Louise's daughter? What's her name?"

"Honey. And there's a little girl that I didn't see at all."

"I bet all the parents are keeping their kids close."

"From what I've seen of the werewolves, I don't blame them. Who knows what they'd do on a hunt?"

Lonna shuddered. "That's not a pleasant picture."

"Since we're on the topic of unpleasant pictures, she got a phone call while I was there, and the junkyard guy told her they'd found Louise's car, and it was messed up pretty bad."

"Ooooh, any chance we could see it?"

"I got her permission."

"Good." She sipped her coffee, her mind seemingly a million miles away.

"And how did things go with Matt?" I prompted.

"He wasn't there. His secretary said he hadn't been in all week."

I lowered my voice. "But hasn't he been on the hunt?"

She shrugged. "We'll have to ask the guys. But first, let's go see the car."

I didn't ask where she'd been while I spoke with Louise, but I could guess. Talking to Matt's secretary would only take so long. I glanced out the window as we drove out of the square. Peter Bowman, his eyes narrowed, watched us from the door of his office.

## 12

Ricky's Junk Yard lay just outside of the subdivision boundaries and farther along the twisted mountain road we had taken to get up to Crystal Pines. When we pulled up, Ricky himself came out to greet us.

"And what'll you ladies be wantin' to look at?" He gave each of us the once-over. His narrow face betrayed only polite interest, but I got the feeling he figured we'd be a waste of time.

This time I spoke before Lonna could take over again. "We're interested in a car you just towed back here this morning. It belonged to Louise."

His eyebrows crawled up his forehead. "And how'd you know that?"

"Honey told me."

"Ah, so you'll be the old man's granddaughter. And this is the friend?"

"This is Lonna Marconi, a social worker from Little Rock."

"Pleased to meet you." She held out her hand and turned the full force of her smile on him.

He took it, but his face didn't show the interest Lonna typically caused. "Well, now, I normally wouldn't mind you ladies takin' a look, but Sheriff Knowles said no one was to touch the car 'til he gets his guys out here to check it out. He was already pretty pissed I'd moved it."

"We'll only be a moment," I said.

He chewed on something. Gum, I hoped. "He was pretty insistent."

Lonna tilted her head—full charm engaged. "I'm sure he was. Can you at least tell us where you found it?"

"Honey mentioned it was between town and my place," I added.

"Yep. It was off the road a little ways in the woods. I'd've never seen it if it hadn't caught the glare off the rising sun."

"And what were you doing on that road?" I crossed my arms and tried to look intimidating.

"The old man paid me to drive that way a couple times a week and take care of any dead animals in the road. I thought I'd do it outta respect for his memory."

"Oh. Thanks, then. I appreciate it."

"Are you sure we can't take a little peek?" Lonna pleaded. "We don't even have to touch it, just take a look."

Ricky rubbed the back of his neck. "Well, if y'all don't touch it, I guess I can let you take a peek at it."

"Thank you."

He led us through the wood cabin that served as an office to the "back lot", a dirt slope strewn with vehicles in various stages of disembowelment and dismemberment. Louise's car, a white domestic hatchback, was near the edge. The crumpled front end and dented sides told us it had gone off the road, rolled, and crashed into a tree or other large obstacle.

"Wow," I said. "How in the world did she survive that? That's why she was in such bad shape when she showed up at my place."

Lonna was already scribbling her number on a piece of paper. "Would you do me a favor, Ricky?"

"Sure, ma'am."

"Would you give me a call and let me know what the police say about the car?"

His jaw dropped. "I don't know if I can do that, ma'am."

She looked up at him through her long eyelashes. "It would mean a lot to me if you would."

He cleared his throat. "I'll see what I can do." Something caught his eye at the back of the lot, and his face went white. "I've got to do some paperwork, ladies. The gate in the fence over yonder is unlocked. Remember, don't touch the car."

He scurried back into the office, and I turned to see a woman in a long white dress gliding through the cars. My first thought was that it was the angry ghost of one of the vehicles' former owners, but then Lonna narrowed her eyes.

"Isn't that the chick who was with Leo in the restaurant on Tuesday? What's her name, Kyra? The third—"

"Yep, that's Kyra Ellison." I interrupted her before she could blurt out the word.

Kyra came closer, revealing she wore a white sundress. So much for the ghost. But she looked pissed.

"You!" Her shout was almost a shriek. "You're the one."

"One what?" I couldn't tell if she was looking at me or Lonna.

"Man-stealer!" She reached into the pocket of her dress, and Lonna grabbed my arm.

"Run!"

We ran through the gate, hopped in the Jeep, and Lonna gunned the engine. We peeled out of the gravel parking lot, and when I looked back, I couldn't see her.

"What was that about?"

Lonna relaxed her white-knuckled grip on the steering wheel. "I think she's jealous."

"Of who? Could she be sleeping with Peter, too?"

"I think she was jealous of you, Joanie."

"Me? That's a preposterous idea. Why should she be jealous of me?"

"Because her boyfriend is sleeping at your house right now."

"Yeah, you've got a point there."

"Just what you need, a territorial bitch of a woman who can turn into a predator."

"I think most of us can when we're threatened." Honey Jorgen's red-rimmed eyes came to mind. "Or when our kids are in trouble."

GABRIEL HAD lunch ready for us when we returned. Although the dark circles under their eyes and shadowed jaws betrayed the fact they had only had a couple of hours of sleep, Leo and Ron seemed to be in good spirits.

"How are you so awake?" I looked at each of them as they dug in to the Philly-style cheesesteak sandwiches. "I would be dead after that little sleep."

Leo spoke around the bite in his mouth. "We were in residency, remember? It's no worse than a call night."

"That's right, I'd forgotten." I searched my mind for a topic change. I'm sure they didn't like to be reminded of what they'd lost, especially Ron, who scowled across the table.

Lonna jumped to my rescue. "So I'm curious, do you only have your transformations at the full moon, or is it every night?"

Leo and Ron looked at each other, and Leo motioned for Ron to answer since his mouth was full.

"The full moon is the only time when we *have* to transform. We can transform any night, but the urge is overwhelming at the full moon."

"Right." Lonna scribbled something on her ever-present

notepad. "And how much do you remember the next day of your previous night's activities?"

Leo answered this time. "It's hard to explain. It's like having had a vivid dream to the point that some parts just don't make sense. I know there's stuff I don't remember. It's like the animal part of the brain takes over, especially at the full moon."

Lonna looked at me, and I knew she and I had the same thought: could they have taken the children? The savory sandwich turned to dust in my mouth, and I struggled to swallow.

She kept her tone neutral. "What do you do on those nights when you transform?"

"We run, howl at the moon. You know, wolf stuff."

"Do you hunt? Joanie said she saw your pack."

"Sometimes. It's harder than you'd think. There's a certain amount of learning that goes into it. We didn't have wolf parents to teach us."

"Do you remember what you've caught the next day?"

Leo put his sandwich back on his plate and fixed Lonna with a cold, dark stare. "Why don't we cut the crap, Ms. Marconi? What, exactly, are you trying to ask? Are you implying we took the children?"

She met his glare with her own. "My job is to find out what happened to them. I have to explore every avenue of possibility."

"Need I remind you my own nephew is one of those children who is now missing? I can assure you, whatever my frame of mind, I wouldn't be able to harm him." He threw his napkin on the table and stalked to the porch. Ron followed him. Leo had eaten all the meat from the middle of the sandwich without touching the bread.

Gabriel came in from the kitchen and picked up the plates. "I guess they won't be having coffee?"

"Probably not. Thank you, Gabriel."

"We didn't even get to ask him about Kyra." Lonna picked her sandwich up and ate with dainty bites.

"I think you got him wound up enough." I kept my voice low, unsure of how sharp their hearing would be.

"So what did you think about Louise's car?"

"It looked pretty banged up. Do you think Ricky will call you after the police have been there?"

She smiled, and I envied the confidence she had in her power over men. "I believe he will."

I SAT in the office and looked at the medical charts again. There was something in there; I knew it in my gut, but what? I opened the laptop, got back into the database, and entered data until it swam in front of my stinging eyes. Still, I was so close I couldn't give up. I decided to curl up in a chair and rest for a few moments.

I closed my eyes on the office and opened them to a clearing in the woods, each tree trunk, branch and leaf illuminated with the silvery-gray light of the moon. My breath came in ragged gasps—*it's after me!* It rustled in the brush to my left, so I gulped air as quietly as I could and assessed my escape paths. My bare feet crushed the pine needles, which released their sharp, musky scent. Careful not to prick myself, I crept to the other end of the clearing. I looked at the trees to see if I could climb to safety, but part of my mind knew that wasn't an option—my pursuer would follow me. So I continued to crawl inch by inch through the undergrowth, careful not to make a sound. The dirt caked my hands, the rocks scraped my knees, but I crept on for what seemed like hours, toward what should be safety.

Just when I thought I could rest, a low chuckle made my skin crawl, and it was upon me—sharp claws in my shoulders and hot breath on my neck. I rolled and grappled with it into another clearing, and as I lay on my back, pinned by its weight, its sharp fangs caught the moonlight, the tongue lolling as it panted over me. Not a black wolf, but a wolf-man in ragged khaki trousers, its chest finely muscled and furred.

I struggled, but it held me with one claw/hand around my throat. It reached into its pocket with the other paw and drew forth a long silver wand. The thick needle flashed in the moonlight, and I knew if he jabbed me with it, I would become one of them. I opened my mouth to scream as he brought it down toward my left shoulder, but no sound came out. I woke covered in sweat.

"Joanie?" Lonna knocked on the door and poked her head in. "Are you okay? You whimpered."

I pressed the heels of my hands to my eyeballs until stars appeared. "I just had a weird dream." Why were they always after me?

"Tell me about it."

She came in, and I recounted as best I could. When I got to the part with the needle, I jumped up. "That's it."

"What is it?"

"Hang on." I pulled the computer out of rest mode and collapsed some of the data so I had two columns side by side: Tdap vaccination date and symptom onset date. The symptom onset was clearly two to three weeks after the Tdap, or tetanus/diphtheria/pertussis vaccine, commonly given around age eleven. "That's the dream. The CLS—it's getting to the victims through the vaccines."

She clapped her hands. "Brilliant! Who would suspect the vaccinations?" Then her expression turned fierce. "And what bastard would do that? It's not like we don't have enough problems with the anti-vaxxers."

"Right?" I'm sure the tension in my face mirrored hers. As a public health scientist, albeit a disgraced one, nothing infuriated me more than someone tampering with one of our most important tools for infection control. "But it's not common enough to be showing up in every single pre-adolescent. There have to be some other factors." I stood up. "I've got to get out of here—I'm pissed. I can't breathe. I'm going to take a walk."

"Do you want me to come with you?"

"No, but thanks for offering. I need to be able to think out loud and talk to myself to work this out. Having company would only distract me."

"Be careful, then."

I looked at the clock. Two thirty. I had only been asleep for an hour? It had felt like several. "If I'm not back by four, send a search party."

"Right. Werewolves to the rescue. Are you sure you'd feel safe with that?"

"It depends on which one you send."

The puzzled look on her face as we walked out of the office told me she would ponder what I meant for a while, but I didn't care. I had finally made progress in solving the mystery of the missing children...and that I now had a ticking clock on unmasking the villain before they hurt anyone else...or the public's trust.

I WALKED across the lawn and resisted the urge to look back and see if I was being followed, or at least watched. I found the trail leading into the woods and took the north fork, which would bring me to a bluff over the river and my grandfather's "thinking spot". It was amazing how quickly my feet remembered the terrain, the dirt path with underlying rock exposed by the rain and erosion. I wondered if anyone else had been this way recently, if my grandfather had gone out to his thinking spot soon before he had disappeared. The sunlight made dappled patterns through the leaves, but the slight metallic smell in the air told me a storm was building close by. I didn't care—a little rain wouldn't hurt me.

I stepped on to the bluff and walked to the front, where a boulder with an indentation that was just the perfect size for an adult bottom stood and looked over the woods and the land below. To the left, a few small trees held on, but there was mostly a drop-off. Across the hills, the trees made a patchwork of green with fading that hinted at autumn but no true color yet. Below me, the river whispered, but I could only see glimpses of it through the greenery. I sat on a rock and watched the clouds, breathed in the fresh air, and was reminded this was the first time I'd been truly alone in almost a week.

I let my mind wander over the past few days, the revelations about the guys and the suspicions I had about my own family and the Landover Curse. Up there, alone, I knew I would have to face memories I'd avoided for years. I would have to read the contents of the box my grandfather had pointed out to me as well as the letters from my childhood.

"Oh, Andrew," I moaned, and a drop plopped on my jeans. I went to wipe the tear from my cheek, but another one fell, then another. I buried my face in my hands as all the grief from the past—and the past week—welled up and spilled out in great, heaving sobs. The biggest insult was that Robert wasn't there to hold me and comfort me, to let me cry on his shoulder. Lying bastard.

I raised my face to the sky, which had gone dark. The clouds had turned gray, and an ominous rumble sent me scurrying off the bluff and back toward the Manor. Soon sheets of rain fell, and I had to stop to get my bearings as the path seemed to taper off into the woods. Had I taken the wrong path off the bluff? I didn't know if there was more than one, but then, things may have changed since my childhood. Righteous indignation welled up. I'd been through enough, and now the forest would betray me?

I picked my way along the path that narrowed, then widened, then practically disappeared. The whole time, raindrops so big they may as well have been small water balloons pelted me and soaked my clothes. I couldn't ignore the misery of the situation. It was all Robert's fault. If he hadn't screwed up my appeal to keep my job, I wouldn't be in this mess.

*But then*, the little voice at the back of my head told me, *he would be the most welcome person to you right now*. For the first time, I questioned it—would he? Or would he laugh at how I'd really screwed up this time?

I continued to walk through the forest, completely lost, and then the rain let up enough for me to hear something behind me. It matched me step for step, only a beat behind. I quickened my pace, and it did as well. The image of the black wolf came to mind, the way it had stalked me and driven me into hiding on the night of the fire, and then how it had reappeared the night of Louise's death. Had it played with me enough? Was it waiting to finally drag me to my doom?

Strong arms wrapped around me and tackled me to the ground on a bed of pine needles. The smell, the same as in my dream, burned my nostrils. I screamed at the top of my lungs and brought my knee up to my attacker's groin. He grunted, but laid on top of me, which completely immobilized me. I squirmed anyway.

"Will you be still?" asked a familiar voice.

I stopped writhing. "Leo?"

"Who else?" He raised himself up on his hands and looked at me through rain-soaked hair. I became acutely aware of his thighs across mine, his face only inches away, and his hair dripping into my eyes.

I turned my head away. "Okay, okay, I surrender." Then a thought crossed my mind, and I giggled.

"Oh, for God's sake, what are you laughing at?"

I rolled on to my side, now laughing so hard I couldn't speak for a moment. He sat back on his heels and watched me.

"I'm sorry," I said as I sat up. "The thought just hit me that I'm very glad you don't smell like wet dog."

His lips twitched. "Actually, it's a good thing I do smell like a dog, otherwise I wouldn't have found you. Do you have any idea how far away from the Manor you are?"

I looked around as though I could divine my location from the trees. "I'm completely lost."

"Well, it's going to be a long walk back. Come on." He stood and held out his hand to me. I took it, and he helped me to my feet. He didn't let go when I achieved balance, and I stepped closer to him. The rain pelted us, but the heat between our bodies didn't turn it to steam.

"Are you cold?" Desire flared in his eyes more than concern.

I shivered and nodded. He drew me to him, and I tilted my head back. "You could help warm me up."

"How?" He didn't close the distance between our lips, but he didn't let go, either. The corner of his mouth curled, and I knew he teased me.

"Like this." I stood on tiptoe and brushed my lips against his. He swiped the raindrops off my cheeks with his thumbs and clasped the back of my head with one hand while supporting me with the other. Then he captured my mouth with his, and I opened to him with my lips. Something loosened in me, a worry that I wasn't desirable and that men would always leave me in the cold like Robert had. I reached around his head and allowed my fingers to play in the damp curls at the base of his skull as our tongues danced. But when I pressed myself into the evidence of his desire, he released me.

For a moment, he didn't speak, and the cold of the rain and his rejection slammed into me. He steadied me with one hand.

"We shouldn't." He said and gestured around us with his other hand. "This is no place for..."

"Right." I turned. "Which way to the Manor?" I asked, my tone light so he couldn't tell how much he'd hurt me.

"Don't be angry." He squeezed my hand, then let it go. "And it's this way."

I followed him and tried to allow the rain to wash away the sting of unfulfilled desire.

"How is your wrist?" he asked as we walked back the direction I had come.

I held it up. "Fine. You didn't damage it when you tackled me."

"Good. I was trying not to."

At least there was that. "Did Lonna send you?"

"No. I saw you leave the Manor and was worried when the storm blew in and you didn't."

A small smile escaped my pouting. "Are you my guardian angel now?"

He glanced over his shoulder at me. "Now that is one job I would *not* want. You're little, but you get yourself into some big messes."

"This is actually the lesser of the two today." I remembered Kyra's running after us at the junkyard and wondered if that's why he'd broken off the kiss. "I think your girlfriend tried to shoot me earlier."

"Who?" The shocked expression on his face seemed genuine, but I couldn't be sure.

"Kyra. She came after us today when we talked to Ricky, the junkyard guy."

"I know Ricky. He's a good guy. Kyra tried to shoot you?"

"She ran after us yelling something about a man-stealer."

He brushed leaves off his jeans. "And she had a gun?"

"Not that I could see, but she reached in her pocket."

"If she was fresh off the hunt, who knows what she was thinking?" He shoved his hands in his pockets. "She lost a lot when she developed CLS. We all did, but it really screwed up her lifestyle."

I crossed my arms. Was he defending her? "And what did she lose?"

"Her business. Her home. Her life. She ran a modeling agency in Memphis and Little Rock. Her main clients were girls whose parents were willing to pay her outrageous fees for classes, but to her credit, she was very good at placing them with companies in New York and L.A. When she started disappearing at night and news of her erratic behavior got around, her contacts dried up, then her clients, and she finally had to close the agency." His voice became hoarse, as Kyra's loss echoed his own. "She moved up here, where her parents had a cabin. She found a place where she wouldn't be bothered and where she could exist as a werewolf."

"Wow." My problems seemed a little better compared to having lost everything. "She shouldn't have come after us, though."

He turned away and studied the gloom ahead. "Who am I to say what she should or shouldn't have done? We all make mistakes, Joanie."

It was my turn to look away as my wrist gave a little throb. Or maybe it was my heart. We walked the rest of the way in silence.

———————

## 13

"Thank God!" Lonna threw open the kitchen door and hugged me close in spite of my wet clothes. "I didn't know what had happened to you. You were gone for hours."

"And you didn't send the cavalry?"

"Ron said Leo had gone after you. I figured he would be best since he knows the woods."

I looked at Leo, but he wouldn't meet my eyes. It struck me that Kyra was his pack-mate, and who was I? Nothing but an ivory-tower princess who may or may not know the secret to their cures. And if they were cured, would they then live happily ever after?

Lonna distracted me from my thoughts by throwing a giant bath sheet around me. "Go on up and take a shower. Gabriel will have dinner waiting when you get done."

The butler was waiting for me at the top of the stairs. "Are you okay?" The concern in his eyes almost made me start crying again, but I steeled myself against the shame of having gotten lost, for falling for the false promise in Leo's kiss, and then for wanting to wallow in my self-pity and grief, especially since others had lost so much more.

"Yes, I'm fine."

"Good, then. I've drawn a nice, hot bath for you and warmed your robe and slippers."

"Thank you, Gabriel."

He inclined his head, and I searched for something more in his smile. His face didn't change, but he squeezed the top of my arm as I walked past him.

I FELT MORE human after my bath and walked down the stairs to find Leo, Ron and Lonna in the sitting room. Gabriel had retreated into the kitchen and into his formal persona. He handed me a glass of shiraz without saying a word.

"Galbraith called while you were upstairs," Lonna said. "I told him you'd call him back when you were available."

"You didn't tell him I was bathing, did you? He's the last person I want thinking of me naked." I caught Leo's glance, and my chest and cheeks heated. "I'll make the call in my office."

I sat at the desk and looked around. Something seemed different, but I couldn't place it. I didn't care. I was tired, hungry, and just wanted to get dinner and go to bed.

"Galbraith." The clipped tone was the same, but it seemed like ages ago that I'd seen him.

"This is Joanie Fisher. I was told that you'd called?"

"Ah, yes, Doctor Fisher. This is regarding the butler your grandfather retained. He apparently has an interesting background."

My stomach clenched, and I put the wineglass on the desk. "What kind of background?"

"One of your colleagues is coming into town tomorrow. He didn't want me to say who because he wanted to surprise you, but he has some interesting information about this Gabriel person."

"Be straight with me, Galbraith. Are we in any sort of danger?"

"None foreseeable."

"Right." Well, this was getting nowhere. "I'd also like any papers my grandfather may have left with you. Are there any files?"

"There is one. He wanted me to hold on to it until you'd seen the Manor and had become acquainted with some of its secrets."

"Right, and now I've got more secrets than I can handle." We set up a time for me to meet with him and this mystery person at two o'clock the following afternoon at his office in Little Rock.

"What was that about?" Lonna asked as I sat down.

"I've got to go into Little Rock tomorrow to meet with Galbraith. He's been holding on to some of my grandfather's papers for me."

"Why didn't he just give them to you when you met with him before?"

"He said my grandfather wanted him to wait until I had been here awhile. Guess he didn't want to put too much on me at once."

Ron and Leo exchanged a look, and Leo asked, "What did he want you to see?"

"I'm guessing it's the big secret that no one is talking about. Or ever talks about willingly."

He dropped his gaze to the butternut squash soup. "There's really nothing to say."

"Actually, I'm fascinated by the whole culture of it. The names, the pack, the fact that Gabriel is a virtual exile for wanting to help my grandfather, but here he is cooking and cleaning for us." That only reminded me about what Galbraith had said. A wave of frustration exploded in my chest. So what if he tried to poison us all? At least I wouldn't have to deal with all the damn secrets.

Lonna cleared her throat. "So Joanie found out the vector for how CLS victims are becoming infected."

Ron's and Leo's spoons clattered into their bowls.

"It's in vaccinations."

Ron's jaw dropped. "We had flu shots right before we got sick."

I nodded. "It's horrible to think someone is tampering with the supply. And it's not just flu shots. We think it's in the kids' Tdap vaccines."

"They're about the right age." Leo sat back and ran his right hand through his hair. "That vulnerable age for development of CLS."

"But was it the same batch?" Lonna asked. "They go through a lot of that stuff, just like they go through a lot of the flu vaccine, I'm sure."

"So there's something in the vaccines, but it's not the only thing."

"Do you mind if I look at those charts?" Lonna offered. "Fresh eyes might help."

"Not a problem. I'll bring them into the library."

Gabriel cleared the soup dishes in preparation for the main course. "Just tell me which boxes you want transferred, Madam, and I'll bring them in there while you finish dinner."

"Thanks, Gabriel. It will be all but the box with the letters and the two really old ones."

Leo smacked both hands on the table, and I jumped. "I'm coming with you."

"Coming where?"

"I'm coming with you. To Little Rock. Who knows what may be waiting for you there?"

"Are you kidding me? I don't need your protection."

"Like you didn't this afternoon?"

My cheeks heated, but I refrained from saying, *"From you?"* Instead, I sounded more sulky than I wanted. "That was different."

Gabriel came in and set a grilled beef tenderloin on the table with horseradish sauce and rolls. "Who would like a slice?"

Leo looked down at the meat and then at me. "Go ahead and start with the ends for the girls. Ron and I like it nice and bloody." He bared his teeth.

I couldn't help it—I laughed, particularly when his facial expression went from ferocious to bewildered.

Lonna cleared her throat. "Ahem, I'd like a rare piece as well."

"Yep, and I'm a medium rare girl, so sorry, Leo, try again."

The corner of his mouth twitched as he tried not to smile, but he failed. "So you're interested in werewolf culture."

"It seems like you have your own. You have your wolf names. I'm assuming there are territories involved, otherwise the appearance of the strange black wolf wouldn't have made such a big stir for you." Never mind why it did for me.

Ron held his plate up to Gabriel for a couple of slices dripping with red juices. "A wolf's territory is where he hunts. Where the pack hunts. And where the pack leader is."

Leo jumped in, but I couldn't tell how serious he was. "That means that this land is the property of the pack. And the last time I checked, you're not a member."

We locked eyes, and my heart beat in my throat, but I refused to look away. A sense of strength and power overwhelmed me, and I imagined what it would have been like if the moment in the woods had continued its sexual turn.

"Hasn't anyone told you never to challenge a predator?" he asked me in a low tone and brought me out of my fantasy into the present moment. Was that a hint of yellow in his eyes?

I remembered our first meeting and what he said to Galbraith about his right to the land. Instead of being frightened, I got pissed. No way was I going to back down from this infuriating but fascinating man. "It doesn't matter about your stupid pack. I'm my grandfather's heir. Sorry, bud, but this is civilized society."

Lonna looked back and forth between the two of us and then put a hand on my arm. "This isn't a productive discussion. Of course the estate is Joanie's, that's what the will said."

"We're sorry, of course you're right." Ron put his hand on Leo's arm in a parallel gesture. "Please forgive my cousin. He's under a lot of stress right now. We really do appreciate all you've done for us." The knuckles of his hand turned white as he squeezed Leo's arm. Leo's face went pale.

"I'm sorry, Doctor Fisher. I do appreciate your hospitality."

I sat back, shaken. That was the first glimpse I'd gotten of the animal Leo since he had hurt my wrist, and I was as troubled by my own reaction as his. *What is this? Doctor Leo and Mr. Werewolf?* It was good Ron intervened when he did, otherwise they would have been sleeping in the woods again. Even so, I wasn't thrilled about having two resentful werewolves in the house in addition to the butler with suspicious credentials and a best friend who seemed to be developing an extra bitchy side.

AFTER DINNER, Lonna and Ron went into the den to play a board game. Having had enough of games of any type, I took a glass of wine out to the back porch. Leo had disappeared before dessert, and I told myself I didn't care where he had gone. Gabriel was in the kitchen cleaning up.

I sat back on the Adirondack chair and looked across the lawn, the edges of the woods inky black outside the range of the house lights. The house would be an amazing place for parties. I could picture it, twinkling lights in small potted trees around the yard, buffet tables on the patio, and a live band set up on the porch. I could see myself walking across the lawn, greeting guests, a tall, handsome man in my wake. I couldn't see his face, for he always had his back to me as I watched the imaginary scene, but I knew he must be with me because a big diamond sparkled on imaginary Joanie's left hand. She had bigger boobs than me, too. Obviously this was a fantasy. The babble of voices dissolved again into the sounds of the evening —wind in the trees and the babble of the stream.

The irony of the situation hit me. This place had been built for entertaining but never had seen a party like I imagined. The ballroom with its strange murals had lain under a layer of dust for months if not years, and who knew whether it was only there to cover up the lab? *Nope, no parties here. Just secrets and closet skeletons with fangs.*

The hiss of a match startled me, and turned to see Leo leaning against the railing in the shadows with a cigarette in his hand. He appeared lost in his thoughts. I thought about leaving, but I decided to stay—it was my house, after all. He didn't hunt here.

"Are you the civilized Doctor Leo or are you the boorish Werewolf Leo?"

He hunched his shoulders as though I'd thrown a rock at him. "Would you believe neither?"

"What are you, then?"

A long drag from his cigarette. "I'm not sure. I get in moods. Then I have those outbursts. It's like the primitive part of my brain takes over."

"Is that what happened in the woods this afternoon?" I tried to hold my breath against the cigarette smoke, but I coughed anyway.

"I didn't want to hurt you."

Would he have? I retreated from the uncomfortable

thoughts that flooded my mind into scientific fact. "It's the impulse control part of CLS—the part that takes over the brains of its victims around the full moon and makes the kids do crazy stuff at night." But those were kids, and this was a full-grown man of tremendous strength.

"Oh, is that all?"

I ignored the sarcasm. "And it's not so bad for Ron?"

"He's different. We've always been like night and day. I was always the one getting him into trouble. He's more of a follower than a leader, but he's also a survivor."

"How so?"

"He'll do whatever needs to be done to preserve that golden hide of his. You know, he's the one who told me about you. That you're the famous Joanna Fisher, CLS researcher and that I had been an idiot to confront you right after my transformation. I knew you'd been watching us. I could smell you on the night air."

"And Ron was watching you? Oh, and I *was* the famous CLS researcher. Not anymore."

"He's never far away." He took another drag at the cigarette. He blew the smoke out slowly, and I watched as it rose and dissipated. "So you lost a lot, too."

"I lost my career."

"And gained a fortune and an estate. Seems like a good-enough trade."

"For all the good it's done me." I exhaled to release some of my resentment. "I don't even know exactly what happened to my grandfather. Until I find out something certain, I only feel like I'm staying here, not that it's truly mine."

He took a drag on his cigarette and blew the smoke out in a lazy plume. "How well did you know your grandfather?"

"Not very. I spent summers out here after my brother died. He took care of me, we'd go for long hikes, and then he'd fix these great, fancy dinners in the old kitchen."

Leo almost smiled. "He did love to cook. He'd feed me and Ron after a long night when we were first learning to hunt. That was before the others joined us."

"Is that why he redid the kitchen?"

"That's a good question." Another pause. "He seemed to be preparing for something those last couple of months. He said he'd need to do some field research and that the house needed to be ready if he was going to be gone for a while."

"Ready for what, I wonder?"

"Who knows? He was pretty secretive."

"And what do you know about Gabriel?"

His lips curled in a sneer. "He appeared around here about a year ago and ingratiated himself to Charles. He tried to be part of the pack, but his British sensibilities just didn't fit in. So then he agreed to be a lab rat for whatever your granddad was working on."

"Any idea what that was?"

"No. Just that it had something to do with CLS. Gabriel had it from childhood, you know." He stubbed the cigarette out on the railing, and I winced for the wood.

"Yes, he told me." *That made for an interesting new angle on the pack...and Gabriel with all his secrets.* "And I thought doctors weren't supposed to smoke."

"They're not supposed to turn into werewolves, either."

"Touché." I realized that we had been conversing like two normal human beings. Of course, the insight then gave way to awkwardness.

I rolled out of the chair since the hard surface had made my butt fall asleep. "Well, I guess I'll go on in, then. I'll tell Gabriel that the two of you will be staying in the same guest rooms. How did you like the ones you slept in this morning?"

"They were comfortable. It's amazing that your grandfather built such a big house for just himself."

I looked back over the lawn, the imaginary party imposing

itself on the broad expanse. "I agree. I'm happy to be able to share it. I don't think he would've minded."

"Thanks."

"You're welcome." *I think.*

I turned back at the door to glance out into the night...and at Leo, who had dropped his customary scowl for a small smile. My cheeks grew hot when I realized I had caused it. I probably wasn't supposed to see his grin, but it helped dispel any doubts as to the wisdom of letting them stay. Now if only I could convince Gabriel. The butler, however, was nowhere to be found, but when I checked the upstairs bedrooms, all of them had been prepared for the night. A wave of sleepiness overcame me, and I decided to turn in.

IN MY DREAMS THAT NIGHT, I was back at Andrew's funeral, his loss fresh in my mind and heart. He had always been by my side, my twin brother. I would say it was like having a shadow, but it was more like I was the shadow, and he was the real thing, the full person, the class clown and center of attention. I was just the shy sister—the studious, quiet one who hung in the background, more than content to let him have the spotlight. His death left a huge hole in more lives than just mine and my parents'. So many people came to his funeral, all of his friends, even ones I didn't know he had.

In my dream, I was there, and it played out in vivid detail. I grew weary of all the condolences, all the tears, the way the people looked at me like they were just now seeing me, the shadow without a body. So I had closed my eyes, put my head on my arms on the table, and hoped people would leave me alone. My mother, deep in conversation with another woman, didn't notice, or I would have been publicly reprimanded and embarrassed for such insolent behavior.

With my eyes covered, my ears picked up more including the conversation behind me. This particular little boy, a redheaded kid whose striking dark orange hair made him stand out, sat with his mother. I had noticed them earlier but didn't recognize him from school.

"See, Michael?" The mother's nasal voice cut through the chatter. "This is what can happen when you go running alone in the woods at night."

A snort. "Andrew'd had his tonsils out. That's what killed him."

"Even if you've always been ridiculously healthy, it doesn't mean you're invincible. You have to stop sneaking out, or the next funeral is going to be yours."

I started awake. Those were harsh words, but the woman had been worried. What had happened to them, to the little boy? I searched my memory for his last name but came up blank. I wondered if he was still alive and if I could talk to him. He would be my age, maybe a little older.

I bit my lip. That would mean a conversation with my mother, something I wasn't ready to do yet. My father had passed away when I was in high school, but by that time, my parents had been divorced and I hadn't seen him in years. He had never had much use for me anyway, especially after Andrew's death.

But there was one thing I could do. The phrase "ridiculously healthy" had sparked my curiosity and connected another strand to the web in my brain. I put on my robe and crept down to the study.

The box with the letters sat on the small end table by the armchair. I pulled out the top one and started reading.

*Dear Grandfather,*

*Something awful has happened. Andrew had his tonsils out, and he ran away the day after. I went to his room to bring him ice cream, and he was gone. They found him in the woods, covered in blood, and he was dead...*

Tears pricked my eyes. It had taken me, a child of nine, weeks to be able to write that letter. I couldn't read that one yet, not with the new grief on top of the old. I pulled out the next one.

*Dear Grandfather,*

*Mama says I may spend the entire summer with you this year! I'm so excited! Ever since Andrew died this spring, I have been so lonely. There hasn't been anyone to talk to besides the dog, and he doesn't talk back. I'm looking forward to lots of long walks in the woods and pretend balls with Mr. Bear. You don't have to do anything special for me, I promise you I'll be good company, just wait!*

*Love,*

*Joanna*

That was the summer after Andrew had died, the summer my grandfather had bought Mishka for me. He had known that my parents' marriage, never good to begin with, was on the rocks because my father's friend had operated on my brother. My mother never forgave him even though the cause of death was some strange reaction Andrew had to the anesthesia.

*Dear Grandfather,*

*It's actually snowing for once, and I'm stuck in bed with a fever of 102, and Andrew said he would bring me a snowball, but he's still outside playing with his friends. It's not fair—we probably won't get any more snow for years, and I'm sick! Mama says it's because I have a delicate, ladylike temperament, but I know it's because Andrew is "ridiculously healthy", like Dad always says. Is that normal, for doctors to have a sick kid and a healthy one? I think this is the fourth time I've been sick since school started! I want to take some of my snot and look at it under the microscope you sent me for Christmas (thank you, thank you, thank you!), but Mama says that's gross, and Dad says that being a pathologist doesn't pay like it used to, what-*

*ever that means. I think I might wait until they're not home and try it.*

*Love,*

*Joanna*

"Ridiculously healthy…" There was that phrase. An idea formed in the back of my mind, something that my grandfather had figured out and was trying to tell me. I kept reading, but most of the rest of the letters were childish things, news of my school and science-fair successes, and Andrew's escapades.

*Dear Grandfather,*

*Last night Andrew showed me how he likes to climb out his window at night and go running through the woods behind our house. I told him there are snakes out there, but he doesn't care. He says he can't breathe in here when it's a pretty night. Last night the moon was so big that it was almost like a cloudy day instead of nighttime…*

*Dear Grandfather,*

*Andrew got to play the Big Bad Wolf in the Second Grade play, Little Red Riding Hood, and he was so excited he wanted to sleep in his costume. He said his teacher told him it would help him to "get into character". I think it's silly. I'm just a forest flower, so it doesn't matter much anyway…*

Reading the letters reminded me I hadn't had a very interesting childhood, but my twin brother had. He had come home from the hospital with a wild streak, Mama said. He had been the one to climb out of his crib, to run before he walked, and to get in trouble at school.

I put my head in my hands. *Impossible! Not my brother.* I tried to think back to the night he disappeared—a cold, clear February night—when the full moon made everything stand out in silvery relief. I had been downstairs watching TV with my parents and tried not to succumb to guilt because I got to stay up late, and Andrew, having just come home from the hospital after having his tonsils out, had to go to bed early. They had never gotten infected, but they were so big that the doctors were worried anyway. I went to take him some ice cream, and he was gone.

The full moon.

He had just come home.

Could Andrew have had CLS? Was that the root of my obsessive interest in it? I put my head in my hands. It made sense, crystal-clear, full-sun, spotlighted sense.

"Joanie?" Leo stood at the door. "Are you okay?"

Of course he would be the one to find me. "My paradigm has been shifted."

He crossed his arms and leaned on the doorframe, a smile on his lips. "I know the feeling."

"I think my brother may have had CLS. That that's what the Landover Curse is. My grandfather must have had it, too."

His lack of surprise made me want to throw something at him. "We were wondering when you'd catch on. You're no dummy, but there's no messing with denial for some people."

"Oh?" I realized that we were alone, the rest of the house asleep. The thought gave me a thrill along my arms that made all the little hairs stand on end. He took a cautious step in, and I held my breath, willing him to come closer.

"So this is the old man's study?" He looked around at the books.

"Yep. Actually, it's my study."

"I guess it is now." He walked in and stood beside my chair so as to get a better view of the bookshelves.

Once again, I was aware of how he towered over me, his heavy black brows moments from drawing over his eyes in stormy anger. A flush warmed my face, but I didn't reach for him. What if he drew away again?

"Don't you have a ton of books at Peter's house?"

He ran a finger along my jaw and then picked up my left

wrist, almost as though studying it. It was still bruised, but the pain had subsided.

"I'd rather be doing than reading." His voice was so quiet I almost didn't hear him.

"Is that why you were going into orthopedics?"

He chuckled. "Maybe." He leaned down so that his face was only inches from mine. "You know they call us the cavemen of medicine?"

"Oh, really?" I could feel his breath on my nose and cheeks. The image of him bonking me over the head with the Encyclopedia of Magic and Witchcraft and dragging me upstairs to have his way with me came into my head.

"Oh, really." His eyes locked on mine. A little thrill moved in my chest—he'd had the same thought, *I knew it!*

A knock startled us, and Lonna poked her head around the door. "You guys couldn't sleep either?"

Leo stepped away. I shook my head, my cheeks hot. "We were just discussing the, ah, charts and the vaccinations."

"I may start looking at them since I can't sleep. Leo?" She arched an eyebrow at him, and the familiar resentment stabbed through my chest.

"I believe I can go back to sleep now, but thanks."

I tried not to look at Leo, but I couldn't resist a small glance. Laughter danced in his eyes as he wished me sweet dreams and walked out of the study.

"I think I'll go to bed now, too."

Lonna shrugged, but a smile played at the corner of her lips. "Suit yourself."

"Good night." The library door closed, and I exhaled, happy to be left alone with the shifting sands of insight.

Andrew had CLS. My grandfather might have had it as well. So where did that leave me? Still with more questions than answers, one of which was why Lonna tended to appear whenever things were about to get interesting with me and one of the werewolf men. It was like she was trying to protect me from myself while she was the one with the bad taste in men, and that was the nice way of putting it.

I powered down my laptop, piled the papers into neat stacks, and turned off the desk lamp with its green cover. *Why is it that only one of us gets to have fun?* As I waited for my eyes to adjust to the moonlight streaming in through the windows, I closed them and thought I caught a whiff of Leo's scent, soap and rain and woods. Nothing of dog, thankfully.

*"It's a good thing I smell like a dog,"* he'd said. *"Otherwise, I wouldn't have found you."*

I smiled at his quip and at the thought that he'd been looking for me. Him, not Gabriel. Had they argued over who got to come rescue me? Or had Leo just made his decision and struck off, all dark energy and determination?

*Don't kid yourself, Joanie,* I told myself. *He's way out of your league... Or is he?*

I crept into the hallway, careful not to step on any of the creaky boards I remembered from my childhood, but a few new ones had appeared. The reawakened scientist in me asked the questions: *How old is this place? Did Grandfather build it or buy it? Why didn't I ask these questions when he was alive?* Grief swept over me like nausea, and, eyes blurry, I banged my ankle against the umbrella stand by the front door. I caught it just before it fell and waited a moment for the silence to reassert itself, my heartbeat in my ears and throat. I cringed, sure one or all three of the werewolves would come charging down the stairs and tear me apart before I could get out, *"No, no, it's me, it's Joanie!"*

But there was nothing, just a breeze outside chasing the first of the fallen leaves across the driveway and a chorus of crickets.

I put the umbrella stand back in the spot it had occupied for decades and swallowed the tears that came to my throat. This stupid four-sided brass bucket had had more stability than I ever would. I sat on the bottom step and sobbed quietly into my hands, not wanting to wake anyone. I couldn't take Lonna's pity or Gabriel's questioning or Leo's guilt trips. The day's conversations came back to me, how others had lost so much more.

"Fuck you, Leo," I muttered into the darkness and wiped my cheeks with my hands.

"Is that an invitation?" He stood over me, leaves in his hair, and I could see from the look in his eyes that he had just come back inside.

I gasped and tried to crab-crawl up the stairs, which didn't work with my injured wrist. After scrabbling for a moment, I curled up on the bottom step, my hand cradled against my chest.

"Don't hurt me."

He sat beside me and gently helped me to a sitting position. "Let me see."

I arched an eyebrow at him.

"I had just changed when I heard a crash in here. What did that poor umbrella stand do to you, anyway?"

"Probably not enough to deserve being kicked," I admitted, but I gave my wrist and hand over to his gentle tug. He examined it, poking and prodding, and I imagined his hands were investigating something else.

If he could sense—or heaven forbid—smell my change in mood, he didn't say. "It's just a nasty bruise, but you need to do a better job of keeping it still. I'll get you some ice."

"I'm fine."

He raised his eyebrows. "If you were 'fine,' you wouldn't be kicking umbrella stands and crying at the foot of the stairs."

I sighed and pulled my wrist away from him. "I'm just tired of people trying to make me feel guilty for not having CLS and for it not taking away everything. So what if I have a manor and a fortune? My grandfather, the only person who cared for me, is gone." I curled up with my knees to my chest.

He ran his hands through his hair, and a few leaves scattered around us like silver tears in the moonlight. "He's not the only one."

I snorted and put my forehead on my knees. "Who else is there?" I let my pajama pants muffle my voice. "Lonna and I can't stop fighting, and I barely know the rest of you." I wasn't going to mention the sparks of lust that occasionally flew between me and the werewolf men—especially him. That wasn't the kind of caring I'd meant, anyway.

A large hand rubbed the back of my neck, and I looked up, startled.

"Just relax." He turned my upper back so I faced away from him.

I tried to do as he said, and he massaged my neck and shoulders. I closed my eyes and pictured his hands as I followed the caresses of his calloused fingertips through my shirt and on my skin. He found knot after knot, smoothing them with deep yet gentle touches until I was so relaxed I slumped against him.

"That's even better than Gabriel's pills."

"I don't want to know," he replied and picked me up.

That woke me. "I'm not a child." I thumped him on the chest. "Put me down!"

He laughed, a rumble against my shoulder and hip. "Just relax. I'm taking you to bed."

"Oh. All right, then." I snuggled against him and grinned at the thought of what would happen in the bedroom.

When he brought me to my room and put me on the bed, he cupped my cheek, and I turned my face to his. His dark eyes met mine. He traced my cheekbone with his thumb and leaned in until only a whisper of air separated our lips. He opened his mouth like he wanted to say something.

"No words," I told him. Although he was the werewolf, I was the one to inhale his smell deeply before closing the gap. It hit me at the same time his mouth crushed mine and sent a lightning bolt to my core. His lips and tongue combined with the freshness of forest air and the heaviness of the desire between us to make a thunderstorm, and I had to draw back before its power crushed me.

*You always run from the storm.*

*Not this time.* I took a deep breath and went in for more, but he placed his hands on my shoulders and held me away from him. We both panted, and I strained against his palms.

"I can't stay." He put his forehead to mine. "The wolf is just below the surface, and he's hungry."

"We'll finish this later, Doctor Bowman," I promised.

He caressed my cheek again, and then he was gone. I didn't think it would happen, but I was fast asleep within minutes and dreaming of running through the woods, the dirt and leaves like velvet under my paws.

I woke from some very naughty dreams, although I couldn't see who the male partner in my early morning fantasies was. At different times, I thought it was Robert, then Leo, and maybe even Gabriel. Finally, when I woke in a sweat, I just gave up, got out of bed, and took a cold shower.

The enticing aroma of Gabriel's homemade blackberry scones lured me out of my room, and I was the first one downstairs. I sat at the table and had just finished my second scone when Lonna walked in, Leo and Ron right behind her.

"Any luck?" I asked.

She looked like she'd been up late, the circles under her eyes dark. "I think so, but it's hard to tell because we don't have any charts for non-CLS patients."

"Really?"

"The serial numbers and lot numbers of the Tdap vaccinations match. It looks like there were a couple of batches."

"Do we know who the manufacturer was?"

"It's a small company that I've never heard of, but I can call one of my colleagues who handles vaccination neglect cases for DFCS and see what they know."

"That works."

"Seriously, are you okay? You look like you've seen a ghost."

"I think I may have... I think I may have seen two."

She rubbed her arms as though chilled. "What do you mean?"

"Galbraith said something about the Landover Curse and how it skips a generation. I think Andy had it, and I think it may have been CLS."

"Your brother?"

"I can't explain it right now, but stuff is fitting together differently this morning."

Leo shot me a sympathetic glance, and I tried not to think about the lustful dreams I'd had after going to sleep.

I couldn't handle their drama as well as my own. "I'm going to finish my coffee on the balcony." I stood on wobbly legs.

"Do you want some company?" Lonna asked.

"No, but thank you."

I walked out on the balcony, sat in one of the Adirondack chairs, and took a deep breath. The sun peeped through a thick layer of clouds, its light watered down by the atmosphere. Every leaf and pine needle seemed extra green in the forest beyond the lawn. No ghostly parties filled my imagination this morning. Instead, my mind strained to recall small things, clues that would confirm or disconfirm what I had just figured out about Andrew. And then there were the vaccinations, the serial and lot numbers pointing in one direction. Had Andrew gotten a bad vaccine? Had it been something that he ate? Or was it something that would have shown up anyway? Finding out that he had CLS was like losing him all over again.

My solitude lasted five minutes at the most. That's when I knew from the prickling at the back of my neck that trouble had arrived.

## 14

A black convertible car stood in the driveway. The sporty car's low-slung body had sleek, European lines, and the tan top was pulled back to reveal a plush leather interior, the dashboard mock-antique. Kyra Ellison stood in the door and argued with Gabriel.

"Kyra?" I asked. "Is there a problem?"

"Ah, Doctor Fisher." She raised her eyebrows in mock friendliness.

"What brings you to my home?"

The fake smile grew bigger, her ruby lips drawn back in an almost feral grin. "I believe that one of my friends has come up here, and I'm just looking for him. I have an important message from his brother."

"Which friend would that be?" I couldn't help it, I sneered through "friend" so as to imply that it was actually more of a client. Probably not fair, but the woman's attitude immediately put me on edge.

"Leo Bowman. Or his cousin Ron. Have you seen them?"

"Not recently." As in, not in the last ten minutes. "Perhaps

Gabriel or I could pass along the message if they do appear here."

"Just tell him to call Peter. I'm afraid that's all I can say. It's a matter of the utmost discretion."

"Who is this?" Lonna appeared in the door, and Kyra immediately snapped to full attention and charm mode.

Kyra held out her hand. Her not perfectly manicured hand. Running around in the woods at night could be rough on the paws. "I'm Kyra Ellison. I live here in Crystal Pines. And who might you be?"

"Lonna Marconi. I'm a social worker, I'm staying with Joanie."

"Ah, a social worker." Independently wealthy versus overworked and underpaid: Kyra 1, Lonna 0. "And no, I don't remember meeting you."

Lonna didn't bite. "We didn't meet. Not that it's any concern of yours. What do you want with Leo and Ron?"

"I have a message from Leo's brother, Peter. Have you met him?"

"Briefly."

I smirked. *As in, in his briefs.* Ouch. Kyra 1, Lonna 1.

The fake smile disappeared from Kyra's face. "I'm not sure what kind of little scam you all have going on here, but I will find the guys. And I have ways of doing it that you can't even begin to suspect."

I couldn't resist saying, "Actually, the thought of you growing fur is very funny." She wheeled around and was in my face so fast I didn't have time to step back. Up close, I could see the ring of yellow around the pupils of her deep green eyes.

"And do you know what a she-wolf does to little flat-chested ivory-tower brats who interfere with her chosen mate?" Her voice was almost a growl.

"No."

"Trust me, you don't want to." And with that, she whirled around, jumped in the car, and roared out of the driveway.

"Did she just threaten you?" Lonna was at my side.

"I think so."

Gabriel, a pensive expression on his face, followed the sports car with his eyes until it disappeared from sight. "She's been a little unhinged since she got up here. She used to run a modeling agency in Memphis until she got sick."

"With CLS?" Lonna asked.

"Yes, Madam. Maybe she had a flu shot from the same batch that infected Leo and Ron. She arrived in Crystal Pines shortly after they did."

"That reminds me." Lonna turned to me. "I need to go back to the office in Little Rock to access the vaccination database. I called, but no one has time to look it up for me. I think they want me back down there."

"I can't say I blame them. You were busy before you came."

She gazed out over the mountains. "It's more peaceful here, in a sense."

I wondered if she was thinking about the fights we'd had, and my old friend guilt appeared, this time telling me it was my fault she was here.

"I don't have to be down there 'til two. Come with me. You can pack a bag if you want, grab a change of clothes."

"You won't mind if I tag along with you?"

"I never do. The more, the merrier." But in truth, the thought of the city with all the noise, people and traffic made my heart lurch.

"Is she gone?" Leo found me in my room packing an overnight bag. Lonna and I planned to stay at her place and then drive back up to Crystal Pines the next morning.

"Who, Kyra?" *I'm not jealous, I'm not jealous.* "Some brave wolf-man you are."

"I don't have to be brave. That woman just doesn't give up."

"You seemed to be getting along well last week." The mental image of him tucking her hair behind her ear popped into my mind.

"I give in every once in a while. She'll leave me alone as she makes plans, then when she notices I'm not following at her side, she comes back."

"She said to call Peter."

"Not right now. He wants to blame me for what happened to Lance. He probably has a trace on the line or something so he can find out where I am and send the cops."

"Because you weren't there watching him?"

"I guess."

He appeared as though he wanted to say something else.

"And?"

"I'm not sure, I feel like there's something missing, some piece we're not seeing."

"Welcome to my life." I balled a shirt up and threw it in my suitcase.

"Right. Sorry, I forgot."

"You don't sound sorry." But I sounded sulky, and I hated it.

"Well, what do you expect? My life changes, and I get stuck with a strange disease that causes me to turn—not comfortably, mind you—into a wolf every so often. Your life turns upside down, and you end up with an estate in the mountains worth hundreds of millions of dollars and an interesting intellectual challenge."

I narrowed my eyes. "How do you know how much this estate is worth? Is that what you were in Galbraith's office for that day?"

He sat down and ran his hands through his hair. "No, I was in Galbraith's office that day trying to convince him not to bring

Gabriel back. I thought your grandfather wanted to have me watching over you."

"What?" I didn't believe him. "You were arguing with him over who got the land."

"And I lost. But that's not what's important. Your grandfather was close to something; that much you do know. He said he had to do some field research and was going to bring you here to help work on it. Then he disappeared."

"Field research? You mentioned that last night." I sat on the end of the bed. "Is that why he was killed? To keep him from finding whatever is out there?"

"I don't know."

We were interrupted by the doorbell. Gabriel answered it, and I cringed at the condescending tone of Sheriff Bud Knowles.

"Is Miz Fisher in?"

"*Doctor* Fisher is in, but she may not be available."

"He's a good butler, I'll give him that," muttered Leo.

I put my finger to my lips. "I would be careful if I were you. I don't think he's looking for me."

Footsteps on the stairs, then in the hall. Even if I hadn't heard the exchange at the front door, I would have been able to tell from Gabriel's disgusted facial expression that he'd had to deal with Knowles.

"Doctor, the sheriff is here."

"Great."

"What do you want me to tell him?"

"I'll talk to him. Just don't say anything about Leo being here."

"Understood."

I found Sheriff Knowles in the foyer. "Can I help you, Sheriff?"

"Well, Doctor, I was wonderin', since you've got your finger in so many of the pies around here, if you could help me find someone."

"Who?"

"His name's Leonard Bowman. A couple of people saw you hangin' out with him and his cousin Ron in town a couple days ago."

"I see. And what business would you have with Mr. Bowman?"

"I need to bring him in to the station and ask him some questions about where he was when his nephew disappeared."

"If I see him, I'll let him know you're looking for him."

"So you don't know where he is?"

"Not right at this moment, no." He could have left the bedroom.

"You know, Doctor Fisher, I wouldn't want to have to bring you to the station and ask you about a crime called obstructing justice."

He looked at me with his beady eyes, and I struggled not to look away. This wasn't friendly Bud Knowles, mountain country sheriff. He was letting me see the shrewd character that had survived all those years in the worst parts of Little Rock.

"That would probably be more trouble than it's worth, Sheriff."

"Then you won't mind if I let one of my boys watch the house in case Leo Bowman shows up here. He might be a dangerous character, if you know what I mean, and I wouldn't want him to hurt you or the lovely Ms. Marconi."

"That would be fine, Sheriff. Ms. Marconi and I are actually traveling to Little Rock this afternoon and plan to be gone for the night, so an extra pair of eyes on the house would suit me perfectly."

"And what is the nature of this trip?"

"Not that it's any of your business, but I'm going to meet with my solicitor about some estate affairs."

He chuckled, a wheezing, grating sound. "As you recall, a woman died here under suspicious circumstances this week, Doctor Fisher. Remember that little agreement we had? You were going to notify me if you decided to leave."

"Consider this your notification."

"And when will you return?"

"Probably tomorrow. You may reach me through my solicitor, Lawrence Galbraith, if you need me before then." I'd be damned before I gave him my cell phone number.

"I'll do that." With a tip of his hat, he was gone.

"What are you going to do about..." Gabriel inclined his head up the stairs.

"If he knows what's good for him, he's already gone."

Gabriel smiled and watched the sheriff's car pull out of the driveway. "You should go as well, then."

"I guess I should."

"Please be careful."

"Can't watch over me down there, huh?"

"I shall be miserably bored while you're away."

I stood on tiptoe and kissed his cheek. "I'll be careful, I promise."

LEO CAUGHT up to us in the garage. He carried his duffel bag and walked with a determined step.

"What are you doing here?" I glanced outside to see if the sheriff's deputy's car was there yet. "You know they're looking for you."

"I said I was coming with you."

I glanced at Lonna, but she held her hands up. "I'm staying out of this."

I fixed him with my sternest stare. "Are you out of your mind?"

"If the sheriff is looking for me here, then it makes sense for me to be somewhere else."

I couldn't fault his logic.

"Besides," he added. "I need to go by UAMS and get Ron's and my medical records. I have a release-of-information form from him in my bag. That way we can see if we got flu shots from the same batch."

"Didn't you get them at the same time?"

"No, we were on different rotations and had opposite schedules."

"Okay, so you have a valid reason to go. But what about me? Knowles said something about obstruction of justice."

"If we get caught, I'll tell them I forced you to take me. Look, I'll hunch down in the back of the car until we're out of town."

"There's no way you'll fit."

"Then put my duffel in the trunk." He unbuttoned the top button of his shirt...and kept going.

"What the hell do you think you're doing?" I couldn't help it, I watched him undress. Fine black hair covered his chest and stomach, but I could still see the tense muscles underneath. Running through the woods might not be good for the paws, but he was in excellent shape. I'd never been much for hirsute men, *but damn!*

"Ah, Joanie? Perhaps we should give him a moment of privacy." Lonna grabbed my arm, and we walked back into the hallway.

"There you go, ruining the show."

She rolled her eyes. "I don't think I want to see that show."

Something whimpered, and a moment later, a wet tongue licked my hand. I looked down into Leo's eyes but with golden irises in a black canine face. The world tilted, but this wasn't the black wolf I'd seen earlier.

"I guess we're going to have to take you now, aren't we?"

The wolf's lips parted in a snarl.

"Okay, okay!"

He barely fit in the backseat, let alone the well, but we covered him with a blanket. A casual glance wouldn't reveal too much, I hoped.

"Are you ready to do this?"

Lonna nodded. "Ready as I'll ever be. Leo?"

A noise between a bark and a yip came from under the blanket in the back.

"Does this mean I'll be able to say whatever I want to you, and you can't talk back?"

*"Not necessarily, elf-girl."* The words brought me back to seeing them that night on the lawn with the deer, and I remembered that I was dealing with a predator whose animal brain was now in full gear.

"Gotcha. And don't call me elf-girl."

"What?" Lonna looked from me to the blanketed lump in the backseat. "I didn't call you elf-girl."

"No, but he did." My heart skipped a beat. "What did you hear?"

"Just a woof or something."

"So I can understand them and you can't." Just like I had understood my brother from the cradle. I remembered my father yelling at him, telling him to speak like a human boy. I had tried to protect Andrew because his speech sounded muffled, but I could still make out what he said.

I didn't breathe easily until we got out of the Crystal Pines gates and on the road. Even then, our passenger and the trip in general, made me uneasy, especially with this new revelation. Did that mean I was genetically predisposed? Or did I have some other, more sinister talent?

## 15

G rief has a funny way of sneaking up on you. It's like one day you're out getting groceries or something, and then *wham!* It punches you in the middle of the chest, or maybe the solar plexus, and it would bring you to your knees if you weren't afraid of dropping the eggs.

It's a good thing Lonna was driving when it happened to me. Leo snoozed in the backseat, still in his lupine form. I watched the road signs as I did when I was little, looking at the towns we passed, their posted populations, and trying to remember which had been the smallest when I had been a lot smaller. For a moment, I was back there with my mother, her perfectly manicured hands tight on the wheel, her knuckles white, and her teeth clenched with the desire to be away from "that godforsaken place." It seemed like every town, no matter how small, put a new obstacle between me and Wolfsbane Manor, the only place where I felt loved and protected.

I snapped back to the present when Lonna asked if I needed a bathroom or coffee break.

"You looked like you were in another world there."

"I was."

"What were you thinking about?"

"Nothing." But the images crowded my mind, and the words caught in my throat in their rush to be the first ones out. Would I tell her about the pretend balls my grandfather and I held, when we would go down into the ballroom and dance with our candles, which would cast weird shadows on the ceiling and make the eyes of the painted woodland animals glow? Or should I tell her about the long hikes we'd take down to the river and the stories he'd tell me about the trees and bugs? What about his patience for my hundreds of questions? It had always taken me a few days to wind down and get used to being quiet again after my visits up there.

"We'll be going back soon," she promised me with a pat on my arm.

I nodded, too choked up to say anything. Leo gazed up at me with expressive canine eyes, his sadness echoing my own. It seemed that we had all lost something up there. Or had maybe found something but hadn't been able to hold on to it. The only question would be what Lonna would have to sacrifice.

Lonna dropped me off at Galbraith's office at five minutes until two, then drove off to take Leo to her apartment, where he could transform back to human and dress. Then she'd drive him to UAMS and go to her office, which was right down the street from the hospital complex.

The air inside Galbraith's foyer was stuffy—was the air-conditioning broken? If so, that would motivate me to get this meeting over with quickly. I hesitated at the door, all too mindful of what had happened the last time I was early. Leo seemed to be a different person every time I encountered him, which made dealing with him unpredictable...and oh-so-exciting. I allowed myself a smirk of satisfaction at the one-sidedness of the relationship between him and Kyra Ellison, as much of a bitch as that made me.

Galbraith opened the door himself. "Doctor Fisher, there's no need to stand outside in the heat. Why don't you come in?"

I un-smirked my face, my cheeks warming. "Um, thanks."

"I apologize. The air is broken in the foyer. I've called the maintenance crew, but there's no telling when they'll be here."

"Typical."

"There's someone who's been wanting to meet you."

"Actually, it's to see her again," said a familiar voice from my past.

"Iain?"

A tall figure emerged from the gloom in the back of Galbraith's office, where three chairs sat around a low, round table with an antique coffee service.

"Iain McPherson." I put my hands on my hips. "I haven't seen you since, when, the International Behavioral Genetics Society meeting in London a few years ago?"

"Joanna, you still haven't managed to hit five-two have you?" he taunted as he enveloped me in a bony hug. Between us, we may have had enough body fat for one normal skinny person. He'd always reminded me of a greyhound with his lanky build and long nose.

"Iain, you're as obnoxiously British as ever."

"That's Scottish, young lady."

"Uh-huh. Technicality. You're still part of Great Britain. At least for now."

He rolled his eyes. A few more wrinkles had appeared around them, and a little more gray at his temples, but he had hardly changed at all. He was still the same old Iain, whom I'd joked was my conference husband even though he didn't share his bed with women.

"What are you doing here?" I asked as we sat down.

Galbraith passed me a white porcelain cup and poured coffee out of a silver pot.

"Your grandfather and I had been corresponding. He said he was close to a breakthrough and would let me know how it shaped up soon, but then he went silent."

"He's, ah, deceased, we think."

"I'm so dreadfully sorry." He leaned over and squeezed my hand. "Galbraith had seen the letters I sent Charles and had contacted me to that effect. Of course I had to come and see if he had left anything, if I could pick up where he stopped."

"Right. That's what I'm trying to do as well."

"You're no longer with Cabal?"

"They got bought. There was a fire. Just bad timing all around. I got laid off."

"Why would a company that has so much to gain with new gene therapies lay off their most promising epidemiologic specialist in CLS?"

I looked away. "I don't know. I don't really want to talk about it."

"What about that chap you were working with, Robert?"

"He's still there." I didn't say anything else and hoped he would get the hint. He had known there was something going on between the two of us, but I didn't want to discuss that in front of Galbraith.

"I see."

Galbraith cleared his throat. "So you had some questions for me?"

"Would you like me to step outside?" asked Iain.

"No, that's okay. I think I may need your help with this matter soon." I took a deep breath. "I know that the circumstances surrounding my grandfather's death are somewhat suspicious."

Galbraith inclined his head.

"I was wondering if he'd actually made arrangements recently. Did he seem to think he was in danger?"

"He essentially told me that he was going into the field and would likely encounter peril there. He wanted it to be expressly stated that he wanted you to have the bulk of the estate. I had the impression he counted on you to continue his work."

"Were there any safe-deposit boxes or anywhere else he might have left papers or notes for me?"

Galbraith frowned. "Not that I can recall, but I will look through the documents again to see if, in my dotage, I misplaced something. There was one folder that he wanted me to hold for you until you had become more acquainted with the Manor and its secrets."

*And the werewolves.* "What do you know about this butler he arranged for me? You said there was something I needed to know."

"Yes, Gabriel…" He tapped the arm of his chair. "His last name escapes me at the moment."

Iain scowled. "It's McCord, Gabriel McCord."

I resisted the urge to ask if Gabriel was a spy like Bond, James Bond. "You know him?"

"If it's the same bloke I'm remembering. He was a member of the Society in the UK, sort of a research assistant, but he wasn't at the meeting you came to. He was interested in your work, though. He made copies of all the slides and notes I brought back."

"When was that?" Galbraith asked.

"Five years ago, to the month." I did some mental calculations. "You're missing the meeting right now, aren't you?"

"I am, but it's worth it to see you again."

"Flatterer."

"That's interesting." Galbraith stood and moved around to his desk to pull out a file. "I believe your grandfather had me start looking for domestic help at about this time last year, and this Gabriel person contacted me in response to the advertisement we placed."

"My grandfather looked for a butler?"

"He was planning on having some renovation done on the house, and he wanted someone to keep the mess and chaos at bay while he worked. He had a woman from the village who would cook and clean for him occasionally, but he needed something a little more permanent."

"That must have been Louise." I tried to block the memory of the last time I'd seen her. "Who died under suspicious circumstances."

"Really?" Iain raised an eyebrow at me. "Does death always follow you, or is this a recent development?"

"It has ever since the fire." I fingered the tip of the scar at my collarbone. "That's when the chaos started."

The braying of a car alarm startled the three of us.

"That's my rental!" Iain jumped and headed toward the door. "What could have set that off?"

My mind flashed back to the night my lab burned. The sound of my car alarm had broken my concentration and called my attention to the smoke that crept under the door.

But there was something else, some small noise I couldn't identify. My heart thudded and sent roaring waves through my throat and skull. Iain opened the door to the lobby, and I ran after him.

"Don't go out there!" I gasped and held on to the sleeve of his jacket.

"I have to see what set it off. It's going to eat up the battery."

"Give it a minute. Maybe it'll go off."

"Don't be ridiculous, Joanna. All I have to do is click the lock button to stop it."

My stomach clenched as he opened the heavy wooden door and pointed the remote at the black Lexus. I forced myself to watch as he pushed the button so I could yank him inside as soon as the alarm stopped. We tumbled to the floor just inside the door and knocked over an end table.

"Joanie, what the hell?"

The wooden door with its metal core saved us from the brunt of the explosion. The whole building rocked with its force, and the windows shattered inward. If we had been farther into the room, we would have been shredded. Smoke poured under the door, and we coughed, holding each other tightly as we cowered by the wall. We didn't dare move.

After a few minutes, he asked, "Are you okay?"

I almost didn't hear him over the ringing in my ears. "I think so. You?"

"Yes." The stubble of his chin scraped against my forehead. I picked up my hand from the floor and hissed in pain—it was the same wrist I'd fallen on a few nights before.

"You're hurt."

"An old injury."

"Is everyone okay in there?" a voice called from outside. "It's the fire department. Please respond."

"We're fine," Iain called back.

"Don't move. We're concerned you may be injured. Someone will get you out in a second."

Iain raised his eyebrows, and the expression almost looked comical on his soot-covered face. "That was fast."

"I guess they don't get many big explosions in Little Rock. And the fire station is just down the road."

"I didn't hear the sirens. Must be the ringing in my ears."

The inner door opened, and Galbraith looked out, his expression one of concern, then shock.

"Doctor Fisher, Doctor McPherson? Are you all right?"

"I think so. Don't come any further—there's glass everywhere."

The outside door swung open, and a fireman in full gear came through. "Is everyone all right in here?"

"Yes. Can we get up now?"

He held out his hand and helped me up first—by my unin-jured hand—and then Iain. Galbraith picked his way across the debris, and the fireman directed his attention to him.

"You the building owner?" When Galbraith nodded, the fireman continued, "We have to make sure the building is still sound. And the two of you should get checked out at the hospi-tal. The paramedics are here if you want to talk to them."

Why he didn't say the same to Galbraith? Right, Iain and I both had soot on our faces and dust in our hair. My left hand throbbed.

"I'm fine, but Doctor Fisher has injured her wrist in the fall." Iain stopped when he noticed the smoldering wreck of what had been his car. "My god!"

"Was anyone on the road?" I asked, craning to see.

"No, luckily there was a lull in traffic when the car exploded."

A policeman walked up to us. "Was this your car, sir?"

Iain ran a hand through his hair. "It was a rental."

"And when did you pick it up?"

Something still didn't add up. I let the paramedic look at my wrist as Iain answered the policeman's questions. No, he hadn't let anyone else have the keys to the car, no he hadn't valet parked it anywhere, yes, the rental place would know the history of the vehicle better than he would, yes, he had called ahead and requested a luxury vehicle...

I started, and the EMT apologized for jarring my wrist.

"No, it wasn't you," I told the earnest young man.

"Well, you should put some ice on it. It's swelling."

I nodded but was too busy following my own train of thought to hear him. There had been a noise outside the window, a noise I'd heard before. It was what had warned me of the impending explosion. But that was as far as my memory would go.

Again, that feeling of being watched, of those invisible fingers across the back of my neck raised all the hairs on my body. I tried not to be obvious about it as I looked around. A shadow at the corner of the building detached itself from the other dark places and moved into the alleyway beside Galbraith's office. The shadow turned, its tongue lolling out at me, and my heart stopped. The black wolf. Before I could be sure, it was gone. Louise's warning echoed in my mind.

*The black wolf knows.*

That was the noise—the sound of an animal prowling outside the window. It was the same sound I'd heard the night of the fire before my car alarm went off and before the explosion in the hallway that started the fire.

"What happened?" Lonna pulled up with Leo in the car, and he leapt out of the passenger seat. He stopped short when he saw Iain.

"Who's this?"

"Iain McPherson. He's another CLS researcher."

"And you are..." Iain raised an eyebrow.

"Leonard Bowman." He looked straight into Iain's eyes. "Doctor Leonard Bowman."

"Leo, that's enough." I pulled him aside. "Do you remember the black wolf?"

His nostrils flared. "Why?"

"I think he's here."

"Give me five minutes, then get my clothes out of the alley."

"What are you going to do?"

"Track him."

"Isn't that dangerous?" I glanced over my shoulder to find Iain watching us. Poor guy, he had no idea what he'd just gotten himself into. But he'd be so excited to hear about what we'd found if he could get past the shock.

"No more dangerous than letting him roam around and making cars explode."

"Touché. Fine. Good luck."

He made sure that no one watched him, then darted into the alleyway and disappeared into the shadows.

"Is he...?" Lonna asked when I returned to the group alone.

"Yep."

"You'll have to fill me in later."

THE REST of the day passed in a whirlwind. First we had to talk to the cops. Then to the bomb-squad guys. Then to another policeman, this one in plainclothes, at the station. Iain had to make a call to his travel-insurance company and straighten out things with the rental-car company as well as replace everything that had been in his suitcase in the trunk. Luckily he'd taken his laptop as well as his wallet and passport into Galbraith's office, so the difficult-to-replace items had been spared. Lonna had left us at the police station to go to her office and finally rescued us just as the sun was setting. She suggested that we go out for dinner, but I wanted to be safely indoors if the black wolf was prowling about.

"So who do you think wants to kill you?" Lonna asked Iain as we sat with Italian take-out in front of us and glasses—big ones—of Chianti in hand.

Iain leaned forward and snagged another calamari ring. "Are you always this direct?"

"Yes. And you're evading the question."

Here we were again, Lonna taking the lead, and me just sitting quietly and keeping my mouth shut. Back in the city with the same old patterns. I couldn't concentrate, though, not with the black wolf prowling around out there and Leo trying to track him.

"I have no idea. I haven't received any threats. I haven't noticed anything suspicious. The first inkling I had of something being out of the ordinary was when my car alarm went off while I was in Galbraith's office talking to Joanie." He raised his glass to me. "I can't thank Joanie enough for saving my life."

"She's got a knack for self-preservation." Lonna grinned, and the red wine gave her purple teeth. She looked like she'd been sucking the lifeblood out of a wine barrel. "Don't you, Joanie?"

"I guess." I swirled the wine in my glass. "I just knew something was wrong. Just like the night of the fire. Just like the night Louise died."

"Wait a second." Iain set his glass on the table and turned to look at me. "You mentioned her earlier, and it slipped my mind. Just how did she die?"

"She showed up one night bloody and hurt, badly hurt. She died on my suede couch. Or maybe it was microfiber. Either way, they took it."

"She died in your house?"

"She knew my grandfather, was helping him at the house. I guess she knew how to get there from the village. It's not like it's a difficult path, just straight up the hill."

He arched an eyebrow, his expression serious. "Then maybe I need to get as far away from you as possible."

"That's not nice, Iain."

"Oh, forgive me, Doctor Fisher." He stood up and shoved his hands in his pockets as he paced back and forth. "If you may recall, I just survived an explosion, one which you also witnessed. I lost my favorite luggage set, my rental car, and likely a few years off my life! I don't know if I'm in the mood to be nice."

Lonna opened her mouth, but I held my hand up. "If you're not in the mood to be nice, then I'm not in the mood to deal with you. I suggest you call a cab and go find a hotel for the night. Then you can skedaddle right on back to Stirling tomorrow."

"Skedaddle?" He frowned, then the corner of his mouth twitched. "I don't think a Scotsman would skedaddle."

"Whatever. You can leave whenever you want to."

He sat back down. "You know I can't do that."

"Why not?"

"Because that bastard Robert should be here to protect you, not me. He's the real reason you're in this mess. If he'd stood up for you at Cabal, none of this would have happened."

My nervous wine-swirling stilled at the sound of Robert's name. "And what do you know about that?"

He looked down at the glass cradled in his hands. "Robert didn't want to fire you, but he said he was under a lot of pressure from his bosses—who were getting heat, if you'll forgive the pun—from the bigwigs at the pharmaceutical company that bought Cabal."

"Wait a second. Cabal was bought by a pharmaceutical company? I thought it was another research organization."

"It was the research arm of one of the big ones, I forget which one. I think it only has one word in the name. The information should be online." He opened his laptop and waited for it to boot up.

"Lonna, did you have any luck figuring out where those vaccines came from?"

"I'd almost forgotten. Yes, I talked to Jasmin, who looked in the state database. I could only get an idea of which ones were distributed in the region. The only company that had both the flu vaccine and the Tdap vaccine came from..."

"Hippocrates Pharmaceuticals," she and Iain said at the same time.

I wish I could say that everything became clear at that point, but the meaning of the revelation punched me in the stomach. My foe—and the threat to me and my friends—had just gotten a lot bigger. I also knew with certainty that I was going to have to talk to Robert and find out what this "pressure" was and how my projects had changed since I had been "terminated".

I DIDN'T THINK I would be able to sleep that night considering the events of the day, so I was surprised when the ringing of my cell phone woke me up. I answered to find a different Scotsman on the line.

"Doctor, is everything okay?"

I rolled over and looked at the clock. Midnight.

"Yes, Gabriel, everything's fine."

"I was just checking the news and saw the piece about the explosion in the Local/Arkansas section. Your name was mentioned." He didn't say anything about Iain's, although surely his must have been as well. "Were you injured?"

"Only my left wrist again. You weren't there to save me this time." I couldn't keep the resentment out of my voice.

"That is something I will always regret."

The genuine sorrow in his voice tugged at my heart, particularly since I had meant to tweak him, but then the conversation with Galbraith and Iain popped into my head.

"You knew Iain McPherson? He said you were on his research team and left, then you showed up when my grandfather started looking for domestic help."

"You sound suspicious."

I noted how he didn't answer the question. "Something doesn't quite add up."

"Did Doctor McPherson also tell you I had collected everything I could find on your work? That I was your 'biggest fan', so to speak?"

"He mentioned that you were very interested in it."

"What would you say if I told you I took the position for the chance to be near you?"

"I would say that that's creepy, almost stalker-ish. How do I know you weren't trying to use me for my knowledge? Or my grandfather? Leo said you were a lab rat."

Silence. I could tell that I'd really hurt him. Gads, I hated how those late-night conversations stripped away the facades we put up. But he had kept information from me, and right now I couldn't trust anyone, not even Lonna, whom I heard in the living room. At least I thought it was Lonna. Maybe it was Iain because whoever it was bumped around like they didn't know where everything was. I held my breath and listened hard.

"Doctor Fisher? Is everything okay?" My heart broke at the formality in his tone, the new wall between us.

"Someone's in the apartment."

"Just stay where you are. I'm calling the police."

"No, don't do that yet. I'll keep you on the phone. Let me just peek my head out and see if it's Lonna or Iain."

"Is that wise?" *Aha!* Still that note of concern.

"I promise, you'll hear everything I do."

I opened the door just wide enough to squeeze through, and cell phone in hand, I crept down the hallway to the living room. The front door stood wide open, and something lay crumpled in a pile in front of it. I knelt down and found Lonna's crimson Razorback T-shirt and boxers—the ones she had gone to bed in.

"Gabriel, I'm not sure what to make of this," I whispered into the phone.

"Of what?"

"Lonna seems to have left the apartment."

"She lives there, doesn't she?"

"Yes, but I think she left naked. Her clothes are by the door."

Gabriel sighed. "I had a suspicion, but there was no way for me to know with certainty. I would have told you had I been sure."

All the pieces to that puzzle fell into place. Lonna's moodiness, her strange illness, and the way the male werewolves had reacted to her. "There's something you haven't been telling me, isn't there? Something else."

"I don't think I need to tell you, do I?"

"No." My best friend had become one of them. "I have to go."

"Be careful. A new werewolf can be difficult to control."

"I'll wake Iain."

A pause. "That's probably a good idea. But good luck getting him to believe you. He never accepted CLS as more than a mental illness."

"He's going to have to. At least I've got compelling evidence."

"You and I can have a long conversation when you get back. I promise to explain everything to your satisfaction."

"I hope so. I think he's coming with me."

Another pause. "I'll prepare a room."

"Gabriel?"

"Yes?"

"Thanks. Whatever tonight and the next few days bring, I'm really glad you've got my back. Even if you're a creepy stalker Scot."

"You're welcome, I think."

# 16

The door creaked on its hinges as the wind picked up, and I moved to shut it. With the door closed, in the silence, I could almost believe I was in a waking dream—that it would be over when I went back to bed and shut my eyes. But then my feet found the discarded garments. What had Gabriel said? That a new werewolf was hard to control. It had never been possible to control Lonna. Just look at the mess she'd made with Peter Bowman. This wasn't going to be easy. I closed my eyes and wished for Leo to return.

A footstep startled me, and I ducked the wine bottle that came swinging toward my head.

"What the hell—"

"Oh, it's you, Joanna." Iain flipped on the light, and the discarded pile of clothing came into lurid view, as did the toppled end table and coffee table. The sofa and chairs, while still upright, sat at odd angles. "What's going on? Someone was moving around in here. I think they bumped into everything."

"Lonna's gone out for a run."

He looked at the clothes by my feet and arched an eyebrow. "Naked?"

"If you weren't gay, I'd swear that idea titillated you."

"If I wasn't gay, I'd allow it to distract me. You're not telling me something."

I took a deep breath. "This is going to be hard to believe."

"Someone tried to blow me up today for no logical reason. I'm up for believing anything."

I gave him the quick-and-dirty explanation of CLS as we put shoes on. He listened, but I could tell he didn't buy it.

"So you're saying that we're dealing with true werewolves, not just delusions?"

"I know it sounds crazy, Iain, but it's true. I've seen them. I saw Gabriel transform, and it wasn't a trick of the light. I've dealt with them post-metamorphosis and after a long night of hunting. I've heard them argue over who got to kill a deer with human voices in canine mouths."

"How is that physically possible?"

"I suspect it was telepathic—I can understand them when others can't—but still, you've got to believe me."

"Whether Lonna has what I know of as CLS or what you're telling me doesn't matter. How did she develop it?"

Good, he'd returned to scientist mode. I released the breath I'd been holding. "With some help. I just need to figure out who and how. But first we have to find her."

"And just what, exactly, are we looking for? Is she still part human?"

"I don't know." I handed him a flashlight, and we walked out the door. I locked it behind me and put the key in my pocket, then hesitated. What if she came back and ended up being locked out, naked on her front step?

"Hang on."

I dashed inside and hung the boxers and T-shirt on the outside doorknob. "Just in case."

Iain gestured for me to precede him down the stairwell. The

lights illuminated a ten-foot radius, but beyond that, inky blackness.

I stopped and squinted into the dark. "Um, why don't you go ahead?"

"Now you're afraid of things that go bump in the night?"

Before I could answer, a howl split the air, reached a crescendo of triumph, and then tapered. The vacuum of sound momentarily sucked all noises into it.

"What was that?" Iain searched the darkness with wide eyes as we walked down the stairs side by side.

"I hope it was Lonna."

"Who else might it be?"

"I don't know." I didn't really feel like going into the whole black-wolf mystery right then. He'd really think I was mad. Still, my heart rate picked up. Was it Leo? Was he trying to warn me?

"Where do you think she might go?"

"Hmmm..." I flicked on my flashlight. "There's an Italian place around the corner. Why don't we check the dumpster?"

"Werewolves go dumpster diving?"

"She might be hungry."

"You don't think she's hunting?"

My stomach flipped. "I don't want to think of her like that."

"The jealousy in your voice is priceless."

I stopped and he bumped into me. "What do you mean?"

"You sound sulky, like you wish it had been you."

"Do not." We moved onward again and headed toward the patch of woods behind the apartments and beyond a small lake. The path around the pond was treacherous during the daytime with loose gravel and places where the path may slide out from under unwary walkers, so we stuck to the ground above it. We searched the area for footprints, but the wet grass kept its secrets.

"This is pointless," Iain groused, but I held my hand up. "What?"

"Do you hear that?" A faint scraping noise reached my ears.

"Hear what?"

"Follow me."

We crept around to the right of the pond and the sound became clearer, like someone—or something—scratched in the dirt. Something pawed at the spent coals in the barbecue pit. Our flashlight beams hit it at the same time: a wolf with tawny fur ticked in black. It glared back at us with topaz eyes, a bone in its mouth.

"Iain, that's her."

"Ah, and how do you know?"

"I could make some smart-ass comment about that being how she always looks if you try to take barbecue away from her, but it's the fur. It's her coloring. And the eyes."

"Right now she's looking at us like we're dinner."

But she recognized us, didn't she? "Running away from a predator is the best way to get it to chase you."

"So what do we do now that we've found her?"

"Good question."

She answered it for us by spitting the bone out and loping down the hillside to the woods, where she vanished among the trees.

"What now? Go after her?"

I nudged the bone with a toe. "We're never going to be able to keep up with her. We're going to have to wait until dawn and then try to find her before she gets taken to the loony bin for running around naked."

"I had no idea hanging out with you would be so interesting."

"Me neither. Or should I say likewise? Until I saw you today, no one had tried to blow me up."

"Is there someone else who could help?" he asked as we

made our way back up the slope and picked through the weeds at the side of the lake.

"Like who?"

"Another werewolf?"

"The only one who's nearby is busy on another hunt."

"How many are there?"

"Five, er, six now. That I know of, anyway."

He shook his head. "That's incredible. It's the advance we've been looking for, the one we didn't dare think would happen, but which defines the disease."

"What do you mean?"

"Do you remember my book, the one about Hillary Baehr, the woman who escaped from the asylum?"

"Yep. It's required reading at Cabal now."

"I didn't want to put it in there for fear someone would refuse to take it seriously, but the guard on duty that night said that the only strange thing he noticed was a 'large dog' that dashed through the yard and then disappeared."

I swung my flashlight so that the beam hit him in the face, his pupils narrowing before he put a hand up to block the light. "Now I know you're kidding me."

He squinted. "Think about it. Say you're an orderly doing your rounds, and you look into a patient room, but you don't see her. So you open the door, and a wolf dashes out. You look inside the room, no patient, so you sound the alarm. But who is going to believe you if you tell them a wolf came out of the room? No one, and they'll probably stick you in the room next door."

I turned my flashlight away from him, and we trudged back to the apartment. "But how would a wolf get out of an asylum?"

"If she was a patient there, she would know the nooks and crannies that a human may not be able to access or hide in, but an animal might, particularly a petite one. And who cares if the patients see you? They're all crazy anyway. You just wait and slip out behind someone who can open the doors."

"I guess that's plausible."

"Now that you know I'm not kidding you, perhaps we should call one of your friends. Dawn won't be for another few hours. They could follow her trail and find her before she hurts herself."

"They're all up in Piney Mount, er, Crystal Pines. It will take them hours to get here."

"What about the one who's not? The good Doctor Bowman?"

"He's chasing another werewolf."

"So that makes seven?"

"Yep. At least, I think that one's a werewolf. I don't know the human behind it."

He rubbed his eyes and with a sigh, suggested, "Call Gabriel."

"What?"

"He's one of them, right? That's why he was so interested in your work."

That did make sense... "I guess."

"Joanie, it's better than nothing. Your friend could hurt herself or someone else."

"Are you really concerned about Lonna or more interested in finding a research subject?"

Iain shrugged. "Would you hate me if I said yes to both?"

I sighed as I turned the key in the lock to let us in to the disarranged apartment. "No, I guess I would understand."

I TRIED THE HOUSE, but Gabriel wasn't answering, and his cell phone went to voice mail. I had no idea how to find Ron or Leo

—Ron may be at the house, but he wouldn't answer the phone. Leo could be anywhere.

So we did the only logical thing. We made a large pot of coffee and waited for sunrise. In spite of the caffeine, I had difficulty staying awake. So did Iain, and we were both startled when someone pounded on the door.

A shot of hope made me bolt upright. "Is it her?"

He held up one finger and reached for the heavy flashlight as I tiptoed to the door and looked through the peephole.

"It's Gabriel." I hoped he didn't hear the relief in my voice, but there was no missing the sarcasm in his tone.

"The research assistant turned butler has arrived to save the day."

I shot Iain a dirty look and opened the door. Gabriel's expression turned from concern to carefully neutral when he saw his fellow Scot.

"Doctor McPherson," he said and held out his hand. "It's good to see you again."

"Likewise. I suppose. So I understand you have CLS. That explains a lot, admittedly. But why didn't you tell me?"

"I wanted to, but I couldn't find the words, and I didn't want to compromise my perceived objectivity."

I stepped between them. "Guys, can we save this discussion for later? Lonna is out there."

Gabriel studied the apartment with dark-circled eyes. "Do you have something of hers I can mark the scent from?"

"Her pajamas are by the door."

"Fine. If you two will, ah, excuse me."

"Transformation is very private," I explained to Iain as I led him down the hallway.

"I see." His facial expression told me he wondered if I was going to drag him into my web of insanity. This would be the ultimate test for him: would he believe, or would he try to have us all committed or arrested for an elaborate hoax?

A noise between a bark and a yip alerted us that Gabriel had changed and was ready to go. A large brown wolf, his tongue lolling to one side, sat by the door. I held my breath and looked at Iain.

"That. Is. Amazing," he whispered, the hint of a smile on his patrician lips.

I could finally exhale fully. "Yeah, it is."

We opened the door, and wolf-Gabriel dashed down the stairs and made a beeline for the barbecue pit. We had to run to keep up with him, the flashlight beams bouncing ahead of us. He took a cursory sniff at the bone Lonna had dropped earlier and, with a glance over his shoulder to make sure we followed, trotted toward the woods. We had to go single file as he wandered back and forth, finally coming out on the other side near Chenal Parkway, a busy thoroughfare that ran from the retail area near I-430 to the neighborhoods off Highway 10. My heart clenched—had she been hit? But no large lump lay moribund in the road or median. Instead, Gabriel took us along the side of the road, and back into another wooded area. He stopped, and Iain opened his mouth, but before he could say anything, a low growl made us freeze.

Wolf-Gabriel gave a whine and tucked his tail as he approached wolf-Lonna, whose snout was bloodied by the rabbit she'd killed and had just disemboweled.

"Oh God," Iain muttered and fainted in a heap behind me. I knelt beside him and gently nudged him.

"C'mon, Iain, this is no time for you to be passing out." I shook a little harder and looked at wolf-Gabriel. Could a lycanthropic face display amusement? I swore he had a grin, and his eyes danced with laughter. Wolf-Lonna nudged him with her cold nose, and he joined her in polishing off the rabbit.

I wrinkled my nose as the metallic stenches of blood and offal wafted on the slight breeze. "Would the two of you mind burying that when you're done? I don't think Iain could take waking up to the mess you've made."

Iain's breathing came regularly, and his heart rate was strong so I knew he would wake soon. That was the good thing about theoretical and literature-based research—not much in the way of blood and guts. I wasn't that squeamish, not since Andrew had died and my father had explained everything in cold, clinical terms that put tragedy safely in the realm of science, but I'll admit the sight did disturb me.

Dawn streaked the sky with fingers of red on the horizon, and Gabriel and Lonna raised their heads as though something had called to them. He touched her nose and started the transformation process. I turned away to give them privacy, and when I looked back, they both sat there, naked, with blood on their faces.

"What?" Lonna asked just before her eyes rolled back. She would have hit her head on a rock had Gabriel not caught her and helped her to the ground.

"Common reaction to the first transformation as the human brain, the cortex, reasserts itself over the animal brain. It's kind of like a teen learning to drive a standard transmission for the first time. It takes practice to find the clutch and not stall." He smirked at the reclining Iain. "So much for the brave Doctor McPherson."

He stood and stretched, and I couldn't help but notice his erection. I glanced away and blushed.

He looked down and tried to cover himself with his hands. "It's not uncommon upon transformation back to being human. And there is a naked woman right here. And part of the animal brain is still very active." He scratched the back of his head.

"I see." Sexual tension crackled between us.

Iain stirred and rolled up on one elbow, the heel of his hand to his temple. He looked at me, at Gabriel, and at Lonna, who also stirred.

"I'm sorry, did I interrupt something?"

"Nope." I tried to sound cheerful. "Nothing at all." But my body thrummed with the energy of the dawn and the desire to run my fingers down Gabriel's soft chest hair, to feel the hard muscle underneath, and to show him exactly what I wanted him to do with his impressive equipment below.

Iain, ever the practical one, observed, "There seems to be a shortage of clothing here."

"No shit." I hoped he didn't see me sneak glances at Gabriel, who stood as though greeting the dawn naked was the most natural thing for him.

"Perhaps we should fetch their clothes from the apartment so they can dress?" Iain suggested. "I doubt it would go over well with motorists for them to stroll along the side of the road in their birthday suits."

"You have a good point." I stood and held out a hand to him. "Why don't you go, and I'll stay here to make sure Lonna is okay?"

Iain rolled to his feet with a graceful maneuver. "I would prefer not to go alone, particularly after yesterday. If something untoward happens to me, I want a witness."

A pang of guilt stung me, and I didn't blame him for being uneasy. After all, if I'd been almost blown up, I'd not want to go walking around alone, either. Actually, I *had* almost been blown up, and I could definitely see where he was coming from.

"We'll be back in a few minutes," I promised.

Gabriel's smile was wry and regretful, but he sat down to wait.

"Is there something going on between the two of you?" Iain asked as we made our way back along the road.

"Nope, just a lot of gloriously unrequited sexual tension."

"Really? I would never have guessed."

"Ha ha."

He shook his head, and when he spoke, his tone conveyed

his wonder. "This is incredible, really. I don't think I believed you until I witnessed what I just did."

"How much did you see? The transformation is their most vulnerable time, so they may not be happy that you watched."

"I saw enough." He held up a hand. "And that is all I'm saying. I'm still processing this."

"I know it's a lot." Something nagged at the back of my brain, but I ignored it, the desire for denial stronger than the idea's will to push through. My left wrist throbbed—I hadn't put on the brace before coming out—and it appeared more swollen than my right one. I'd have to put ice on it before driving home.

The idea came through. Leo, just post-transformation, the look on his face as his territorial feelings about Wolfsbane Manor and its grounds overcame his better judgment as a doctor and caused him to hurt me. Ron's story about the professor's daughter and how it had cost him his fellowship popped into my head right behind it. My interlude with Gabriel the morning after Louise died and how we had almost made love right there on the island, the desire so thick I could taste it. Passion, lust and greed: the animal part of the brain on overdrive. And I had just left Gabriel alone and naked in a clearing with my best friend, whose state of mind was as yet unknown, but who had been known to dally with the occasional unsuitable male, even to hunt him.

"Oh God."

"What?"

"We need to go back." I turned around and was surprised to feel Iain's iron grip on my right wrist.

"It's already too late."

I shook my head, tears stinging my eyes. "But it would ruin everything." The image of the wolf from Cabal's letterhead came back to me— *"Unfair, unfair,"* indeed. I knew it would sound silly to him, how she'd always been taller, prettier and more confident than me, but we were still best friends in spite of it. She'd had her pick of boys in college, and I would never date them after her because if I did, I'd wonder if I fell short—literally and figuratively. That I'd kissed Gabriel first wouldn't matter. I couldn't compete with the passion of the perfect woman or the new werewolf.

"If you're going to live with them, you need to be able to accept the limitations of the disorder. You need to realize that they can't be held completely accountable for their actions."

I knew he was right, but I didn't have to like it.

"It's already too late," he said again and gently tugged me after him up the hill, past the barbecue pit, and around the lake. We gathered their clothing and trudged back, only to find the clearing empty, the only sign of what had happened a flattened area in the pine straw on the ground and traces of the dead rabbit.

"Where are they?"

The black wolf lunged at us from the trees. It snarled, and Iain and I took the hint and ran the other way. We made it to the road just as the clearing exploded and knocked us to the ground. The earth rocked, and black smoke poured over us.

"Are you okay?"

I opened my eyes and found Leo's dark brown ones looking at me with concern. "You were out for about five minutes."

"Iain?"

"I'm all right." His voice sounded shaky, but at least he was alive.

"Can you move everything?" Leo asked.

I tested my fingers and toes. Everything worked fine. "Can I sit up?"

"We need to wait for the paramedics. You got thrown back a few feet. I don't know if there's any spinal damage."

"You're the orthopedic doctor."

"It's hard to tell by just touching sometimes."

That reminded me. "Are *you* okay?"

"I was still in wolf form. If I'd transformed..." He gestured to himself. He was naked and vulnerable. His wolf-hide had probably saved him.

"The black wolf was there."

"It warned you. I would have, but it dashed out there first and snarled at you. I couldn't follow it—I had to make sure you were okay."

"Thank you."

He raised his head as the sound of sirens floated through the broken trees. "I'll be close by, but I don't want to be seen."

"I don't blame you. Go find some clothes." I gestured to the ones we'd brought, which wouldn't have fit him even if they had been wearable.

He melted into the shadows.

THE PARAMEDICS ARRIVED with the police, checked us out, and declared us to be generally unharmed, just shaken and bruised. We declined to go to the hospital for X-rays and other diagnostic tests. Then we had to deal with the police again.

"I don't know what you've done, but someone wants you to stop doing it. Badly," the detective said to us as we sat in his office. Again, we were bruised and dirty, and I still clutched the tattered remains of the clothing.

It was a rehash of the day before, this time sleep deprived, exhausted, and with something to hide. I couldn't deny that the black wolf had warned us, and my head spun as the implications sunk in. It had warned me the day before, although I hadn't realized it, but enough of the warning had sunk in to make me pull Iain back in the nick of time. Then there was the night Louise had died. Had it brought her to Wolfsbane Manor to give me the message, *"The black wolf knows"*? And had it set my car alarm off and broken my focus so I could escape that night from the fire in the lab? What if the black wolf wasn't my enemy, but rather some sort of twisted guardian angel?

What if the black wolf wasn't a wolf, as I suspected? Leo and Ron said they'd tracked a strange werewolf back to the Manor. Leo hadn't said anything that morning, but it's not like we'd had a lot of time to chat.

"We have to go," I said and stood. "You can contact me at Wolfsbane Manor in Crystal Pines if you have any more questions."

"Now, Doctor Fisher, we haven't finished talking yet." The detective motioned for me to sit down. His drawl as well as his condescending tone reminded me of Bud Knowles, and something inside me snapped.

"Are we under arrest, Detective?"

"No, but—"

"But it's ten o'clock, and I've been up since three without any coffee or breakfast, and don't you even try to tell me that the swill and donuts you have in the break room will do. My blood sugar is dropping, and unless you'd like to give me an escort to UAMS when I crash out, I suggest you let me leave, get something decent to eat, and then get back to my estate. My solicitor, Mr. Galbraith, will know how to get in touch with me. Frankly, I'm tired, injured and ready to go home."

The detective's mouth worked, and he struggled to say something. I ignored him, and with a sharp incline of my head, told Iain it was time to go. Again, his lips twitched as though he was trying not to smile, but he followed me out without a word.

## 17

"I'm seeing a side of you I had no idea existed," Iain told me as we rode in a taxi back to Lonna's apartment.

"What can I say? Death threats and kidnappings tend to bring out the best in me."

The police had beaten us back to Lonna's apartment. They didn't indicate that they knew we walked out on the detective. Two members of the bomb squad checked the apartment, then my car, and declared them to be clear.

"Doctor Fisher, Doctor McPherson." The voice was Galbraith's. He slammed the door of his antique black sedan and hurried up the stairs in front of the apartment. "The police just contacted me and told me what happened."

"We're getting out of here, Galbraith. Someone's after us."

"It appears so. I wanted to tell you I did find those papers of your grandfather's we discussed. In all the excitement yesterday, I forgot." He handed me a manila folder. "And I wanted to make sure you are, indeed, unhurt."

"Generally, yes," Iain put in. "Doctor Fisher has hurt her wrist yet again."

"Have you had it attended to?"

"There's a good orthopedist in Crystal Pines. I'll talk to him about it."

"I would recommend you stay here until you know you're safe."

I didn't show my frustration at yet someone else trying to tell me what to do, but it took some effort. "I appreciate your concern, but I think that will happen at about the half of never."

"Then Godspeed on your journey. Do you know what route you'll take?"

"Not yet. It depends on construction."

"Please give me a call when you arrive."

Galbraith followed the bomb squad and patrol car out of the apartment complex. His car reinforced my initial impression of him as the creepy undertaker in some old B-movie.

"Was that a little much?" I looked over the grounds of the apartment complex for a large black wolf to appear. Where was Leo?

"I believe so. He seemed very concerned."

"A little too concerned. Or am I being paranoid?"

"After surviving two explosions in two days? I would say you haven't been paranoid enough." Iain put his hands on my upper arms and squeezed gently, which stopped my trembling.

"You're probably right. We still have to find Lonna and Gabriel."

"So why are we going back to Crystal Pines? Shouldn't we revisit the scene of the crime? Look for evidence? See if they were, indeed, kidnapped?"

"Nope." I hoped that my impression had been correct and that the clearing had been empty before the explosion. "It's all been obliterated. And we're not going back to Crystal Pines."

"I see." That's what I liked about Iain—he understood that sometimes good research needs tangents. "Where are we going, then?"

"I'm paranoid, remember? I won't tell you until we get there. But first we have to wait for Leo."

"I always told that cad Robert that you would be the better boss."

We walked inside and straightened up the mess the bomb squad had left. If—no, I chided myself, when—Lonna came back, I didn't want her to find the place trashed.

Iain yawned. "I haven't had a good night's sleep since getting here. Would you mind if I take a nap while we wait for Leo to reappear?"

"That's fine."

Iain went to rest. I sat on Lonna's couch and flipped through a magazine, but I didn't really see what was in it. Leo stumbled into the apartment a few minutes later. He wore his clothes from the day before.

"Forget something?"

His clothes. From the alley. I put my palm to my forehead. "Whoops, I forgot to get those. I'm sorry."

"Yeah, good thing I hid them pretty well. Otherwise, my wallet may not have still been in my pocket. I was able to use what little cash I had for a cab. So what's the plan now?" Although he hadn't had any more sleep than Iain, he looked as alert and ready for action as he had the day before. His rumpled appearance with his wild hair and a day's growth of beard reminded me of our very first encounter, when he'd blasted out of Galbraith's office like a dark energy fireball. I blushed when I remembered his kisses. He was dark and dangerous, and all I wanted to do was jump him, wrap my legs around his waist, and run my fingers through his hair while showing him I could be just as good a kisser as he was.

"You have an interesting expression on your face, Doctor."

I'd always sucked at poker. The heat in my cheeks intensified. "I'm not at liberty to say why, Doctor. That's classified information."

For a moment, I imagined what the two of us must look like standing there in Lonna's living room: him rumpled and wild—yes, that word kept coming to mind—and me looking disheveled and forlorn.

He took my hand, examining my injured wrist again. "This doesn't look as bad as I thought it would after all that." He moved his gaze from my wrist up my arm to my shoulder and my torn shirt, where the edge of my bra peeked out, up my chest to my neck and finally my lips, and I shivered like he had actually touched me.

I could barely speak between the heartbeat that seemed simultaneously lodged in my throat and between my legs. "It's feeling pretty good right now."

He pulled me against him, and I leaned into his strength and steadiness. "Someone tried to blow you up."

"Twice." A hysterical giggle escaped.

"Most women, most people, would be crying puddles on the floor."

At his words, a tear escaped from each eye, but I refused to let him see me cry again. "I'm not most people."

"No," he said and tilted my face up with his index finger. "You're stronger than anyone gives you credit for."

His echoing Lonna's words on the first day of this horrible adventure made the lump in my throat grow to a burning coal, but still I struggled to keep the tears in check. His lips on mine, soft and questioning, brought me back to the present, and I opened to him. I felt the hardening in his pants between us, and my pelvis seemed to press into it on its own. He groaned and tightened his fingers in my hair and on my butt, trapping me to him.

*He's just been off the hunt*, the rational, scientific part of me said. *He could be dangerous. Remember your wrist.*

*Shut up*, I told it. *I'm not threatening him.*

But again, he pulled away and walked across the room.

"Okay, now I feel like melting into an emotional puddle on the floor." I crossed my arms so I wouldn't shiver with the sudden absence of his warmth. "What the hell was that? Why won't you finish what you start?"

"It's my brain." With a heavy sigh, he sat on the recliner and put his head in his hands. "I don't know if wanting you is me or if it's the wolf instinct trying to protect you and claim you."

The image of him dragging me off somewhere and... *Not now, brain!* "Why do you need to claim me? It's not like there's a bunch of suitors vying for my hand."

He shook his head. "Do you remember where I was all night until the explosion in the clearing?"

"Tracking the black wolf."

"And do you know where I tracked him?"

"No. How could I possibly know that?"

"Joanie," he said, his tone serious. "The black wolf followed every one of your moves from the police station to the Italian restaurant to your chase after Lonna."

"Wait a second. If you knew we were following Lonna, why didn't you help?"

"Because I thought the black wolf was a threat, and..." He sighed again. "My brain wouldn't let me leave it until it warned you away from the explosion at sunrise."

This time I couldn't suppress the shiver, and I sat on the sofa. It warned me twice, but what did it want?

Iain walked into the room and stretched. "There, now, much better. Oh, good, you're back." He stopped and looked at us more closely. "Did I interrupt something?"

"No." I stood and looked out the window to the east. "We don't have time to be fooling around, anyway."

"Right," Leo agreed, but was that a trace of regret in his tone? Or wishful thinking on my part? "So what's the plan now?"

"She's not saying." Iain's lips twitched, and I could tell he was amused. "But I have a suspicion."

"We're not going back to Crystal Pines?" Leo asked.

I turned and gave him what I hoped was a wicked grin. "Nope."

We piled in the car, Iain in the passenger side and Leo in the back. When I turned on I-40 toward Memphis, Iain smiled. That was the other thing I liked about Iain: his mind worked very similarly to mine. He held up his cell phone in a query.

"Go for it."

I didn't read the text he sent, but I knew that it said something to the effect of, *Doctor Robert Cannon, be prepared for visitors. Tell us where to meet you.*

❡

Iain and Leo snored in harmony by the time we crossed the river into downtown Memphis. Not that I blamed them. It was a long, flat, boring road, and none of us had slept much. Adrenaline—and the breakfast burritos we'd stopped off for—kept me going.

I rehearsed what I would say to Robert in my head. Now that I knew he'd only fired me because he'd been forced to, it gave me hope that we may be able to get something back. I was surprised that my thoughts turned to the research partnership rather than the romantic one, but it seemed indecent to remember the episodes on the office sofa with one of my colleagues in the car. Or with being in such close proximity to the man I couldn't resist.

Before I could follow that train of thought, a semi passed us, its horn blaring, and the noise startled the guys awake.

Iain bolted upright with a, "What in the hell?" Leo blinked sleepily in the backseat.

"Just a lorry," I said, using the British term for large truck.

"Did you come up with any good inspirations while you dozed?"

"Not a one." Iain checked his cell phone. "Oh, bugger!"

"What?"

"Robert texted me back. He said he's out of town on business."

"He's not here?" Frustration and relief warred in my chest at the delayed confrontation and possible reconciliation.

"That's not all. He said that he'd like to meet you at your manor this evening at midnight."

"Oh, crap. That means we have to turn around and drive all the way back."

"Wait a minute," said Leo. "He's out of town on business but can meet us in Crystal Pines? Where is he?"

"Didn't say, but you make an excellent point. I think that we'll find more from our Doctor Cannon than we expected."

I spotted an exit, but I had to think fast. This one or the next one? The impetus of seeing Robert again made up my mind for me. Without worrying about my turn signal, I swerved into the next lane and on to the exit ramp.

The blast of a horn startled me, and an out-of-control tractor trailer swerved into the lane where I had just been, crashed, and burst into flame on the other side of the bridge.

"Son of a..." I looked at the plume of black smoke and pressed my foot to the gas, running the red light to get away on the access road as fast as I could. I couldn't get the image of what my car could have looked like out of my mind. *If I hadn't taken the exit, I would have been trapped by the bridge supports, and we would have been crushed.*

Iain twisted around to get a better look. "Should we try to help him?"

"Are you nuts? He was after us." Instead of left to get back on the interstate, I turned right and headed into town, hoping that amidst the smoke, no one had seen us. I wiped my shaking hands one at a time on my jeans to make sure they wouldn't slip off the steering wheel, and I was grateful for that rest stop a half hour before.

"How do you know?"

"Because it's the trailer part of the truck that burst into flame, not the cab."

Leo's voice still had a gravelly quality from having been asleep, but he sounded alert. "She's right. I watched it. I took an oath to help people, but I'm not itching to go back. They tried to squash us."

We darted through quiet neighborhoods, careful not to drive too fast or attract attention. My tag was still for Shelby County, Tennessee, so no one would have reason to notice us.

"Are we going back to Crystal Pines?"

"Yes, but we're taking back ways. I'm going to use the I-55 bridge, not the I-40 one to get back into Arkansas, and then we're staying off the highway. Hopefully they think they did us in back there. It'll take them a while to figure out they didn't."

"How did they know we were here? Did you see anyone follow us out of town?"

Another shot of adrenaline hit my heart, and I slowed the car. "Good question." I thought for a moment. "Robert may have set us up. Or someone's cell phone is tapped, and they can intercept messages. Turn your phone off."

Iain did as I suggested, and I turned mine off as well. Leo didn't have one. I pulled into a small road between two new neighborhoods and stopped the car in the shade of an oak tree.

"What are you doing?"

"I need to think for a moment." I spotted the manila folder from Galbraith and opened it. Inside, we found a sheaf of papers in my grandfather's handwriting. Iain looked over my shoulder.

"Joanie, this is—"

"Just what I had asked him for."

"We have to get back. This work is incredible."

I put my hand on Iain's arm, which trembled with excitement. "That is just what they were hoping we'd do. And I bet we'd have found a nasty surprise when we got there."

Comprehension dawned on his features. "Galbraith set us up yesterday."

"And again today. I bet they have Lonna and Gabriel, too."

"How do they know how to find us?"

"It may be the cell phones, or I bet there's a GPS in the car or on the car. The bomb squad could have planted it while Galbraith was talking to us."

"So they'll know that we weren't killed by the tractor trailer." He licked his lips and looked out the window.

"We need to find the GPS and hide it here."

"Why here?"

"This is Robert's neighborhood. They'll think we're headed to his house."

We searched the car, lifted seat cushions, and emptied the glove compartment. We emptied the trunk, checked under the spare tire, and lowered the backseat in case it was nestled in the space under the bottom of the seat. Finally, with the help of a flashlight, we found it: a black box with a blinking red light magnetically attached to the underside of the car.

"So it wasn't the phones." Iain reached for it, but I stayed his hand.

"Think about the explosives. What if it's designed to trigger something if the magnetic seal is broken?"

He looked at me as though he was trying to decide whether I was crazy paranoid or very shrewd, but he didn't move. "What do we do?"

"Get our stuff, walk around the corner, and rent a car. How much cash do you have?"

"Barely any. I didn't have time to change much."

"Leo?"

"Used all mine this morning."

I checked my bag. Inside, a strange envelope peeked out, and I recognized it as the one Galbraith had left me for expenses. I had stuck it in a drawer in the night table in my bedroom. I opened it, and several hundred dollar bills fell out. I hadn't packed it, but I didn't have time to worry about who had.

"This should cover it."

Leo shook his head. "No one's going to rent a car to you without a credit card, and what do you want to bet that all of ours are being tracked?"

Iain pulled out his wallet and flipped through his cards. "Not this one."

"What is it?" It looked like a regular Visa card to me.

He smiled. "This is my university faculty 'emergency' card. My chair gave it to me in case I needed some cash quick." He shrugged, and I refrained from pointing out the similarity to Gabriel's favorite gesture. "I have a tendency to get into sticky situations. It goes back to the university, not to me, so it's unlikely that it's being tracked, particularly since the account is overseas."

"I think this qualifies as an emergency."

Within half an hour, we were on our way on the back roads to Crystal Pines.

Our trip proceeded without incident, but it occurred to me that they might be watching the roads around Crystal Pines. Whoever "They" were. Minions of Hippocrates Pharmaceuticals, most likely. I had a feeling that Galbraith was in on it, too. I had fixated on Peter Bowman as my enemy, and he may well be, but I had focused on the wrong lawyer.

I pulled the car over and parked it behind some trees about a mile beyond the gatehouse. We hadn't come across another car for miles, and although I couldn't see too far back from the road, I didn't think anyone had spotted us. However, darkness was falling, and I didn't want to be caught by surprise by another vehicle.

When I turned off the engine, Iain asked, "What now?"

I got out and slung my backpack—manila folder and money envelope safely inside—over my shoulders. He stood up and stretched. It had been a long, twisty ride, and he looked a little green. Leo, exhausted from running the entire night before, had slept on and off.

"Try not to hurl. Gads, Iain, I had no idea you were such a wimp."

"I had no idea you were such a feared and reviled human being to attract so much trouble."

"You haven't talked to my mother lately. For all I know, she might be in on it, too."

No smile, not even a twitch. "Let me guess, we get to walk now?"

"My grandfather and I used to know every inch of this mountain and the ones near it. The trails were old hunting trails, and I bet they're still in good shape." I gazed into the dark woods and tried to convince myself it would be a pleasant hike, but my mind turned to the unknown that might lurk around every bend, specifically the creature that made those awful screams.

"I can guide you," Leo offered. "Just let me change." He ducked behind a tree and emerged in canine form.

Now Iain's lips curled into a small smile. "I don't know if I'll ever become accustomed to that. So you don't think we'll be targets in a hunter's scope?"

"Nope, it's not deer season yet, and Leo will be able to smell anything that might try to surprise us." We set off through the woods and found a trail that wound down the side of the mountain.

"Shouldn't we be going up?"

"Will you hush? And no, we're headed for the river. I want to approach the house from the back side."

Wolf-Leo bobbed his head and darted on. He stayed a few feet in front of us. A waning moon lit our way, and I found my way to the river. We had to go off trail for the last hundred yards or so because the trail led up the mountain again. Iain didn't say anything, just watched where he stepped and occasionally shot me a look questioning how much of a madwoman I must be and whether he would be better off on his own. I couldn't blame him—until a week ago, I had been the same, an industry-employed scientist who, at heart, held on to the attitudes of an academician who expected others to do all the dirty work for her. Trudging through the woods at night wouldn't have been my idea of fun, either. I would have sent some poor trainee or graduate student to do it. But now the fresh air soothed my lungs and only the sounds of our crunched footsteps on the gravel bank, the whispering breeze, and the murmuring river disturbed the quiet. The thoughts of my old, comfortable lab and even the beautiful, shiny one at Wolfsbane Manor made me feel stifled.

We continued to walk upstream, and the sound of the water took on an echo such that it drowned out other noises. Leo stopped, his nose to the air. I held my hand up to Iain, who moved closer and bent his ear to my mouth.

"Something's not right," I whispered. "Let's move back into the brush. Try to be as quiet as you can."

We stepped off the riverbank and into the woods, where we eschewed the path paralleling the river for the pine needles and undergrowth. We continued to move along and found a split. The main river continued north toward the edge of Wolfsbane Manor land, and part of it had been diverted toward the west, where formerly only a small canyon with a trickling stream and a few caves had been.

I beckoned for him to come closer again, but as he bent, a scream split the air—the horrible, tormented noise that I had heard before. He straightened, his eyes wide, and I reached up and clapped a hand over his mouth before he could exclaim anything in the silence that followed. Wolf-Leo took off like a shot, and the shadows swallowed him. If the noise was painful to human ears, I couldn't begin to imagine what it sounded like to his super-sensitive canine ones. The sound had made my hair stand on end, if for no other reason than it was very close. And this time, something about it triggered a sense of familiarity and overwhelming sorrow.

"Are we near the mouth of hell?" Iain murmured in my ear.

"We may very well be." Tales of the Gowrow, who lived in caves and ate anything that wandered too close, came back to me. People had seen strange things in these hills.

Something splashed into the water. I beckoned for Iain to follow me, and we crept toward the river, where we could barely see a small head bobbing in the current. It seemed to try to swim toward the bank, but every time it got close, an eddy would sweep it back to the center of the river.

Iain gasped, "Good lord, it's a child."

"Quick!" I grabbed a branch, and we ran to the edge of the river. Iain held on to my left arm above the wrist as I reached the other one out with the branch and steadied myself in the cold water. I braced myself but didn't expect the tug at the branch as the child caught on to it. I stumbled, regained my footing, and held on with all my strength as Iain pulled us both to shore.

The child, a boy of about twelve, looked at us as though he thought we might be ghosts. His eyes widened in fear, and his lips worked as he decided whether to say something or to scream. I placed my hand over his mouth and held a finger to my lips. He glanced over his shoulder, and we crept into the bush again as two figures emerged from the woods on the other side of the bank. One of them wore a white lab coat, the other one a dark suit. Both men scanned the river.

"Simon," the lab-coated one called out. "Simon, there's no use running. If you don't have your treatment, you may die!"

I held the boy tight, my arms wrapped around his shivering frame. I couldn't tell whether he reacted to the cold water or trembled with fear. Or both. The other man talked into a radio, and with a nod, he and the one in the lab coat headed down the opposite bank calling and looking at the river.

Simon... A child in early adolescence who appeared in the middle of the woods on a dark night chased by a man in a lab coat. Could this be one of the lost children of Piney Mountain?

"Simon Van Doren?" I whispered in his ear. The boy nodded but didn't take his eyes off the two men until they disappeared around a bend in the river.

"Iain," I said in as low a voice as I could and still be heard above the water, "this is one of the missing boys."

Simon turned to me. "You're not one of them?"

"No, I'm here to help you."

"Then you have to help the rest."

"The rest of who?"

"The other boys. And the grown-ups. They hurt us. They put things in needles, and it makes us scream." Indeed, his voice sounded hoarse, and it wasn't because he was whispering. The most recent scream still lingered in my ears, and I imagined that such a horrible noise being forced out of a small throat would cause some damage.

"Which grown-ups?" I asked. Could we have found Lonna and Gabriel?

"They brought a man and a woman today. The man has an accent. And the old man was already there."

"What old man?"

"The one in the big house."

My eyes filled with tears of sorrow and relief. "Iain, my grandfather—he's alive."

"Alive or not, I don't think that sitting here waiting for them to come back is going to do us any good." Iain held out his hand to the boy, who took it.

He looked up at Iain with wide black eyes. "You talk like the new guy."

"Aye." He thickened his accent a little. "We're both from Scotland." The corners of his eyes crinkled, and he smiled. "We've got some good werewolf legends in Europe, you know."

The boy shook his head. "Mister, you're living in one."

I stifled a laugh and gestured that we should keep moving. We walked as quickly as we could without making too much noise. I imagined, if there were any cooperative werewolves in the rogue lab, they would soon send them after Simon, and it wouldn't take long for them to sniff up the other bank of the river.

The trail forked to the right, but we stayed on the river path. I strained my eyes ahead to see if I could make out the bulk of the boathouse and wished I had the wolves' night vision. To me the forest was all shadows and slivers of silvery light with moonlit outlines of trees and plants. We didn't see the boathouse until we were almost right on it.

"There's someone in there." Simon's nose twitched. "A wolf-man. But I don't know him."

We skirted around the edge of the place, and then it occurred to me. *Leo.* He must have ducked in there after the scream.

"Leo," I hissed. Something moved around inside.

"Joanie, are you sure?" Iain asked.

"No." I wasn't sure about anything. But I needed somewhere to put Simon, and fast. It was past eleven, and we still had a good forty-five minutes of hiking straight uphill. The boy might be hardy, but I couldn't drag him along with us. He needed a good meal, medical attention, and lots of rest.

The door opened, and Leo came out. He had dark circles under his eyes. "What the hell have you been doing? I was about to go back and look for you. I had to get out of there—that scream, it tore up the inside of my head." Then his eyes fell on the boy.

"Who's this?"

"It's Simon Van Doren. He's one of the boys that went missing from Crystal Pines."

"How did you escape?" Leo asked.

"The black wolf drove me out. When the doctor and the guards were busy with the new people, he showed me a crack in the wall I could fit through."

"The black wolf?" My head spun. What—or who—was the black wolf? Why was it following me? Why had it given me this child?

"They got Gabriel and Lonna," Iain said.

"Wait a second." I fixed Leo with my best "no bullshit" look. "How did you know Simon had 'escaped'?"

He ran his hands through his tangled hair, and leaves and pine needles fell out. "We knew that the place was there, the cave of the Gowrow. We couldn't get close because we didn't want to be caught. He smells like that place, like chemicals and fear."

"Why didn't you say something when we were down here?" I took a deep breath, reminding myself to focus on the most important matter. "Wait, we can sort that out later. Can you keep an eye on him? They're looking for him. Iain and I have to make it to Wolfsbane Manor by midnight."

"I guess." I thought at first he was just being rude, but he gazed at Simon with searching dark eyes. "Was there a little boy there? About two, with curly blond hair?"

"Yes, but they don't do anything to him. He just cries."

Leo held out his hand and Simon took it. Then he jerked his head in the direction of the path. "Go ahead. I'll take care of the boy."

I should have been happy to have Simon's care out of my hands, but the way Leo looked at him made me wonder if maybe the boy would be safer with us, particularly with Leo not being so psychologically adept at the animal-human transition. I didn't have time to worry. Iain tugged at my arm, and we hiked up the trail. The murmur of voices, Leo's bass and Simon's rasping tenor, faded behind us, and I wondered what they could be plotting. I only hoped they wouldn't act rashly and give us away before we could figure out who was ultimately responsible for creating that hell in my childhood playground.

## 18

W e reached the edge of the lawn with five minutes to spare. My heart pounded in my ears, and I bent over with my hands on my knees to catch my breath.

The house made a dark silhouette against the starred sky. The waning moon lit some of the corners and planes, and it looked like a movie set, two-dimensional with the shadows painted wrong unless you saw it from a certain angle. No light shone in any of the windows, and the manor seemed desolate and abandoned. I thought back to returning there that first night with Lonna, how we'd been unsure of what we'd find and how Gabriel had come down the stairs to welcome us. Some Lady of the Manor I turned out to be. Both of them were now held captive by mad scientists who would do God only knew what to them.

The usual night noises of the last of summer's crickets, the wind rustling through the trees, and the occasional car on the road below the front gate rushed to fill the sound vacuum left by the water and by Iain's gasping and my own pounding heart as we climbed the hill. Although all seemed safe, I felt reluctant to step into the open. All my instincts screamed at me to run, that there was danger here—and underneath it all, the half-hope and half-fear that Robert would, after all this, want me back. I had fallen for aspects of him in the wolf-men, Leo's intensity and Gabriel's cunning, but now, watching the second hand move around my watch face, I realized they paled in comparison to him, my mentor and best friend. Earlier that day, I'd been ready to toss him aside as a lover and focus on rekindling the professional relationship. Now, in the dark, that familiar longing for his arms as well as his brain welled up. He would know what to do, how to sort this out.

A twig snapped behind us, and Iain and I crouched behind some blackberry bushes at the woods' edge. A large black wolf —*the* black wolf—ambled up the path we had just taken, sniffed at our footsteps, and stepped into the moonlight. Once there, it lifted its nose to the light and closed its eyes, and a fine mist wreathed it. We watched, transfixed, as the wolf shape blurred and resolved into the shape of a man with his face lifted to the moon, his arms outstretched at his side. His body —oh, how *my* body ached with longing for it. During the month since I'd seen him, he'd become lean, muscular, and more hirsute.

"Joanie? I know you're there. I can smell you. Iain, too." He turned and looked straight at us, so we made our way to the path and to the lawn.

"Robert? You're..." I held up my hands.

"Naked, yes."

Tears clogged my throat, and I couldn't speak, only look at him and let the knowledge of what he had become sink in.

Iain pointed out the obvious. "You're a werewolf. You've got it, CLS."

"The phenotypic expression, yes."

"How?" I choked out.

"I had hoped you would find that out by now. You must be close."

"Did you have a vaccine? A flu shot?"

"They shot me up with something, but I don't know what it was. All I know is that I lost a few weeks. When I woke up, I had it. Remember when I was supposedly in Atlanta for the final merger briefings?"

"Who did this to you?"

"Hippocrates Pharmaceuticals." He crossed his arms, and I wondered if the chill in the air was getting to him. "They would have done it to you, too, if they'd had the chance. That's why I had to get you out of there. Oh, Joanie, it hurt so much to lose you."

"I thought that's why you let me go, because you thought it was my fault."

He shook his head, but he didn't hold his arms out so I didn't run into them. This was not how I pictured our reconciliation.

"You were there. At the fire."

"I was. They set it, but I made sure to distract you so you'd get out of there." He reached over and brushed a tear off my cheek. I grabbed his hand and held it to my face. "I just didn't expect you to get caught on the stool. How's your arm?"

"The shoulder is fine. The wrist is hurt from other things."

"Why did you want to see us?" Iain broke in. "You're one of them now. What could you possibly want with us?"

"To give you one last warning."

My heart skipped a beat. "What?"

"You have to work fast to isolate the ingredient in the vaccines that's causing this. Your grandfather was close to finding out something, but they got him before he could."

"Why do we have to work fast?"

"Isn't it obvious? They're trying to kill you so you can't. And they've just gotten a contract for the new bird flu vaccine for the whole nation, not just this area."

I caught my breath and heard Iain do so as well. With the public now sensitive to any possibility of a new pandemic, that would be a very popular vaccine, even more so than the regular flu shots.

Iain frowned. "Why create a problem without a cure? Or were they planning to cause an epidemic and then have the only way to treat it?"

Robert didn't answer, but I knew it was true. He was stuck with them, but I wasn't.

"Listen, Joanie, they've already killed Louise."

I remembered the terrible night she died and the black wolf outside the kitchen window. "You brought her to the Manor. Why?"

"I found her by her car. She needed help but was so far off the road, there was no way I could get medical attention to her in time. I thought you might be able to help her, so I changed and explained it to her, and I carried her most of the way there. I couldn't let you see me because I knew it would frighten you. I didn't mean to walk by the light near the kitchen."

That explained the intense look on her face when she'd told me, *"The black wolf knows."* It hadn't been fear; she was trying to make me understand. Had he told her we'd been lovers?

I had so many questions, but I had to stick with the most important ones. "Why are you doing this? Why are you warning us and telling us all of this now?"

"Because they're on my heels waiting for me to lead them to the van Doren boy. And because..." He shook his head, his turn to be choked. He pulled his hand away. "Because I shouldn't have. That is, we shouldn't have."

"No, it's okay, I wanted it to happen. I was happy there, with you. I've missed you terribly."

"You helped me feel like a young man again, Joanna Fisher. That's why I kept you around long after you could have gone on to your own lab."

His words hit me like a splash of icy river water. "You kept me around after what?"

"I got a letter before I went to Atlanta. GeniTech was interested in you, but they didn't want to seem like they were poaching you, so they approached me first and asked about you."

I caught my breath. GeniTech was the big dog in the industry. Going to work there would have been the next step to the shining career I'd wanted.

"I told them that you wouldn't be interested." His eyes locked with mine. "I wanted your brain, your body, and your talents, and I couldn't stand the thought of you having the opportunity I'd wanted for most of my professional career."

"You sabotaged me." I clenched my fists as though I could stop the image I'd built up of him as a mentor and lover from unraveling.

"I used you, and it's something I'll never forgive myself for, especially since I could have spared you from all this."

I noticed then how the lines around his mouth, evidence I'd previously ignored of the eighteen years separating us, had grown deeper. "But you didn't. And now we're here."

"I won't be for much longer. I made sure there's no one at the house, only the sheriff's man out front in his car."

"Oh, so they're in on it, too? I should've guessed when they took everything after Louise died."

"Knowles is taking orders from someone, but I haven't been able to find out who. Probably Hippocrates." He reached over to brush my cheek again, but I flinched away.

"I can't believe you did that, sabotaged my career for a little fun so you could use me."

"Joanie, there's no time to argue now. Go in there and don't come out until you have something. I'll lead them away."

My chest tightened with the shame of knowing I had to follow his orders, even after I knew he'd betrayed me. I wanted to say more, to scream at him or claw his eyes out, or at least his throat so that we'd have matching pain. I'd forgotten how much I hated it when he ordered me around. The mist enveloped him, and the black wolf reappeared and bounded into the woods. I looked after it and bit my lip to keep from crying.

"Did he really mean it, Iain? That he used me? Did you know about GeniTech?"

Iain wouldn't meet my gaze. "Let's get to work."

ARMED with my grandfather's notes and equipment, Iain's background knowledge and theoretical research, and my experience, we set up in the underground laboratory. First I made sure that all the doors were locked, and we avoided turning on any lights or giving any other indication that the house was occupied until we were inside the windowless room. I didn't want Sheriff Knowles to turn up and insist that he urgently had to question me. I was surprised to find that Ron wasn't in the house, but perhaps he'd decided to make himself scarce.

My grandfather had, through his own research and experience as well as reading my work, isolated a genetic component to the expression of CLS. The Landover Curse, it had been called in our family. In other families, it had been called other things, and some didn't have a name for it. I guess that sort of information tended to be swept under the rug when it could get you and your family burned.

It was more common, I had found in my research, in families of Germanic and Scandinavian descent, which made sense considering that part of the world had spawned the best werewolf legends. Other cultures might have similar tales, for example, the dolphin-men of the Amazon, and they might carry through as well, but there was something about CLS that made it more common, at least in the U.S. This area, with its Dutch, German and Scandinavian heritages all intermixed, would be the perfect area to find subjects, which is likely why the local kids, and not the newcomers, were the targets.

"So what can make a genetic trait more likely to express?" I asked after we'd hashed all this out. "This has to be complicated considering all the parts of the transformation, several genes at least."

He steepled his fingers and sat back. "Whoever came up with this has to be a genius in the field. They took your heredity and epidemiology work as well as our work in the genes themselves and found a way to make the traits express in a temporary fashion."

"Do we know anyone with that capability?"

"We know several, but the question is who would be unethical enough to do it and to 'experiment' on children as well as other victims of the tainted vaccines?"

"It depends on how much money is involved, I guess. To create a problem so you can monopolize the cure..." I shuddered. "It's hard to say. Let's get back to the question of how they tainted the vaccines. What could be in them?"

"Some sort of chemical? I'm just guessing what could be transmitted through vaccinations."

"Maybe, but what?"

We once again turned to my grandfather's notes. He had been working with—*surprise!*—wolfsbane, also known as aconite, which could either be used as a topical anesthetic or a poison if taken internally or if too much is absorbed through the skin. He was in pursuit of the legendary use, which was to bring on a state of lycanthropy or to banish it. He hoped for the latter. His aim, according to his notes, was to use my research on the causes and spread of the disorder to figure out how wolfsbane may act on the nervous system of the CLS victims.

And we could ask him about it when we found it. I couldn't keep the excitement out of my voice. "So if he was looking at wolfsbane to prevent the expression of CLS, what could be the cause of it?"

"Let's think of what one finds in vaccinations," Iain suggested. "Perhaps it's something that's already in there or that could be tweaked rather than something that's introduced that the FDA would be able to trace."

"Good call. There's the active ingredient, which is a dead virus, part of a live virus, a less problematic but similar one..."

Iain's eyes unfocused, and I could almost see the calculations going on in his head. "And what do viruses do?"

"They inject their DNA into a cell and cause it to replicate little viruses."

"So what if a virus was to be engineered to do that, but to cause the cell's DNA to express CLS symptoms if that propensity were there?"

"As in a viral vector? You know, that makes sense. Instead of using the viral vector to inhibit the patient's CLS gene expression, it enhances it. CLS is recessive, but with the vector, only one of parents needs to have the gene."

"So why kidnap the children?"

"Because adolescence is when the CLS really takes off along with the expression of secondary sex characteristics, acne, the works. All the victims were pre-adolescents."

Everything fell into place then, like a perfectly arranged Tetris grid. I only had two more questions. One was how my grandfather had gotten hold of records from a pediatrician's office. The second was for Peter Bowman. Why had his son been taken? Sure, the family had the gene, but little Lance was too young to participate in the CLS "field research". His kidnapping had to have been for other, more sinister purposes.

Iain broke me out of my reverie. "I have some friends at the FDA, and I'll give them a call first thing in the morning. They'll probably be very interested in these ideas as well as possible contamination of the vaccines with viral vectors for a genetic disorder."

"But what if the viruses are so cleverly engineered that they won't be able to detect them?"

He drummed his fingers on the metal tabletop. "I wish there was some way we could get a sample of it. Without it, we don't have any proof, and I'm sure they've got clean materials to give to the FDA if requested."

The hopelessness of the situation struck me. "You've got me there. I don't know how to get a contaminated vaccine or a sample of the viral vector."

"Still, I'll call in the morning."

"Just stay hidden until then. If you need to go upstairs for anything, try not to turn on any lights."

He looked up from the notes in his hands. "I'll also try not to kill myself stumbling around in the dark."

I ignored his grumpy response. "Good call. And stay away from any explosive devices too."

"That's not funny, Joanna."

"None of this is." I moved toward the door, but he stopped me.

"And where are you going?"

"I have to speak with a mother and a lawyer."

Both his eyebrows lifted. "You're going to sue Robert?"

"Nope. I'm going to find out why Peter Bowman's son was kidnapped."

Iain elected to catch a few hours' sleep, his jet lag and the adventures of the past two nights having caught up with him. I put him in one of the guest rooms down the hall at the Manor, changed into clean clothes in my room, and ignored the siren song of my own bed.

I STOOD outside the apartment complex where Honey Jorgens lived. It seemed like I had questioned her a lifetime ago. The light in her apartment living room shone red through the curtains, and someone moved around inside.

I took a step forward to go up the stairs and knock on her door, but a large gray wolf bounded in front of me, its lips curled in a snarl.

"Easy there. Matthew, isn't it?"

The wolf sat back on its haunches and studied me.

*I'm not as young as the others, so changing is tough.* I recognized the voice as the wolf who had complained that they needed to figure out how real wolves hunted.

"It's okay, I can hear you just fine."

*You have the talent. Your grandfather did, too.*

I didn't have time to talk about my family abilities. "Why won't you let me pass?"

*Because she's been through enough. The shame of knowing that you figured her out may kill her.*

"She knows her son is still alive because you told her. And you called Lonna up here because you knew what was going on, but you couldn't report anything without outing yourself as a CLS sufferer. You wanted her to do the dirty work for you."

*I wanted her to find out with human methods. No one would believe me. I got close to the lab once, and they did this to me.*

"So H.J. is Honey Jorgens? She got the records for my grandfather from the pediatrician's office, and that's why her son was taken and why her mother was killed."

*How did you figure it out? There are many people here with those initials.*

It had struck me as strange the first time I'd been here that in a poor community, Honey wasn't working—not even to take care of other people's small children. It didn't click until later that she'd lost her job and was probably having difficulty finding another one, especially if she was under suspicion by a powerful entity. Louise had wanted to talk to me about something, likely the tough time her daughter was having or to encourage me to become involved in the search for the missing kids in my grandfather's place, and so had headed up to the Manor before work to talk to me in private. I bet she was being followed, and when They figured out where she was going, They ensured she would never reach the Manor alive. And then after she had, They took every bit of evidence she'd been there.

"I'm good at figuring stuff out."

The wolf gazed at me with suspicious eyes.

"Fine, I'll leave her alone. You've confirmed what I suspected anyway. Are you here on your own or did They send you?"

*A little of both. Don't worry, I won't tell Them you were here. If you leave now.* The intent behind his snarl was unmistakable.

I glanced up at Honey's window one more time. Someone had to have tipped Them off that Louise and I had talked about meeting, and I knew just who that Someone was. Rather than try to fight my way through Matthew or risk him blackmailing me to keep knowledge of my snooping away from the sheriff, I decided to cut my losses and go visit a lawyer.

DAWN TINGED the sky as I walked up the circular Bowman driveway. I was afraid I'd have to rouse the household, but a light shining from a bay window on the side of the house told me someone was awake. A quick inspection revealed a library and a disheveled, unshaven, bleary-eyed Peter Bowman sitting at a desk in the middle of it. A green-shaded desk lamp cast unflattering shadows over his face as he struggled to keep his eyes open to pore over the documents in front of him.

I rapped on the window with my fingernail, and he straightened and looked around. I tapped again, and he came over and scowled into the darkness. A third time brought his face to eye level with me. I had to stand on tiptoe and balance myself with a hand on the wall as his holly bush got fresh with my backside.

"Who's out there?" he snarled.

I resisted the urge to intone, "The grim reaper." Just the thought was almost enough to put me into a fit of giggles. Thank goodness for that holly bush. It's hard to be funny when your rear end is getting pricked.

"It's me, Doctor Joanie Fisher. I know where your son is."

He scowled but pointed toward the rear of the house. "Back door's that way. I'll let you in."

I found the back door just as the light came on, and he let me in through the mudroom. A small pair of galoshes and a little red wagon reminded me the house had been missing its youngest inhabitant for a couple of days. He looked at them and ran his hand through his hair in a gesture reminiscent of Leo.

"You said you had news of my son?" He kept his voice lowered, so I only nodded. "Come with me, and quietly. Marguerite has finally fallen asleep, and I can't take any more of her shrieking and crying."

"She's taking it hard, is she?"

"She blames me." He pinched the bridge of his nose, and I noticed his red-rimmed eyes. "Not that it matters who's to blame. I could blame her for wanting this big house in the nice, new neighborhood."

He led me into the library and shut the door. I made a quick inventory of the shelves—several legal books, leather-bound and thick, but also other things I hadn't expected such as a

Physicians' Desk Reference and other medical manuals. I also spotted piles of familiar journals.

"Who do you work for? I thought it was the town's developer."

"I do. But that's not my main job." He gestured for me to sit in one of the overstuffed leather armchairs and picked up a square glass half-filled with amber liquid from the desk. It sloshed as he flopped in the chair across from me, and I wrinkled my nose at the burnt tire smell. Scotch.

"I'd offer you some, but you don't look old enough to drink."

"There's no reason to be rude. I'm here with news, remember?"

"What? You're going to tell me that Lance is being held in a cave in the middle of the woods by the river? And that you can help me to free him if I only do one thing for you?" He waved his hand in dismissal. "Been there, had that conversation."

"With whom?"

He snorted, and something came out of his nose and hung on the edge of his right nostril. "Wouldn't you like to know? But they're looking for you."

"Who is?"

"See? Now you're trying to trick me. Maybe you're one of those wood spirits who's only taken on the form of the sylph-like Doctor Fisher, PH fucking D who's so smart and independent she can't even let her best friend help her out."

"They have Lonna, too." My voice was barely above a whisper.

"What?" His hand trembled as he set the glass on a side table with a checkerboard surface.

"They have Lonna. They got her yesterday just after she'd transformed back."

"So it worked."

"What worked?"

"The spell. And a little something in her drink. And a little nibble from someone with an attenuated version of CLS."

"You have it too?" I flopped back in my chair.

"A partial expression. At least that's how I explain the fact I can't get enough of what my wife won't give me."

I remembered Lonna mentioning something about his dissatisfaction with his marriage. It sounded like bullshit to me, but then again, I wanted answers. I could sort out the truth later.

He took another drink of his Scotch. "They wanted me to try a spell, she presented herself. End of story."

"No, it's not the end of the story." Spells from various texts sprang to mind. Some required more than just words. I had forgotten the third way to create a lycanthrope—a curse. "What did you do to her?"

"Mind you, I wouldn't have done it if I'd actually thought it would work. I don't believe in hocus-pocus stuff. But when we had lunch and we ordered drinks, I said the words under my breath."

"There's no way a spell could have caused my friend to become a werewolf. There had to be something else. Did you inject her with something?"

He shook his head. "I'm not that kinky, Doctor."

"Okay, that was a mental picture I didn't need. But you did bite her?"

He only shrugged, but a satisfied look came across his face.

"Okay, ew again. Did you tell your bosses or whoever that you had succeeded with your spell?"

"Of course not. I didn't know I had succeeded."

"But they do now. And they have your son. What if they try to do it to him? You know he's got the genetic predisposition: your brother and cousin are both werewolves. And there are your, ah, proclivities."

"I've been trying not to think about that. You must be some

sort of spirit-wench to keep bringing that up. My poor little boy."

"I'm just trying to find my friend and my butler. And the rest of the children that have been taken."

He looked at the desk, and before he could stop me, I jumped up and ran over to see what he'd been looking at. It was a topographical map of Crystal Pines and the surrounding areas, but it didn't include the canyon Simon had told us about. The bottom of the map told me more than I ever needed to know about how Peter Bowman could be connected to all of it. When he grabbed my left wrist and jerked me away, tears stung my eyes, but I knew what I had clearly seen. In the bottom right corner of the map was a symbol—a howling wolf. In the bottom left corner, another one, a stylized H with a snake winding around the middle bar. Cabal Research and Hippocrates Pharmaceuticals, a match made in hell, a hell they'd created right here in the middle of the Ozark Mountains.

Peter twisted my arm behind my back, and I struggled against the pain that made dots swim in front of my eyes and threatened to overwhelm me into blackness. "Where is it?" he growled, his Scotch breath burning my ear. "Where is the cave? I stole these from the Town Hall today so I could find it, but there's nothing on there."

"Where's the lab, you mean? That's what it is, a research lab, and the genetically pure kids here are the rats. Except your son." His grip relaxed a little. "Why did they steal your son, Peter? What do they need to blackmail you for? You work for them."

He let me go, and I stumbled forward and hit my hip on the edge of the desk as I tried not to catch myself with my hurt arm, which throbbed again.

"They didn't feel like I was pushing hard enough for the Town Hall to be destroyed." He ran his hand through his hair again, and it fell in greasy strands around his face. "The plan was to mess up the demolition date so that it would be imploded before all the records were removed. They didn't want anyone to be able to trace their motives for setting up here and make the genetic connection that you did. That's why they fired you, you know. You were getting too close to the truth." He reached in a drawer and pulled out a gun. "I suppose I should kill you now. You know too much."

I held up my hands and backed away. "I know where your son is, Peter. And I'm the only one who's going to be able to take you to him before they do something awful to him. Have you seen what happens to kids with CLS? They do all sorts of crazy things like climb out windows and run away in the middle of the night. He may do that one day, and then you'll never hear the end of it from Marguerite. The worst part is that you won't know until then what they may or may not have done to him."

"Ah, so now I'm caught between two shrews, not just one. And once I find my son, what then? Will you have my sorry ass hauled off to jail?"

My mind worked quickly. The strands of the spider's web had been there the whole time. Sometimes it's hardest to see what's right in front of you, especially when you find out the man you loved betrayed you. Now that I'd made the connection between Cabal, Hippocrates, and the lab in the woods I didn't really need Peter Bowman except for one thing.

"I'll make a deal with you."

He chuckled and waved me to a chair with his gun. I sat down and crossed my legs, trying hard not to reveal my anxiety.

"I don't really think you're in a position to be making deals, Doctor Fisher."

"Oh, but I think I am." I drew on the insouciance that had gotten the sheriff to buy breakfast for me, the anger that caused me to confront Leo, the frustration that made me tell Iain off, and the pain that Robert's revelations had left me with. I leaned forward. "I'll take you to the cave in the woods. I'll even help you rescue your son. But you have to promise to testify against Hippocrates and Cabal."

He laughed, and it wasn't pleasant. "How about this? You take me to my son, and I'll think about whether to keep you alive or not after I find him."

I opened my mouth to protest, but then shut it. Robert was still out there. So were Leo, Ron, Lonna, and Gabriel. I may not be able to count on them to defend me, but it was a chance I had to take.

As if reading my thoughts, Peter smiled. "And if you think one of those mutt-men may come to your rescue, don't worry." He held out his hand and showed me what he held in his palm —silver bullets.

## 19

Our shoes made tracks in the grass, which the gray early morning sunlight frosted in glittering dew drops. The air smelled sharp, the chill settling into my skin. A mist rose from the ground and wreathed the trees in otherworldly fog, their branches held high in warning or fear at the creatures who roamed among their roots under the moon.

I paused. The light hadn't made it into the woods yet, and shadows still twisted and undulated in the fog. I reminded myself the most lethal shadow walked behind me, his footprints in mine, his hand on the gun he held in the pocket of his navy jacket.

I found one of the deer paths my grandfather and I had explored when I was a child. When I stepped on the crunching rocks, the memory of the trail snapped into place, and I walked forward with confidence. The path toward the river sloped more gently from this side of the mountain. The vapor hung heavily here, and I had to tread slowly so as not to lose the path or my footing. As we got closer to the river, the rocky path turned to dirt, then to slippery mud.

"How much farther?" Peter hissed, his voice coming through the fog from somewhere behind me.

"Not too long," I told him and wondered if I could make a run for it at this point.

"Don't even think of trying to run," he whispered after me. "I can still see you."

*Damn.* I grabbed a tree trunk to keep from sliding the last few feet to the riverbank and thought a twig snapped nearby, but I couldn't be sure. I moved away from the tree, and Peter came after me. He seemed to not be in danger of losing his footing, although his hiking boots were caked with mud.

"What now?"

I held my hand up, listening, but the noise of the rushing water filled my ears. "Follow me."

We headed upstream, and my and Iain's, then Simon's, footprints from the night before made holes on the trail. Surely whoever was in the cave must have seen them, for there were more prints beside them, adult-sized boots and small paw prints. My heart skipped a beat, then rage welled up. They were using the children to hunt us! And I thought it had just been Robert. I worried for Iain's safety, but there was nothing to be done for it now. He'd just have to take care of himself. As for Leo, I hoped he'd gotten the boy—and himself—somewhere secure.

We came to the fork in the river. I pointed down it. "All you have to do is follow that branch to the canyon."

"All *we* have to do," he corrected me. "And how do we get across?"

"Carefully." The footprints on the bank led us to a crossing point, a series of stones in the water. We stepped from rock to rock. I planted my feet and tried not to look at the water rushing between the current stone and my next target. That's how it went: plant, shift, stretch, plant again. I thought about making a run for it when I got to the bank on the other side, but a look back told me Peter still had control of his weapon in spite of his slippery passage. I didn't want him to shoot me or warn anyone who might be near of our presence.

I stopped and listened again but didn't hear anything aside from the water and the usual early morning noises of the forest. We followed the footsteps away from the main river and down the smaller stream. The mist hung here too, but not nearly as heavily. I stopped a few times, sure I'd heard the slow breathing of something watching us from the forest, but every time I stopped, so did the sound.

A rustling in the branches startled me, and I halted. Peter stumbled into me, and the hard rim of his weapon poked me through the material of his jacket.

"Stop doing that," he hissed in my ear.

"We're being watched."

He drew his weapon and leveled it at me. With his thumb, he clicked the safety catch off. "Keep going."

"Don't you hear it? We're being followed."

"That's why I have the silver bullets. Keep going."

I shoved my hands in my pocket to warm my chilled fingers. The terrain to either side of the bank grew rockier, and instead of looking up through tree trunks, I instead found myself walking through the eroded lip of the canyon. Small, scrubby bushes and vines clung to the sides, and time seemed to turn back to the end of night before full sunrise. I could barely see in front of me as we entered the gloom.

"Where's the cave?" I had been so intent on keeping my feet dry on the narrow path by the river I hadn't heard Peter close the distance between us. "It should be in here somewhere."

"Did you bring a flashlight?" he asked.

"No. We came from your house, remember?"

"Here." He passed a small ultralight flashlight into my hand, and I used it to illuminate our way. Above us, I could see blue sky, but the walls of the canyon cast deep shadows.

The river's noise filled the ravine, and if something followed us, I couldn't hear them. The light exposed us, but there was nothing I could do. I only hoped whoever guarded the laboratory hadn't seen us.

"Over there." Peter gestured to the end of the canyon, where the river disappeared into the walls, and a jagged gash swallowed the light as well as the water. "Shine your light in there."

"Are you crazy?" I whispered. "You may as well shoot the damn gun and alert all of them."

He didn't have time to argue. A low growl behind us rumbled through me, and he swung around. I switched the light off, shoved it in my pocket, and ran toward the gash. A gunshot ricocheted off the walls. I hit the ground and covered my head just as a large, furry body crashed into me. We tumbled around, me struggling, and it snapping and snarling at my throat. Then my head hit a rock, and just before I blacked out, Peter screamed in terror.

I came to with a pounding headache and with my wrists tied in front of me. I lay on my side on a sandy surface with hard rock underneath. Peter's mini flashlight dug into my ribs, and I rolled to my back. I found the sore spot where I'd hit my head and couldn't suppress a groan.

"Doctor Fisher?" The accent and the voice were familiar, albeit a little hoarse.

"Gabriel?"

"Aye."

"Is it her? Is she all right?" This voice, older, familiar, one I never thought I'd hear again.

"Grandfather?"

"Are you okay, Joanna? Did they hurt you?"

"I don't know yet." I rolled on to my side again, then sat up on my knees and rubbed my head, checking for injuries. I found a huge knot that made me see stars when I touched it.

"I'm a little shaken up, that's all." My left wrist throbbed, and I could feel it swollen against the binds. "I'm tied up."

"We all are." This voice, rueful, was Lonna's.

"What happened to you? We went to get clothes, and you were gone."

"She remembers nothing," Gabriel explained. "It's not uncommon after the first change. You wake up, usually naked and sometimes in a compromising position, and ask yourself what the hell happened."

"Yeah, like your first time getting smashed at a frat party," Lonna added. I was relieved to hear the usual hint of humor in her voice.

Something shuffled toward me, and I shrank back, unsure in the absence of light what it could be. Then I smelled sweat, dried blood, and river water, and calloused fingers caressed my face.

"Grandfather?"

"I'm here, Joanna."

"I'd hug you, but I'm incapacitated."

He chuckled. "I understand. We'll get our hugs in later."

"Let me see you."

"There's no light in here."

"Where are we?"

"In a side room off the main cavern." This voice was younger and unfamiliar. "There's a metal door they keep closed during the day and night and only pull us out when they want to draw blood or experiment on us."

"Who is that?"

"Johnny."

My throat tightened with tears. "Louise's grandson?"

"Yes." The voice sounded small and afraid.

"How many of you are in here? Wait a second, shut your

eyes." I twisted until the flashlight was in my hands, and I turned it on. The powerful beam, even aimed toward the ceiling, was enough to illuminate the prison and its inhabitants. Everyone squinted.

Lonna and Gabriel, both naked except for dingy white lab coats, leaned back against the wall. Ropes ran from their tied wrists to large iron rings bolted into the walls. Three boys ranging in age from ten to twelve were also tied up. My grandfather, his cheeks sunken and covered with stubble, sat beside them. His shrewd, knowing eyes were the same. We were tied to adjacent rings.

"Why hasn't anyone untied themselves? Or the others, rather. You can all reach."

"They make us change too fast, so our fingers don't work as well as they should," Johnny explained.

A horrible realization broke to the forefront of my brain, and I flexed my fingers experimentally. Stiff and numb, all of them. I'd thought it was from being tied so tight.

"Pull up my sleeve, please." My grandfather obliged, his fingers cramped and unwieldy as well. As I feared, on my forearm just below the ropes, a small red puncture wound stood out against my skin. I had been infected.

Data, I needed data... "How soon is the first transformation?"

Jonny answered. "Usually it wouldn't be until the next full moon, but the formula they use is different. It may be tonight."

"What time is it?" But there was no way to tell—they had taken my watch. How had they missed the flashlight? Or maybe they wanted me to know and to fear. I looked around the room, but no one would meet my eyes, not even my grandfather. I remembered the heartrending scream and Simon Van Doren's hoarseness.

"What's going to happen to me?" My voice, small, echoed in the stone chamber. No one could—or would—answer.

I DIDN'T SPEAK to anyone, and they left me to my despair. I knew what was happening to me, could picture the physiological process as the viral vector raced through my bloodstream and replicated, attacking my cells and finding a certain combination on a specific genetic strand. It wasn't comforting.

I wanted to deny I had the CLS potential, but there was the Landover Curse, the one that skipped a generation. I knew now what it was.

"Did you read those books I gave you, Joanna?" The voice was my grandfather's.

"I was familiar with them already."

"So you read the one by Lecouteaux, on shapeshifting?"

"It's a classic. I've practically memorized it."

"Use it." With those cryptic words, he bowed his head and fell silent.

I'd had enough of silence. "Why didn't you tell me you were a werewolf? Why didn't you let me in when you knew I was studying it?"

"Would you have believed me if I had?"

"I don't know." The lab seemed so far away from this cave, this despair. So did the Manor. I wondered if Iain was having any luck, if he'd missed me yet. Even if he did alert his friends, what proof did we have? Werewolves and kidnapped children? You can't build a legal case on a fairytale, no matter how gruesome.

The air changed, and a hum vibrated through the cave floor and walls. Spots floated at the edge of my vision, and something squeezed my lungs. I gasped for air but couldn't fill them and wheezed. I doubled over and toppled from my knees to the floor in the fetal position as pain shot from my heels through my hamstrings, my lower back, my shoulders and my neck—like giant hands were wringing me out and shaping me into something I wasn't. My clothes, which had been comfortable, loosened and tightened in all the wrong places, and I strained against the fabric, panting and moaning.

"Use it!" my grandfather yelled. "Use the book. And open your mouth."

I opened my mouth and stuck my tongue out as I remembered what I had found in the study, books about how rather than physically changing into werewolves, people would fall into a trance and allow their spiritual aspect to roam free. Some called it a doppelganger, others an astral projection. Something bitter melted on my tongue: aconite. My shuddering stopped, and I shrank in from my body, like it was a shell. I pulled away from my skin and my bones until I was hidden inside.

"What did you do to her?" Lonna's voice, laden with tears, seemed so very far away. "Jo—"

"Don't say her name. Don't touch her. She's in a trance. If you call her or touch her, she may not be able to get back into her body."

My lungs breathed deeply and at an even pace. I curled inside my chest, ready to be expelled. With an exhale, I emerged into the cave and stretched my unfamiliar, awkward body. The disorientation only lasted a moment. Then my heart filled with elation as though I had been waiting my whole life for the transformation into a creature of mist and spirit with four legs, a long tail, and brown eyes.

"She's a wolf, a ghost wolf." I looked at the boy who had spoken and at the others, and the lupine aspects in each of them became evident.

My grandfather nodded, and he gave me the encouraging smile I remembered from my childhood. "Go. We shall guard your body until you return."

For a moment, panic welled up in my heart as it occurred to me I might not know how to get back, how to wake myself up.

And what if someone did say my name or touch me? It might break the tenuous connection I still had with my physical form.

"You don't have time for concern. Just go."

I knew Iain would need proof for the FDA, and the only way to get it would be for me to bring it to him. And hope he didn't ask any questions.

WALKING through walls proved to be no problem. I went through them as though they were mist, and I willed myself to be invisible as I entered the cave proper. Halogen lights stood propped up on poles, and the cavern resembled a movie set of an underground laboratory rather than the real thing. Two men in white coats worked at a long metal table. One of them measured a silvery liquid into vials with a dropper while the other one peered through a microscope.

"Do you think it's happened to her yet?" the first one asked. The light flattened the reddish-gold of his hair and goatee, and I imagined the flame it would be in sunlight.

"No. We'd've heard her scream. Just keep working. They need this prototype in Memphis by tomorrow afternoon." This one looked like some sort of modern medical monk with his receding black hair and long white coat. He blinked beady black eyes.

"Another all-nighter." The first one sighed. "You'd think they'd understand between the experiments and the babysitting we have to do, especially with them bringing in new people lately. One of us is going to have to feed the kid at some point."

"We'll send the lawyer for food. It's about all they're good for, anyway."

Peter Bowman huddled in the corner with a small blond boy asleep in his arms. The child had the beginnings of his father's straight, narrow nose. Before I realized it, I was right beside them, peering into the toddler's face. He opened large brown eyes, and I saw my reflection in them even though I still willed myself to be invisible. He could see me. Maybe he and I had similar gifts, and he understood the wolves' silent communication. I imagined he had heard one of the boys as a wolf and crept out of the house to see the other child, not recognizing the trap. He didn't cry, only smiled sleepily, murmured, "Doggie," and dozed off again.

"Hey, lawyer. Bowman."

Peter jerked awake, and blinked his eyes—the one that hadn't been blackened—open. He'd been roughed up pretty good. I couldn't help but feel a little satisfaction.

"What do you have in your house for food?"

"You're letting me go?" His good eye narrowed. "For what?"

"We're not letting you take the kid, dumbass. You bring food, and we'll think about it."

"Right."

"Perhaps you could have your wifey whip something up for us. She's French, isn't she?"

"You'd be disappointed. She's a horrible cook."

"Ah, well, those European women make it up in other ways, I bet."

The ribald joking continued, and I willed for Peter to do something, anything, to distract them so I could grab one of the vials of "prototype". They didn't say what it was, but I could only guess it was a vehicle—complete with viral vector—for the bird flu vaccine. Finally, I'd had enough and gave the kid's knee a little nip. Not enough to break the skin, but it definitely got his attention.

His cry reverberated off the stone walls, and I jumped away, the noise harsh in my newly hypersensitive ears.

"What the hell?"

"Shut that kid up!" The tall one with the hook nose and

beady eyes hauled Peter to his feet and ushered him outside the cave. The other one followed to help control the kid, and I took my chance. I grabbed one of the sealed vials with my mouth and dashed out of the cave behind them.

A low growl stopped me in my tracks. Peter, the two scientists, and Lance had been cornered by two wolves, one yellow wolf and one smaller black one. They crouched on the bank, their eyes aglow. The breeze brought me their scents, and amidst the musky odor of wolf, I recognized Ron's familiar scent, and the other one must have been Kyra. Now I knew who had attacked me and Peter. But why had they attacked? I didn't have time to think about it. I leapt over the stream and followed the other bank. They were so distracted by Lance's cries and the commotion made by the three men they paid no attention to me. I wondered if a spirit-wolf such as myself would have a scent.

The moon, waning but still bright this far away from the city, dappled the path. The night forest proved to be a gauntlet of intriguing rustlings, wisps of scent begging to be followed, and glowing eyes that blinked shut when I looked directly at them. I had to consciously focus my attention on the task at hand so I wouldn't drop the vial. My stomach growled, but I dared not hunt, at least not until I delivered the solution to Iain.

*So they got you, too?*

The familiar voice reverberated in my head, and I stopped, confused. Where did it come from?

*Who's there?* I asked, trying out my mental voice. *Robert?*

He stepped on to the path, a lean wolf with glossy black fur. His tongue lolled to the side as he sat and looked me over. I sat on my haunches and watched him, unsure of what to do next.

*Where are you headed, pretty wolf lady?*

*I have a delivery to make.* I tried to remember who I was and how hurt I had been, but in my wolf form I was mercifully separated from all those silly human emotions.

*So I see. To whom?*

*Who do you think?*

*Iain, I presume.*

*Yep.*

*I'm afraid I can't let you.*

I tried to gauge his seriousness as well as a possible escape route.

*Why not?*

*You got your one chance earlier. My loyalty, although forced, is with Cabal. If the FDA finds out about the viral vectors in the vaccines, the higher-ups will kill my wife.*

I narrowed my eyes. *And that would be a bad thing?*

*Don't let the wolf take over your humanity, Joanie. She's pregnant.*

The statement hit me in the gut, the force of this second betrayal almost enough to knock the vial out of my mouth.

*How far along is she?*

*Three months.*

I did some calculations with my eyes closed. *That was when we were still together.* I opened them to find him breathing in my face.

*She wanted a baby. I thought it would help keep her distracted and out of the way so I could carry on with you. Then all this happened.*

*You were supposed to be separated!* I backed up until my tail brushed against a tree. *You did use me. You're no better than sleazy Peter Bowman.*

*C'mon, Joanie. We could get out of this together, and then they'd let Sarah go, and it would be just as before.*

For a moment, I was tempted. I could almost smell the faint chemical odor of the lab, the scent of his leather sofa as he lowered me on to it so we could make love again, just as before. Wasn't that what I had been missing, yearning for ever since our fateful meeting?

But married men always go back to their wives. This was a lesson I had learned all too well. And this one had ruined my career so he could keep stringing me along. With a growl, I leaped aside just as he lunged for me, and his skull cracked against the tree. I didn't look back to see if he was hurt—if he was, well, I could let the wolf take over that part of my humanity, because I didn't want to admit to my broken heart and the fact he'd almost fooled me again.

## 20

I returned to Wolfsbane Manor and realized, although I had meant to give the vial to Iain—and as far as I could smell, he was still alone there—I had one small problem: I didn't have opposable thumbs, and all the doors were closed and likely locked. So I did the next best thing—I went around to the side door by the kitchen and rang the doorbell with my long nose. I heard Iain pad through the kitchen and pause by the window by the sink. I had told him to be careful, but I hadn't counted on it working against me. The door opened. He looked down, and his eyes widened in surprise.

"Well, hello there," he crooned. "What's a pretty girl doggie like you doing here?"

I carefully placed the vial on the mat and sat on my haunches.

"What's this, then?"

*It's a sample of the serum, idiot.* But all that came out was a whine.

"Have you been to the lab in the woods? Did you see Joanie? Is she okay?"

*As okay as one can be separated from one's body.* I hoped his saying my name wouldn't keep me from being able to return, but he was likely too far away from my physical self to have an effect.

Iain still didn't pick up the vial. Instead, he glanced behind me and gave it a quick nudge with his foot. It rolled until it rested in a crack between the mat and the threshold stone with a clink.

A sense of *wrong* overwhelmed me, and I turned to see the barrel of a gun pointed straight at my head by the charming Sheriff Knowles. All trace of friendly mountain cop was gone, his expression determined.

"You know keepin' wild animals as pets is illegal, don't you, Scotty? Especially ones not indigenous to the area."

I tried not to growl. *Good for you, Sheriff, that's a big word.*

"My name is Iain, and it's not a pet. It just appeared."

"Now a wild animal would never just show up at your door if it didn't know you. Have you been feedin' this pretty wolf?"

"No, officer."

I didn't know with certainty, but I could guess that Sheriff Knowles' gun didn't have the regulation lead slugs in it. I wondered if they made silver hollow-point bullets and how badly it would hurt.

I forced myself to sit on my haunches and give Sheriff Knowles a lupine grin. *See? I'm a friendly wolf-girl. Don't shoot me.*

"And did this animal bring anything to you?"

"Nothing, officer."

"Then you won't mind if I look around?"

*I mind.*

"Do you have a warrant, Sheriff?"

*Yay, Iain!*

"As a matter of fact, I do." He produced an envelope from his pocket and showed an official-looking piece of paper to

Iain. "We suspect Doctor Fisher is harboring suspects in a kidnapping case."

"Then you may perform a cursory visual inspection of the premises, as the warrant states. I'll show you around."

He glanced back over his shoulder, and I debated whether I should wait or disappear. "Go," he mouthed, and I bobbed my head.

I followed the trails back through the forest, but when I came to the spot where I'd knocked Robert into a tree, he wasn't there. Only the disarrangement of the dried leaves showed where he'd landed.

He snarled, *You little bitch,* just before he landed on top of me. We rolled, and I alternately struggled to keep his hind legs from disemboweling me with sharp claws and to prevent his teeth from closing in on my neck.

*That's Doctor Bitch to you.* But I couldn't hang on for long— my strength waned. My still unfamiliar werewolf form was no match for his expert maneuvers. All I could do was try not to let him tear apart anything important. I wondered what would happen to my body if he killed me.

Wait. This wasn't a physical form, although I'd been acting like it was. With a force of effort, I tugged on the wisp of energy connecting me to my body.

I woke and coughed and sputtered in my efforts to spit out the aconite. My body didn't fit right, and something had muffled my senses, particularly hearing and smell. The metallic flavor of blood joined the bitterness of the aconite in my mouth.

"How was it?" asked my grandfather.

"Interesting. How long was I gone?"

"It's hard to say, but I would guess about five hours. Did you accomplish what you needed?"

"I think so." I passed out.

I WOKE A FEW HOURS LATER. Our captors had tossed some bread and bottles of water into the cave within reach of my bound hands. I had dreamed in fragments, of running through the woods, and of Leo as a wolf, his dark eyes in a lupine face.

I ate my provisions and was struggling with the cap on the water bottle a commotion erupted on the other side of the metal door fitted into the cave wall. It opened slowly, the light spilling in bit by bit to illuminate the floor. I squinted against the glare. A young man in a paramedic's uniform poked his head in.

"They're in here."

The next half hour passed in a whirlwind of images that seemed too bright to my light-deprived eyes. People untied our hands, and the paramedics checked to make sure there were no injuries past minor scrapes and bumps. They also checked for problems that would have been caused by partial starvation and dehydration.

"How did you know where to find us?" I asked after I drank an entire bottle of water in one gulp.

"Those two brought us here," the EMT said and inclined his head toward Leo and Simon. "Once we could tear the boy away from his mother, that is. He insisted on coming with us to help rescue the others."

"I'm sure she was glad to see him."

"The mothers of the other boys will be happy to see their sons too. That's why we're checking them here. We don't want them to be away from their families for a minute longer than they have to be."

Iain pushed his way into the cave. "Gentlemen, please do not dismantle any of the equipment. Try not to touch it. The FBI and FDA agents are going to examine it."

A hand landed on my shoulder, and I looked up into my

grandfather's eyes. He had a weary smile on his face. "How's the house?"

I patted his hand. "Still in one piece as far as I know."

"Did you find the surprises I left you?"

"I think so."

"And the cats?"

I pulled the silver chain out of my shirt. "Yep, here's Mishka." He put an arm around my shoulder and squeezed me tightly.

"I thought I wasn't going to be able to do that ever again," he said, his voice gruff. I looked away so I wouldn't see him cry.

"Me too."

Leo came over. "Are you okay? How's the wrist?"

"Decent."

"Sir, how are you?" Leo asked and gave my grandfather a hearty handshake. He cocked his head as if to ask how much he could give away.

"I'm doing much better now I know my granddaughter and all the children are safe. And you can say anything. She's a smart girl—I'm sure she's figured it all out."

Leo grinned at me. "That she did, sir. Are you ready to assume the pack alpha role? We could use you on the hunt."

"In time, Leo, in time. Where's your cousin?"

Leo frowned, his handsome features distressed. "I can't find him."

My grandfather put his hand on my shoulder. "Then it's a good thing we have a spirit-walker among us. She'll be able to find him more quickly than anyone."

"A spirit-walker?"

"It's the term for a shape-changer who does so with spirit rather than physically, like you do. Not everyone has the talent. With a spirit form, you can move much more quickly and silently."

I thought about my escape from Robert, and my stomach

turned when I thought about how, for a moment, I had been tempted.

Leo regarded me with respect and curiosity. "Is it the wolfsbane? How does that work?"

"It both helps and hinders the transformation. It prevents the transformation physically but facilitates the spiritual one."

Leo shook his head. "That's amazing."

We walked out of the cave into the waning sunlight of another day. Iain continued to direct the federal agents, but one broke off from the crowd and followed us.

"Doctor Fisher? Doctor Landover? We have some questions for you."

My grandfather's brows drew together. "Can't we go home, get hot showers and a good night's sleep first? Have mercy on an old man."

"It will just take a moment."

My grandfather turned to Leo. "Can you take care of the others?"

"Yes, sir. I'll get Simon back to his family, and can give Gabriel and Lonna a ride."

The two of them hadn't met each other's eyes the entire time we were in the main cavern, and I wondered what, exactly, had transpired between them before they were kidnapped. But I didn't have time for speculation now. The federal agent led us out of the ravine and away from the river to a clearing, where a lone black SUV with tinted windows sat.

I turned to the agent—a nondescript fellow with sandy brown hair and blue eyes—who I had nicknamed "Buddy" in my head, to ask what was going on, but got the answer even before the words came out of my mouth. He pointed a gun at us and gestured to the car.

"Someone wants to talk to you."

"I'm guessing there are silver bullets in that thing, aren't there?"

"Of course."

The window rolled down to reveal Sheriff Knowles in the driver's seat. "Come on in, Doctors. I've got someone here who's been dying to meet you."

The back door opened. Ron as well as a guy who looked like he'd been up all night waited for us. The unfamiliar man's salt-and-pepper tufts were messy over his ears, and his greasy comb-over zigzagged in disheveled strands across his shiny head. His jowls wobbled as he introduced himself.

"I'm Agent Marius. I have a proposition for you."

We climbed in, and Buddy closed the door behind us. The SUV started up with a purr, its hybrid engine making all the noise of a large golf cart. One more vehicle leaving the scene wouldn't be noticed, especially one as quiet as this one. I didn't know how long they'd been there, but I could guess from the collection of fast food bags on the floor and the empty drink cups it had been several hours.

Ron faced the window and wouldn't meet either my or my grandfather's gaze when he spoke. "That took longer than we thought."

What was wrong with him? "Not that you were any help," I snapped. "And where is Kyra?"

"She's around. She wanted to find Leo."

I tried not to think of Kyra and Leo and how close they had looked that first evening. He had said there was nothing between them, but was it true?

"That was you last night, wasn't it, coming out of the cave? How did you do that?"

I held up my hand. "All in good time. Now, can you guys please explain why we're getting kidnapped—again?"

Agent Marius made a sound combining a cough, harrumph, and sneeze. "This isn't a kidnapping, Doctor Fisher. We just want to have a little conversation."

"About what? And what does Ron have to do with all of this?"

"All in good time." His tone mocked me.

The vehicle went over a rough patch, and we were thrown from side to side. I hit my left wrist, and the pain made me hiss.

"Are you injured, Doctor Fisher?"

I glared at Ron. "As you well know."

Knowles chuckled from the front seat. The road evened out. *So*, I guessed, *this is what happens. Be disagreeable, get jostled. Be friendly, and things go smoothly. And keep in mind if things get too rough, Buddy's gun might just "accidentally" go off.*

"What can we do for you, Agent Marius?" My grandfather's tone held steel beneath his charming words. He'd sounded similarly the last time I saw him and my mother together, and she had told him I wouldn't be spending summers up there anymore. She got her way, but at the cost of losing her inheritance.

"Well, Doctor Landover, we're interested in some of the experiments you've been doing." He pulled a manila folder out of his black briefcase and handed it to my grandfather.

"How did you get these?"

They were my grandfather's notes on his aconite research, copies of the documents Galbraith had given me and Iain.

"Your lawyer was more than happy to cooperate with us when we subpoenaed your records."

"On what grounds was the subpoena served?"

"We were concerned about your research on the grounds of homeland security. A rogue scientist in a mountaintop laboratory might be making things we would rather not have fall into the hands of our enemies."

"How did you find out in the first place?"

Ron's guilty look told me all I needed to know. "They promised me a cure, Joanie," he mumbled, his eyes still down.

"They promised me if I cooperated, I would get my old life back."

"Just couldn't wait, could you?"

He flexed his fingers. "I need to be back in Little Rock, back at my fellowship."

"And back within dating distance of your professor's daughter."

"What we're interested in most is something Ron observed last night," Marius, obviously ignoring us, continued. "A shadowy wolf with something solid in its mouth slipped without a sound through the woods, fended off an attack from a material wolf, and then disappeared when attacked again." He raised one bushy eyebrow. "Would you know anything about that?"

I had been so intent on my goal I hadn't noticed I was being followed. "I don't know what you're talking about."

"Are you sure, spirit-walker?"

"You had bugs in the lab. You knew what was going on." I clenched my fists, and the truck lurched over a pothole or rock of some sort.

"Sorry," Sheriff Knowles called out. "That one snuck up on me."

Marius ignored him. "We've been keeping an eye on Hippocrates-Cabal. We wouldn't have let them contaminate the bird flu supply, of course."

*Wouldn't they?* I wondered. But I kept my breathing even and relaxed my hands with effort. "What do you want from us?"

"We want you to continue your research. We think it has intriguing possibilities."

"We're scientists, Agent Marius," said my grandfather. "You're going to have to be more specific."

"Fine, then." Marius made the disagreeable sound again. "As you know, our military is stretched thin right now, and our enemies numerous, including at home."

"Right."

"We need better, stealthier, ways of quelling insurgency so we can get our soldiers out faster. Then we need the money to bankroll the operations."

I put together what he wasn't saying. "You want to be the ones to make the 'cure' for CLS. You let Hippocrates create the problem, and you'll be the one to fix it. At premium cost."

"And you want to turn your soldiers into werewolves." My grandfather's tone held more steel than before. "You want to take all those young men and women and condemn them to a life I wouldn't wish on my worst enemy. Do you have a plan for what to do with them when they return?"

"We cure them." Marius spread his hands as though it was the most obvious thing in the world.

"But there isn't a cure."

"That's what we need you to find before we can put the program into effect. It's a risk we're willing to take. We'll take care of them in the future if necessary."

My grandfather leaned back. "You have my notes. You have my granddaughter's documentation from her research so you can see who to experiment on. Why do you need us?"

"Because you're the only ones who have made it this far, and for someone to try to replicate and fully understand your work, even for someone like Iain McPherson, would take far too long. This is an urgent situation, Doctors. We don't have that kind of time."

Gravel ground under the tires. We had reached the driveway to Wolfsbane Manor.

"You have a decision to make, Doctors. Will you help us with this?"

"What if we don't?"

"Then you will be treated as rogue scientists, and we will not hesitate to lock you away for the rest of your life. Prison is hard on terrorists."

My grandfather seemed to deflate in his seat. "It appears as though the decision has been made for us."

They dropped us off at the front door and drove away.

"Why did you agree?" I asked as we walked inside. "I would have gone to jail to keep them from hurting any more people, from turning our tools into weapons. This is not how I remembered you."

He shook his head. "Because they might just try the transformation anyway, without a cure. The dosing of aconite is such a delicate process they would likely kill many innocent people before they succeeded in their aims. At least this way, we'd have control."

I looked at him in disbelief. He had always told me scientific integrity was the most important defense we had against the pressures of government. But he seemed too weary for me to argue.

We trudged up the stairs. The noises of the other inhabitants of the house were comforting, albeit sharper than they had been before my transformation. Lonna packed in her room. With the mystery of the disappearing children solved, I guessed she would be heading back to Little Rock, although I didn't know how she would manage to live with her new CLS.

"Go talk to her." My grandfather inclined his head toward the bedroom wing of the house. He had always managed to read my mind—or at least my face. "She told us in the cave things had been...tense...between you two since she arrived. Something about her not learning from your mistakes."

"You could say that."

"I think she learned her lesson. And you learned yours."

"Mine?" But I knew what he meant.

Lonna's suitcase lay open on the bed. She had already folded everything into it.

"Hey," I said. She looked up, her liquid topaz eyes full of emotion.

"Joanie, I should've listened to you," she started, but I held up my hand.

"It's all in the past."

She bit her lip and took a deep breath. "I need to tell you what happened. With me and Peter. You need to know."

The conversation about the spell he had put on her came back to me. "Okay." I sat on the bed. "I'm listening."

She told me how she'd gone to interview him at his request, and he'd made her agree to have lunch with him as the price of his silence as to who she really was.

"He was really nice, you know. He told me how impressed he'd been with my work. But then things got weird."

He had leaned across the desk and taken her hand, turning it palm up. "You have an interesting story on your palm, Ms. Marconi. It says you're in for some big changes." Then he brought it to his lips and kissed it.

"God, Joanie, it went all the way down to my toes. It was the most sensual kiss I'd had in my life—on my hand." So sensual, in fact, she experienced an orgasm right there in his office. She excused herself to go to the bathroom, and when she'd washed her hands, she noticed the hand he kissed had a small cut on it as though it had been grazed by one of his teeth.

"And then we went to lunch, and then back to his office, and then..." She put her hands to her face.

"It's not your fault. You were seduced *and* bespelled."

But my mind raced. Peter wasn't a werewolf, of that I was sure. I would have been able to tell in my spirit-walker form. So how could his bite have triggered the effect? But what if it wasn't just the bite? What if it had been the bite and the spell reinforced by all the sexual energy between them? What if he had been telling me the truth, and he had some attenuated form that looked more like a traditional impulse-control disorder? His son, who had inherited his genes, had been able to see me.

My mind had been slammed by the possibility of were-wolves, but now it seemed there might be some sort of rogue wizard or shaman, with enough of the genetic predisposition toward lycanthropy to inflict it on others.

Lonna sighed. "But all that's neither here nor there. Now we both have this problem."

"We'll get through it. And my grandfather and I will find a cure."

"God, Joanie. I wish I had never come up here."

I went to touch her arm, but she flinched away from me.

"I should never have come up here," she repeated. "Now I have some weird disease that's going to make me turn into some awful creature once a month."

"Maybe the aconite will work for you, too. We can always try it."

"Even so, it's going to mean a day off from work out of every twenty-eight to handle not having slept. It's going to mean strange stories I'll have to tell my lovers. Can you imagine?" She raised her tear-stained face to me. "'No, honey, I can't go out tonight. No, I can't tell you why. Oh, and don't call me tomorrow, either, I'll be asleep all day.' This is going to ruin my career and my love life."

"You'll handle it. I'll handle it. You can have some of my money to make up what you won't earn."

"It's not your money. Your grandfather is still alive, remember? That leaves you with nothing again."

My heart plummeted to my stomach, and I swallowed around the acid in my throat. She was right, and I didn't feel like I knew my grandfather anymore. "I've lost my career and contracted CLS, too."

"But you won't be alone in it. I will."

"No, you won't."

"Thanks, but I'm just still so pissed, and Peter's gone, and it's just too much for me to deal with."

"I'll leave you alone, then, if it's what you want."

"Yes." For the first time in our long friendship, her eyes grew cold, and she turned her back on me. "That's exactly what I want."

"Okay, then." I walked out of the room as slowly as I could, but she made no indication she wanted me to stop. I closed the door behind me, and when it clicked shut, she began to sob. With a heavy heart, I went downstairs.

I found Grandfather and Gabriel poring over the blueprints as well as the electrical and gas-line schematics of the house, which they had laid out on the long dining room table.

"What are you guys doing?"

My grandfather put a hand to his lips and made a crawling motion with his hand. I understood—they didn't know if, while the house was empty, Knowles and his goons had come in and bugged the place. That explained his comments by the front door.

They wrote notes to each other, but all my grandfather would say to me was, "Shouldn't you find the car you rented in Memphis and return it? You should bring Lonna with you. It sounds like she's ready to go home. You can take my car, and she can drive the rental."

"I'll ask her if she wants to go. I think her car is still down at her apartment anyway from when Gabriel drove it."

Lonna agreed to follow me down to Little Rock in the rental car. I found a place I could return it there. After a quick shower and change, I was ready as well.

"Bye, honey," my grandfather said as he kissed me on the cheek. "We'll see you when you get back." In my ear, he whispered, "Spend the night with Lonna at her apartment. She may need you." He pressed a small packet into my hand—two homemade capsules. "You may need each other. And remember, I'm so very proud of you."

I bit my lip to keep from crying. "She's so upset right now

she wants nothing to do with me." I pointed to the packet. "And how do you know these will work on her?"

"I don't know. But it's worth a try. Give her time, honey, she'll come around. Emotions are always unstable soon after the first change. And she was given the formula that made them scream in agony and forced them to change."

I shook my head, angry at myself for not realizing they'd been there long enough to be experimented on. I wondered how Gabriel was recovering, but he wouldn't meet my eyes.

"You need to be gentle with yourself, too." My grandfather enveloped me in a hug and squeezed me tight. He'd showered, and the clean soap smell in combination with the crispness of his cotton shirt stayed in my nostrils and brought back happy memories.

"I'll try."

"Be careful."

I didn't know what he and Gabriel planned, but I knew it couldn't be good. "You, too."

## 21

M y story began with fire, and it ends with fire. Water might cleanse, but fire transforms. It burns away all the dead matter and leaves exposed the bare essence of the field and the forest. And of my life.

The newly transformed CLS sufferer—I still have a hard time thinking of myself as a werewolf—goes through fits and starts before settling into the full-moon pattern. Lonna and I both felt the transformation coming on as we arrived back at her apartment from dropping off the rental car, and we hurried in and locked the door behind us. Then, for good measure, we moved her heavy dining room table against it.

Lonna doubled over in a cramp and slumped on the floor, panting. I remembered the lozenges in my pocket.

"Here." I forced her mouth open with shaking fingers and slid one under her tongue. I took one as well and sat on the floor, waiting for it to begin.

A profound sleepiness overtook me, and darkness closed in on my vision. The sensation of shrinking until the essence of my soul was distilled somewhere beneath my heart, between my lungs, overtook me. Then I caught an exhale and emerged through my open mouth. Lonna was there, both in sleeping human body as well as in a transparent version of her werewolf body.

*This is much better.* She shook herself out. *I don't feel so clumsy.*

A faint whiff of smoke caught my attention, but I couldn't sense any fire nearby. Then I realized what my grandfather and Gabriel intended.

*We have to go.*

*Where?*

*Wolfsbane Manor!*

And with a thought, we were there.

BY THE TIME WE ARRIVED, the entire house was engulfed in flame. The orange and yellow glow lit the edges of the trees around the yard, and even the low clouds seemed to reflect the fury of the fire. In my mind's eye, I pictured the ballroom, the paint of the mural curling off from the heat, the boxes of papers catching quickly and helping the hungry flames into the underground laboratory, where chemicals would explode, glass would shatter, and plastic would melt. A lifetime of work gone in a puff of smoke.

*Did you know this would happen?* Werewolf-Lonna sat on the grass next to me, the flames reflected in her eyes.

*No.*

*Where are the men?*

My heart caught in my throat. *I don't know.*

I darted toward the flames, but a large gray wolf blocked my way. This one was also a spirit wolf, and my grandfather's soul looked at me from his eyes.

*Don't go any closer,* he warned me. *If you inhale too much smoke, it will kill your physical form as well.*

Smoke wreathed his form, and I knew what he had done, the sacrifice he had made to keep his knowledge out of the hands of those who would abuse it. Still, with my last glimmer of hope, I had to ask, *What did you do?*

*I don't have much time. There's something I left for you. It's in the boathouse in a hidden compartment just above the canoe hooks. It's hidden well enough the Feds won't find it.* He touched his nose to mine. *I will always love you and be proud of you. Remember that.* He disappeared.

If I had been in human form, I would have cried. As it was, all I could do was throw my head back and let forth a long, mournful howl. Other voices joined mine, a chorus of grief for my grandfather, the alpha wolf of the Crystal Pines pack. Warm bodies crowded in around me and I knew they were there, even Kyra, who had always hated me, and Ron and Matt, who had betrayed me for their own purposes. I knew the pack would scatter, but on that night, we came together and howled our grief at the waning moon.

TWO MONTHS *Later*

I sat in Peter Bowman's old office, where a fresh young partner went through the formalities to make me the heir to my grandfather's fortune as well as the land on which Wolfsbane Manor had stood. It had been eight weeks and four days, and the process had been held up, first by assertions of insurance fraud, and then by the resulting arson investigation. There hadn't been evidence of any foul play, and the whole thing was ruled a tragic accident.

The fire had been caused by a short in the electrical system, the insurance report said. The house was such a shambles even the arson investigator had a difficult time pinpointing the cause. There had been a spark near a place where the gas line had cracked, and the whole system had gone up in flames. Along with it went the house. My grandfather, ostensibly exhausted from his ordeal, had slept through the alarms and had died of smoke inhalation in his bed before his body had burned to a pile of charred remains. They used dental records to identify him.

My mother sat in the other desk chair, petite like myself, but with iron-gray hair and a mouth perpetually twisted into a sneer. Her bitterness at losing my grandfather's fortune to me was almost palpable. He had left her enough to live on very comfortably for the rest of her life, but he knew her innate self-ishness would never allow her to be satisfied. She signed the necessary papers and left without saying a word.

The lawyer winced when she slammed the door. "Your grandfather was a smart man. This will is ironclad."

"So was his." I signed the last page with a heavy heart. That meant the final papers were drawn up, so he handed me over to the banker, who had come all the way from Memphis to help transfer the money and the accounts to my name. I walked out of the office with more money than I could have ever imagined, but more bereft of family and friends than I had ever been.

Denial that the body in the house had been my grandfa-ther's gave way to anger at him for sacrificing himself, and now grief. It would be a long time to acceptance. I hadn't been to what was left of the Manor since it all happened. The nice, perky Crystal Pines real estate lady had been very helpful in finding me a new house. "It's on the cul-de-sac and very quiet." It turned out to have been Peter Bowman's, who had skipped town with his family the day after the raid on the lab in the woods. They had taken what they could carry and left most of the furniture, which had been included with the house. I still sold off most of the stuff in the office and decorated the room so it looked like my grandfather's. My possessions had finally arrived from Memphis the day after the fire.

Ron had disappeared as well just after the Bowman family had left. I later found out he had gone down to Little Rock and was trying to convince UAMS to re-admit him to his residency program as well as to win the heart of the charming Lisa Temmerson. Iain, meanwhile, had flown to Washington, D.C., to act as a consultant and expert witness for the FDA's suit against Hippocrates-Cabal. Leo had gone after Peter, and I hadn't heard from him since. I sometimes wished we could talk about it, what had happened. Would the aconite lozenges help with his mood swings?

And what of Gabriel? I knew he wasn't dead—he had been beside me in body on the night of the fire. I'd never figured out his true motives or identity, only that he'd come hoping I could finish my grandfather's work. Now I could be of no use to him. It sounds crazy to say it, but his betrayal hurt almost as much as Robert's. They had both shown me a world beyond what I could have imagined.

I had never found out what happened between Gabriel and Lonna the morning after we left them, and I honestly didn't want to know. Lonna and I still got together occasionally. My grandfather had left me the recipe for the aconite lozenges as well as my brother's and my letters in the boathouse. Lonna and I would occasionally hunt together as spirit wolves, but the trust wasn't there anymore. I'd been a hypocrite for being so hard on her about Peter when I'd still lusted after Robert. She would never admit it, but she resented me for having brought her into a situation where she was compromised on every level. That it was partially her fault for being overconfident was something she'd never admit.

So I was alone, the rich heiress in a small town in the Ozarks in Arkansas. I pondered it on the way back to my new house filled with furnishings that still felt like they belonged to other people.

I stopped off for a flu shot on the way home and then ran a couple more errands. As I sat with a cup of coffee in the town diner, I faced the fact that I'd have to go back to that big empty house eventually. I reminded myself it could be worse, and maybe I needed to be alone for a while.

But when I turned the curve to the cul-de-sac, I found someone sitting on my front porch steps. My heart skipped a beat at the sight of the wavy dark hair, the intense black eyes, and the muscular body in blue jeans and a black leather jacket.

"Leo?"

He came and opened the car door for me. "Good afternoon, Doctor Fisher."

"Good afternoon, Doctor Bowman. What are you doing here?"

"I had to disappear for a while—there was something I needed to investigate on my own. But I'm back. They said you live here now."

"I can't go back to the Manor, not yet." I brushed a tear from my eye. "It's too soon. I still can't believe he's gone."

He looked away and bit his lip.

I held my hand out to him, and he took it. My hand looked so small in his, which was warm in spite of him having waited out in the cold for me.

I squeezed. "We both loved him."

"And we'll both miss him. I can't believe I didn't realize he'd been taken to that place. And Ron..." His voice broke.

"Ron betrayed you for love."

"Right." He ran his hand through his hair. "I hope it was worth it. Did you hear they're thinking of starting a CLS specialty at UAMS?"

"Then he's ended up in the right place."

Leo followed me into the kitchen, where I put on a pot of coffee.

"No butler?"

"Nope. Gabriel left after the fire. It wasn't really my style anyway."

A little of the tension seeped out of Leo. "Why live here? Why not rebuild?"

"I'm not ready yet. I have to feel like it's the right time."

He leaned against the counter and crossed his arms. "There's a reason for that. Let's go up there this evening, at twilight."

"Go up to where? The manor ruins?"

"Yes."

Tears stung my eyes, and the kitchen blurred. "Leo, I can't. I haven't been up there since they found his body."

In a moment, his arms were around me, and I cried into his shoulder. It felt so good just to let it out, to let someone else hold me up for a change, especially when one of his tears plopped on the top of my head.

"Don't worry, I'll be with you. Have been from the beginning, you know."

"Oh?"

"Yes. You remember how I told Galbraith he didn't need to bring Gabriel in?"

I raised an eyebrow. "No, I didn't hear that part of the conversation, remember?"

"You heard the end of it. If I couldn't keep Gabriel away from your grandfather's estate, I hoped to at least keep him away from mine."

"I see." I put my cheek against the warm leather of his jacket.

"After I met you, and you were so feisty with Kyra, I couldn't help but fall for you. And then you never let my wild moods intimidate you. It was like you saw beyond all the CLS stuff. You could say I was your greatest admirer. Still am."

The words stung, and I remembered Gabriel had said something similar, but then the recollection of a certain dinner that had been paid for came to mind.

"Would that perhaps be a *secret* admirer?"

He smiled at me and then tucked my head under his chin, where it fit perfectly. "Not so secret anymore. Shall I show you how much I admire you?"

I tilted my head back to look at him, and he pressed his lips to mine, his mouth questioning like I might be the one to draw back. Just in case he had any doubt, I threaded my fingers through his thick curls. With nothing standing between us anymore, this kiss was molten and carried with it the excitement of being the most powerful animal running through the forest. I shivered, and he drew me closer.

"You're not going to push me away this time, are you?"

"No words," he teased and made sure I couldn't ask any more questions or doubt his intentions.

"Let's go upstairs," I whispered the next time we came up for air.

He grabbed my wrist, the one he had hurt, and tugged me gently to the master bedroom. I'd forgotten for a moment he knew the house. Then he proceeded to show me how he could be both a wild animal and a tender lover, switching between the two as I needed. By the end, as we both came, I knew without a doubt who I wanted my second pack mate to be.

"Come to the Manor with me tonight," he whispered as we lay collapsed together.

I drew away, but he pulled me back to him. "Why?"

"Charles made me promise I'd bring you when I returned. He knew you'd need time to heal and forgive, but there's something he wanted me to show you."

I sighed. "I could never say no to him."

SO THERE I WAS, at twilight, sharing a thermos of hot chocolate with Leo and trying not to look at the jagged edges of what was left of my childhood sanctuary and my adult legacy. The trees around the edge of the lawn were bare of leaves, and their branches made intricate lacework against the feathery clouds in the sky. The sun set behind the ruins, and the sky turned pink, streaked with orange and purple, and gilded the remains of Wolfsbane Manor.

I allowed the beauty of the scene to soothe some of the ache in my heart. "It's beautiful."

"That's not all."

A large gray wolf loped across the lawn from the woods and disappeared into the ruins of the house. I tugged on Leo's sleeve to let him know I wanted to follow it, but he held his finger up —*wait*. I waited and watched, and as dusk fell, the wolf emerged again, this time with something in its mouth. It trotted up to us and dropped a key into the grass. It was the old front door key, and miraculously, it hadn't been melted into oblivion. If anything, it was only a little sooty.

Then the wolf disappeared, and a chill breeze froze the tears to my face. I picked up the key. "What is this?"

"When a person dies, it sometimes takes a while for the part of the spirit that animated the body to disappear. He had a reason to wait."

I put the key in my pocket as we walked to the car. "What does it mean?"

But I knew. My grandfather's spirit, or maybe it was the spirit of one of our ancestors, wouldn't be at rest until I lived on our land again, in a house on top of the mountain, the guardian of Piney Mountain and now Crystal Pines. Honey had told me there was a tie between the Landover blood and the land. Maybe she'd been right.

Leo held the car door open for me—I loved this new civilized manner—and even though we didn't say anything, I knew he agreed with the spirit wolf.

"I'll build another Wolfsbane Manor," I told him, "but on one condition."

He kept his eyes forward as he started the car. "What's that?"

"That you'll be there with me. I know sometimes I'm going to want to kill you, especially when your animal brain is taking over, but I need you here."

He grinned, his eyes full of mischief and a little something else.

"What?" I asked, my heart stopping for a moment.

"It took you long enough to realize. And besides..." The grin was definitely a leer. "As you found out this afternoon, the animal part of my brain can be fun."

I blushed and wanted to smack him, but I knew he was right. Everything happens in its own time, and sometimes you just need a trial by fire—or two—to transform you into the right person. And once we got the place built again, we were going to throw some fabulous parties and make it into the house it had always been meant to be.

I rolled down the window, opened my hand to the breeze, and let go of the past.

~

The story continues in book two, *Long Shadows*.

~

THANK you for reading *The Wolf's Shadow*! The best way to help me continue to write fun books by helping others to find them is to take one simple step—leaving a review at the site where you bought the book. Retailers take reviews seriously, as do a lot of other readers. Even short reviews can have a large effect. Thank you!

Also, please continue reading for an important author's note...

# AUTHOR'S NOTE

When I originally wrote *The Mountain's Shadow* (the original title of *The Wolf's Shadow*) in 2006, the anti-vaccination movement had yet to grow into the major problem it is today. Also, at that time, none of us had any idea of what would happen with the pandemic of 2020. I struggled with how much of the book to change with this third edition. I added in a few elements of increased horror on the part of the characters, especially Joanie who is a public health researcher, at the idea of tampering with vaccines. I also sent her for a flu shot at the end of the book, but I didn't want to belabor the point . We're reading to escape right now, aren't we?

Most importantly, I want to assert that I am firmly pro-vaccine, and I plan to get the COVID vaccine as soon as it's available to me. I have also gotten my flu shot. Vaccines are one of our most powerful tools to help keep the public healthy, and if you think about it, it's so simple and worth whatever minor discomfort you may experience.

# ABOUT LONG SHADOWS

*This time, being true to herself could be a deadly mistake.*

Lonna Marconi likes to solve problems. The hard kind. A social worker by day, P.I. in her "spare time," she's figured out how to handle her little "werewolf problem." After a dose of wolfsbane, her physical body stays safe in bed while her wolf goes spirit walking. If only she didn't have a mind of her own...

Deep in the Appalachians, Lonna learns a family secret that means she's unique, even among werewolves. Now she's pursued by a rogue sorcerer with poisonous intentions, other wizards who'd like to throw her in a gilded prison, and a band of ghostly wolves thirsting for her blood.

Worse, there's only one man who can protect her, and even he demands a price: her heart. Even though his own may be forever beyond her reach.

Lonna Marconi likes to solve problems. The hard kind. A social worker by day, P.I. in her "spare time," she's figured out how to handle her little "werewolf problem." After a dose of wolfsbane, her physical body stays safe in bed while her wolf goes spirit walking. If only she didn't have a mind of her own...

Deep in the Appalachians, Lonna learns a family secret that

means she's unique, even among werewolves. Now she's pursued by a rogue sorcerer with poisonous intentions, other wizards who'd like to throw her in a gilded prison, and a band of ghostly wolves thirsting for her blood.

Worse, there's only one man who can protect her, and even he demands a price: her heart. Even though his own may be forever beyond her reach.

Grab your copy from your favorite online retailer, or your local bookstore can order it for you from Ingram Spark. To make it easy for them, you can give them the ISBN 978-1-945074-38-7

# LONG SHADOWS PREVIEW

*Enjoy the first chapter of* Long Shadows, *Lycanthropy Files, Book 2*:

People say I'm beautiful, but they don't see the monster inside.

It was like a fairy tale: a big, beautiful house, a plucky heroine, an evil wizard... But the best friend never fares well, and I didn't. The heroine got cursed too, but she found true love in the end. I got a lifestyle change that wasn't a choice and came with no warning. The worst part? I couldn't even remember the specifics of my first change— only that it was traumatic, so my mind had even less to make sense of.

Yes, ladies and gentlemen, I'm a werewolf. Please hold your applause. It will only make me cry. Big girls don't cry, and when you're a predator, you don't show signs of weakness.

My part of the story started one rainy February morning. I'd just gotten into the office, a satellite site for the Arkansas Department of Family and Child Services, and snarled at the pile of case files on my desk when the phone rang.

"Marconi!" my boss Paul barked. "Get in here!"

I nearly jumped out of my skin. Literally. I had a wicked

aconite hangover. No, I didn't use it recreationally. I used it to "spirit-walk," or create a spiritual doppelganger so I could roam as a spirit-wolf rather than a physical one. I almost kicked my spirit out of my body again when Paul startled me, but I took a few deep breaths to get everything settled in, like spreading batter into the corners of a pan.

Evil cake, that's me.

It's hardest for me to control my temper mornings after hunting, and I struggled not to bare my teeth at Paul when I walked into his cluttered office. The piles of files, papers, and dirty Styrofoam cups made me want to gag into the wastebasket. My nose picked up the scent of dried-out, rancid turkey sandwich somewhere under his desk, and I noticed he wore yesterday's shirt. With his pointy nose, prominent thin ears, and wisps of gray hair clinging to his head, he looked like a sick rodent, and I pushed away the image of shaking him until his neck broke. I had done that to a rat the night before. It had been lurking about, tearing into the garbage bags my neighbors left outside their door, which unleashed an awful mélange of scents into the breezeway and my apartment. I'd complained, but the management hadn't done anything about either the neighbors or the rat. It was generally frowned upon to hunt down and kill one's neighbors, so the rat had to go. Paul was *my* management, and he paid me, so I squashed my impulses.

"Have a seat," he said.

"Where?" Every surface was covered with paper.

He shrugged and sat. "As you can see, we're overworked and understaffed, but we can't afford to keep on dead weight."

I folded my hands in front of me and pressed my nails into my knuckles. "I'm pulling my weight, Paul."

"Right, but where were you last night? I got a call this morning that someone saw you at a club 'shaking your booty' and 'getting shitfaced drunk.'" His air quotes almost made it comical.

"Not that what I do on my own time is any of your business, but I can assure you it wasn't me."

"Can someone give you an alibi?" he asked and leaned forward, a look of concern on his rodent face. "I don't want to cut you from my staff, but the higher ups are after me to get rid of whoever I can. You know we have a code of conduct here and strict policies when it comes to dual relationships with clients."

I nodded. "I'm aware of them. I was at home watching television, and I turned in early." *Into a spirit-werewolf*, I added in my head to make it not technically a lie.

"They said they talked to you, and you recognized them."

My eyebrows shot up my forehead.

"Come on, Marconi," he said and gestured to my face. "You say you turned in early, but you've got dark circles under your eyes, and you keep stifling yawns."

"I haven't been feeling well. Look, Paul, I swear to you I wasn't at any club last night."

"That will do for now," he said and wrote my statement of innocence on a piece of paper. "You didn't happen to talk to anyone on the phone or anything like that while you were at home, did you?"

"Nope. I'm just a boring girl, Paul. Did the mysterious caller say I had mentioned their case or even who they were?"

"No. Fine. Get back to work." He frowned at me once more. "But be aware I'm watching you." He dismissed me with a wave of his hand and looked down at the open file on his desk. I took advantage of the moment he looked away to bare my teeth, then turn before he could see me. *No man dismisses me.*

I frowned all the way back to my office and sat to review cases, but my mind wouldn't focus. Who was the woman at the club? Who looked that much like me? And who called Paul? Probably an unhappy parent. That part didn't concern me as much—when you work for the Department of Family and Child Services, you make enemies, especially if you take kids out of abusive homes. That a parent was at a club didn't shock me. That someone pretended to be me did.

*But who hates me enough to try to get me fired?* I wanted to know who she was and how she knew who I worked with.

I kept my Private Investigator license current to pick up some extra work on the side. Sometimes it came in handy for the job, so they didn't say anything. It looked like I was going to be doing some extra work on my own time.

Oh, I had my suspicions. Apparently the events of the previous summer hadn't resolved yet, and there was only one person I could think of who resembled me enough to impersonate me. I needed to know why Kyra Ellison, former alpha female of the Crystal Pines pack and fellow tall brunette, had come out of the mountains and into Little Rock, and even more, why she was posing as me. I also wondered if it was even her. We shared certain characteristics, but no one thought we were similar once they'd interacted with us.

"You two don't look anything alike," Joanie, former best friend of a certain social worker werewolf, had told me. "One glance is all you need to see how she's mean and spiteful, and you're not."

Yet my spite had ended our friendship.

At the end of the day, Paul caught up to me in the parking deck.

"Going out tonight?" he asked and curled his thin lips into a shape between a sneer and a leer. "I can't imagine a girl like you spends too many nights in."

"No," I told him. "At least not to a club. Again, not that it's any of your business."

"Budget cuts," he said in an ominous tone and tapped his nose. He walked to his ancient hatchback, which had rust spots starting to show through the beige paint. I chose to ignore the pheromones he exuded and the insinuation he was doing me a favor. Men had that response to me now that I had a true animal side, and I hoped he wouldn't cross the line into sexual harassment. Yes, the thought of his attentions repulsed me, but I also liked him as a supervisor because he mostly left me alone, and I would hate for him to get fired over it.

*Or for me to.* His warning about our department's financial situation played back in my mind.

I shook my head, not blaming him for nibbling at the drama like a rat gnawing on chicken bones for a pitiful bit of marrow. It was amazing how these government jobs, especially the ones where we supposedly take care of others, sucked the life and soul out of people. On his desk, Paul kept a picture taken during fishing trip he'd been on just after starting here. It showed he had been straight-shouldered and with a full head of wavy brown hair. Now he was stooped and graying, and the rest of his life seemed to have stopped on that day. Even more reason for him to want to create a little drama with the social worker who seemed to be falling down on her job. *And who doesn't seem to be withering in it. It's not my fault my family ages well.*

I drove my similarly ancient but in much better shape green Jeep Cherokee back to my apartment off Chenal Parkway, but when I got home, I sensed something was not right. At first glance, the building looked the same—a two-story, four-unit brick building with lit stairwell between the units on each floor. Dusk was falling, and the lights had just started flickering on, but there was something wrong with the shadows. I squinted and flared my nostrils. An unfamiliar tropical scent rode the top of the breeze. It threaded through the layers of stale cigarette and the bruise-like decay of takeout containers in the bag of trash by my neighbors' door. *Lazy asses.* The new scent, if it had a color, would be fuchsia over the grays and browns of ordinary life, and a shiver tiptoed down my spine. Whether it was of fear or excitement, I didn't know.

One by one, the lights in the stairwells buzzed, popped, and flickered out. That could only mean one thing—a wizard—and my previous encounter with one had left me with this little werewolf problem.

*Okay, fear it is. Whatever you do, don't show it. Just get into the apartment.*

Sure they had seen me, I played nonchalant and grabbed my purse off the passenger seat. I left the files I'd been planning to work on once Giancarlo passed out after his second bottle of wine. He was due over in half an hour and I needed to make sure he wasn't in danger. Sure, he was an alcoholic, but he was a cute one, and his problems worked for me on a practical level, although my constantly wondering if I was enabling him didn't work for me on an ethical one. I was going to get help for him eventually, but he didn't want it at the moment, so there was no point. At least that's what I kept telling myself.

The internal twisting and folding inward sensations told me the aconite hadn't quite worked out of my system from the night before, although the swill that passed for office coffee had kept my frontal lobes jazzed enough during the day to fight the effects.

*"No, we're not going to change now."* Sometimes sternly addressing my animal side worked, like I had to constantly reinforce I was the alpha of my own mind, especially with the aconite hangover. That was a different kind of fear—it seemed the aconite was taking longer and longer to wear off each time. The animal part of my brain scrabbled in my skull, wanting me to change and hunt down whatever the threat was.

*"Down,"* I told it. *"Maybe the rat I killed last night has a vengeful family?"*

*"No, whatever it is, it's bigger than a rat and is watching you."*

I shivered and cursed under my breath. *"Thanks, really. No showing weakness, remember?"*

*"So change."*

Sometimes these conversations I had with myself were useful. Most often, not, and I was left wondering whether I was insane, and maybe all the werewolf stuff was a wicked psychosis.

I held my keys in my right hand and my pepper spray in my left. My inner wolf scoffed at my puny defenses, inferior to fangs and claws. Each light I walked under flickered back to life, and a warm breeze followed me. Again, the scent of fuchsia, both the color and the flower, teased my nose.

*Someone's toying with me. They know I'm aware of them. Why don't they show themselves?*

I reached my apartment and looked around before I stuck my key in my lock. Again, nothing visible, but *something* was out there watching me. I ducked into the apartment and closed the door behind me, breathing a sigh of relief when my lights switched on without flickering or flashing. I put my purse on the counter next to the postcard reminding me that it was time for my physical and I was scheduled for blood work the next morning. My phone buzzed with a voicemail. The call hadn't rung, although it should have. I touched the little icon and listened to Giancarlo's lilting tones. His cheerful voice sounded odd in the context of my strange experiences.

"Lonna, *Bellissima*, I am so sorry, but something's come up at the restaurant, and I cannot make it. Know you will be in my heart tonight."

"Along with your Chianti." I exhaled with both relief and disappointment at Giancarlo's cancellation. I didn't want to put him in any danger, but I also needed to blow off some steam. The day after the full moon was the worst for wanting to explore other animal impulses once the desire to hunt was satisfied.

*Yet another thing they didn't tell me.*

I went to bed after an uneventful evening with no more electrical strangeness. By the time I ventured out to the Jeep to get
the files I needed to catch up on, the odd odor had disappeared.
That night I dreamed of a tropical beach with a turquoise
ocean at my feet and large-leafed flora all around. Huge fuchsia
plants dripped the scent of their purple and pink flowers on the
breeze. I leaned back in my beach chair, cold drink in hand,
and soaked up the sun, happy I wouldn't have to renew my
membership to the tanning salon. Yes, I knew it was bad for me,
but it was my one indulgence. Never mind that I had on the
skimpiest bikini I'd ever worn and had to keep sipping my
drink so I wouldn't open my mouth and spill all my secrets to
the strange man who sat beside me, but whose face I couldn't
quite make out.

*Wait a second, whose dream is this?*

A buzz startled me awake, and the radio hissed on. I fiddled
with the knob. It settled into its regular morning show alarm
just as the DJ announced the rain and current temperature
with unwarranted perkiness. Something about it reminded me
of the flickering lights the night before and how my phone
hadn't rung when Giancarlo called. I shivered again, but I
attributed it to the damp and current temperature near forty.

My inner wolf laughed at my dismay. *"Those conditions would
be nothing for fur... or spirit fur. Change! We're being stalked."*

*"Tonight. I can't take the aconite too much. It's poison in a
normal human body."*

A snort, then, *"Change for real."*

*"Can't. Too hard to manage doors, and I can't escape tight situa-
tions in an instant by returning to my body."*

No response, but I sensed her sulking. I knew "she" or
"spirit wolf-Lonna" was a manifestation of the animal part of
my brain, or maybe even some sort of spiritual part of me, but
sometimes she seemed oddly separate, like when we had these

conversations. Whatever she was, it put me in a bad mood for my blood work that morning. I would have canceled, but if I did, I'd have to move my physical, which had been scheduled for a year, and I needed to make sure my new weird lifestyle wasn't having any strange effects on my body. Somehow I suspected being an apex predator wouldn't grant me an exception for having to wait forever for a new doctor's appointment.

I arrived at the doctor's office and took a seat just before my appointment time. It was crowded with people with the ends of that winter's illnesses, and although they had been given masks to cover up their coughs and sneezes, I touched as few surfaces as possible. It had been a rough year, and I groaned inwardly—stressful job plus powerful viruses equaled lots of people out at the office, which meant more work for me. That was another side benefit of my lycanthropy: a heightened immune system.

A nurse brought me back to the phlebotomy station, and I caught a glimpse of a new doctor. He ran his hand through wavy reddish-gold hair as he talked to a young mother holding a baby, and his green-blue eyes the color of the ocean in my dream sparkled. He had a tan, too dark to have been hanging around Little Rock recently, and in his words, I heard hints of the islands. The faint smell of fuchsia made my heartbeat accelerate.

"Your blood pressure's up, Miss Marconi," the young nurse said with concern in her tone.

"Rough morning," I said. "It's what happens when I don't get my coffee."

She smiled, her teeth bright white against her dark skin. "I understand that. We'll get this done quickly so you can get you some." She tied the rubber strap around my arm and poked around for a vein. I looked away so I'd only feel what she was doing, not see it.

"Thank you. New doctor?"

She followed my gaze. "That's Doctor Fortuna," she said with a dreamy little sigh. "He's filling in for Doctor Kasdon while she's on temporary bed rest. They went to school together."

"Where is he from?"

"Somewhere in the Caribbean." She wrinkled her nose. "I know he's told me, but I can't remember exactly where. He did his schooling here in the States, though, so don't worry, when you see him next week, he'll know what he's doing. Now," she said, and gave me a stern look, "your chart says you haven't had the flu shot. It's still going around, so it's not too late."

"I'll pass," I told her, a little shot of adrenaline making my heart skip. Although the current vaccines wouldn't be contaminated, I'd never trust them again. Not that they could do anything to me that hadn't already been done by other means, but it was an instinctive response.

"Are you sure?" She put a cotton ball over the hole in my arm and taped it in place. "Keep that there for a little while."

"Positive. I'll talk to Doctor Fortuna about it next week."

That dreamy expression returned. "He's a good doctor," she said and packed up her kit.

Her spacey confidence didn't make me feel any better, and my inner wolf wanted to run around him and sniff him to figure him out. That would have been the only way to catch his scent —the chemical odors of the medical facility drowned out any others.

I was relieved to get back to my car and then to my windowless office, where the files I had taken home to catch up on had been replaced by a whole new set. I looked through them and was listing phone calls I'd have to make when Paul walked by and gave me a wave, a grin on his rat face. When he had just passed my door, he turned around and poked his head in.

"Are you free for lunch today?"

I arched an eyebrow. "I believe the correct greeting in our culture is 'good morning.'"

"Good morning, then." He stood, hands in his pockets. "Now aren't you supposed to reply?"

"Touché, and good morning. What's got you in such a good mood?"

He shrugged. "There's just something in the air these days. Haven't you felt it? Spring is my favorite season."

He had something between his teeth, but I elected not to point it out to him. Honestly, his cheerfulness freaked me out. "It's not spring yet. And no, I'm not free for lunch." I gestured to the pile of files and list of phone calls I needed to make.

"I hope you're not saying that because of our conversation yesterday." His false concern made me want to strangle him.

"No, I always put my work first, whether you believe it or not. Guess what I was doing last night?"

The look on his face made me immediately regret the question. "Clubbing?" Dear gods, he sounded hopeful.

"No, my *boyfriend* canceled out on me, so I stayed home and caught up on some reports."

He sniffed. "Keeping everything secure, I hope?"

"Yes, Paul." *Mostly.* "Unless they changed the rules on us again."

He laughed, and it came out with a wheeze. "You never know, do you?" He continued chuckling as he walked around the corner. "You really never know."

"Okay..." I shook my head. *Maybe he finally lost it.*

A file that should have gone somewhere else caught my attention, and I jumped up to catch up with Paul. He had disappeared, so I went to his office. I paused just outside the door, hearing his voice. His words chilled me.

"Are you sure?" He spoke with the phone cradled to his ear. "She seems so normal. No, I couldn't get her to come out for lunch. Yes, she leaves at around five o'clock, and she's always parked near me. Uh huh, a green Jeep Cherokee, license plate..."

Want to keep reading? Grab Long Shadows from your favorite retailer today or order it through your local bookstore with the ISBN 978-1-945074-38-7

# ABOUT THE AUTHOR

Cecilia Dominic wrote her first story when she was two years old and has always had a much more interesting life inside her head than outside of it. She became a clinical psychologist because she's fascinated by people and their stories, but she couldn't stop writing fiction. The first draft of her dissertation, while not fiction, was still criticized by her major professor for being too entertaining. She made it through graduate school and got her PhD, started her own practice, and by day, she helps people cure their insomnia without using medication. By night, she writes fiction she hopes will keep her readers turning the pages all night. Yes, she recognizes the conflict of interest between her two careers, but she prefers the term versatile to conflicted. She lives in Atlanta, Georgia, with her husband and the world's cutest cat.

You can find her in the following online places:
Newsletter (get a free novella):
https://ceciliadominic.com/booknewsletter

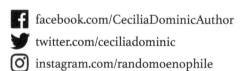

facebook.com/CeciliaDominicAuthor
twitter.com/ceciliadominic
instagram.com/randomoenophile